GW01372453

THE LORD OF THE RINGS
DIARY

Illustrated by
ALAN LEE

1994

Grafton
An Imprint of HarperCollins*Publishers*

Grafton
An imprint of HarperCollins*Publishers*
77-85 Fulham Palace Road
Hammersmith, London W6 8JB

Published by Grafton 1993
The Lord of The Rings Diary 1994

All colour illustrations originally published in 1991 in a new edition
of *The Lord of The Rings* by J. R. R. Tolkien, illustrated by Alan Lee

ISBN 0261 10287 7

Printed in Hong Kong

John Ronald Reuel Tolkien was born on 3rd January 1892 in Bloemfontein in the Orange Free State. He was educated at King Edward's School, Birmingham where he began to develop his linguistic talent.

1914 saw the outbreak of the First World War. Tolkien graduated in 1915 with a first in English language and literature at Oxford. Before embarking for France in 1916, he married his childhood sweetheart, Edith Bratt. He survived the Somme, but was later invalided home.

After the war Tolkien became Professor of Anglo-Saxon at Oxford. He had already started writing the great cycle of myths that became *The Silmarillion*. He and Edith had four children and it was for them that he first told the tale of *The Hobbit* which was published in 1937. It was so successful that the publishers instantly wanted a sequel, but it was not until 1954 that the first volume of his great masterpiece, *The Lord of the Rings*, appeared. Its enormous popularity took Tolkien by surprise.

After retirement Ronald and Edith Tolkien moved to Bournemouth where Edith died in 1971. Tolkien then returned to Oxford where he died in 1973.

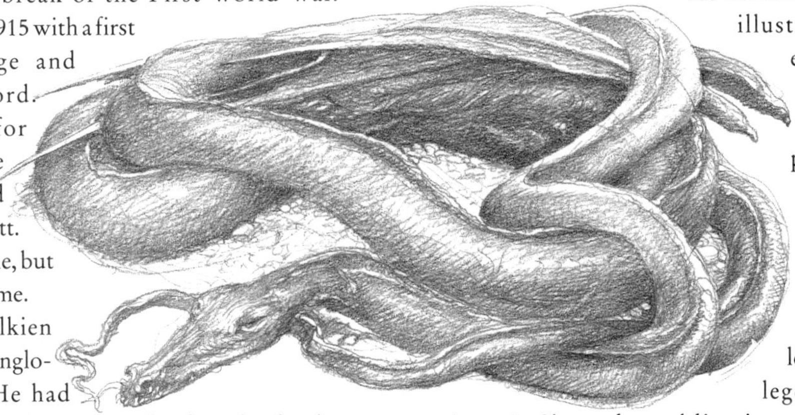

Alan Lee was born in Middlesex in 1947. He studied Graphic Design at Ealing School of Art from 1966 to 1969. As a student he concentrated on the depiction of Celtic and Norse myths and he has remained fascinated by mythology throughout his career. Working as a freelance illustrator from 1970, he established his reputation in 1978 with *Faeries,* a volume of fairy lore produced in collaboration with Brian Froud, and its success enabled him to devote time to a long-cherished ambition, the illustration of the collection of medieval Welsh legends, *The Mabinogion* (1982). Since the publication of Michael Palin's *The Mirrorstone* in 1986, Lee has worked with several contemporary writers of fantasy and myth including Joan Aiken, Peter Dickinson and Rosemary Sutcliff. He has also created the conceptual design for the film version of Terry Jones' *Erik the Viking*.

The illustrations that he produced for the centenary edition of J.R.R. Tolkien's *The Lord of the Rings* (1991) represent the height of his achievement to date.He lives in Devon with his wife and children

C·A·L·E·N·D·A·R

1993

JANUARY

M		4	11	18	25
T		5	12	19	26
W		6	13	20	27
T		7	14	21	28
F	1	8	15	22	29
S	2	9	16	23	30
S	3	10	17	24	31

FEBRUARY

M	1	8	15	22
T	2	9	16	23
W	3	10	17	24
T	4	11	18	25
F	5	12	19	26
S	6	13	20	27
S	7	14	21	28

MARCH

M	1	8	15	22	29
T	2	9	16	23	30
W	3	10	17	24	31
T	4	11	18	25	
F	5	12	19	26	
S	6	13	20	27	
S	7	14	21	28	

APRIL

M		5	12	19	26
T		6	13	20	27
W		7	14	21	28
T	1	8	15	22	29
F	2	9	16	23	30
S	3	10	17	24	
S	4	11	18	25	

MAY

M		3	10	17	24	31
T		4	11	18	25	
W		5	12	19	26	
T		6	13	20	27	
F		7	14	21	28	
S	1	8	15	22	29	
S	2	9	16	23	30	

JUNE

M		7	14	21	28
T	1	8	15	22	29
W	2	9	16	23	30
T	3	10	17	24	
F	4	11	18	25	
S	5	12	19	26	
S	6	13	20	27	

JULY

M		5	12	19	26
T		6	13	20	27
W		7	14	21	28
T	1	8	15	22	29
F	2	9	16	23	30
S	3	10	17	24	31
S	4	11	18	25	

AUGUST

M		2	9	16	23	30
T		3	10	17	24	31
W		4	11	18	25	
T		5	12	19	26	
F		6	13	20	27	
S		7	14	21	28	
S	1	8	15	22	29	

SEPTEMBER

M		6	13	20	27
T		7	14	21	28
W	1	8	15	22	29
T	2	9	16	23	30
F	3	10	17	24	
S	4	11	18	25	
S	5	12	19	26	

OCTOBER

M		4	11	18	25
T		5	12	19	26
W		6	13	20	27
T		7	14	21	28
F	1	8	15	22	29
S	2	9	16	23	30
S	3	10	17	24	31

NOVEMBER

M	1	8	15	22	29
T	2	9	16	23	30
W	3	10	17	24	
T	4	11	18	25	
F	5	12	19	26	
S	6	13	20	27	
S	7	14	21	28	

DECEMBER

M		6	13	20	27
T		7	14	21	28
W	1	8	15	22	29
T	2	9	16	23	30
F	3	10	17	24	31
S	4	11	18	25	
S	5	12	19	26	

1995

JANUARY

M		2	9	16	23	30
T		3	10	17	24	31
W		4	11	18	25	
T		5	12	19	26	
F		6	13	20	27	
S		7	14	21	28	
S	1	8	15	22	29	

FEBRUARY

M		6	13	20	27
T		7	14	21	28
W	1	8	15	22	
T	2	9	16	23	
F	3	10	17	24	
S	4	11	18	25	
S	5	12	19	26	

MARCH

M		6	13	20	27
T		7	14	21	28
W	1	8	15	22	29
T	2	9	16	23	30
F	3	10	17	24	31
S	4	11	18	25	
S	5	12	19	26	

APRIL

M		3	10	17	24
T		4	11	18	25
W		5	12	19	26
T		6	13	20	27
F		7	14	21	28
S	1	8	15	22	29
S	2	9	16	23	30

MAY

M	1	8	15	22	29
T	2	9	16	23	30
W	3	10	17	24	31
T	4	11	18	25	
F	5	12	19	26	
S	6	13	20	27	
S	7	14	21	28	

JUNE

M		5	12	19	26
T		6	13	20	27
W		7	14	21	28
T	1	8	15	22	29
F	2	9	16	23	30
S	3	10	17	24	
S	4	11	18	25	

JULY

M		3	10	17	24	31
T		4	11	18	25	
W		5	12	19	26	
T		6	13	20	27	
F		7	14	21	28	
S	1	8	15	22	29	
S	2	9	16	23	30	

AUGUST

M		7	14	21	28
T	1	8	15	22	29
W	2	9	16	23	30
T	3	10	17	24	31
F	4	11	18	25	
S	5	12	19	26	
S	6	13	20	27	

SEPTEMBER

M		4	11	18	25
T		5	12	19	26
W		6	13	20	27
T		7	14	21	28
F	1	8	15	22	29
S	2	9	16	23	30
S	3	10	17	24	

OCTOBER

M		2	9	16	23	30
T		3	10	17	24	31
W		4	11	18	25	
T		5	12	19	26	
F		6	13	20	27	
S		7	14	21	28	
S	1	8	15	22	29	

NOVEMBER

M		6	13	20	27
T		7	14	21	28
W	1	8	15	22	29
T	2	9	16	23	30
F	3	10	17	24	
S	4	11	18	25	
S	5	12	19	26	

DECEMBER

M		4	11	18	25
T		5	12	19	26
W		6	13	20	27
T		7	14	21	28
F	1	8	15	22	29
S	2	9	16	23	30
S	3	10	17	24	31

1994

CALENDAR

JANUARY

M		3	10	17	24	31
T		4	11	18	25	
W		5	12	19	26	
T		6	13	20	27	
F		7	14	21	28	
S	1	8	15	22	29	
S	2	9	16	23	30	

FEBRUARY

M		7	14	21	28
T	1	8	15	22	
W	2	9	16	23	
T	3	10	17	24	
F	4	11	18	25	
S	5	12	19	26	
S	6	13	20	27	

MARCH

M		7	14	21	28
T	1	8	15	22	29
W	2	9	16	23	30
T	3	10	17	24	31
F	4	11	18	25	
S	5	12	19	26	
S	6	13	20	27	

APRIL

M		4	11	18	25
T		5	12	19	26
W		6	13	20	27
T		7	14	21	28
F	1	8	15	22	29
S	2	9	16	23	30
S	3	10	17	24	

MAY

M		2	9	16	23	30
T		3	10	17	24	31
W		4	11	18	25	
T		5	12	19	26	
F		6	13	20	27	
S		7	14	21	28	
S	1	8	15	22	29	

JUNE

M		6	13	20	27
T		7	14	21	28
W	1	8	15	22	29
T	2	9	16	23	30
F	3	10	17	24	
S	4	11	18	25	
S	5	12	19	26	

JULY

M		4	11	18	25
T		5	12	19	26
W		6	13	20	27
T		7	14	21	28
F	1	8	15	22	29
S	2	9	16	23	30
S	3	10	17	24	31

AUGUST

M	1	8	15	22	29
T	2	9	16	23	30
W	3	10	17	24	31
T	4	11	18	25	
F	5	12	19	26	
S	6	13	20	27	
S	7	14	21	28	

SEPTEMBER

M		5	12	19	26
T		6	13	20	27
W		7	14	21	28
T	1	8	15	22	29
F	2	9	16	23	30
S	3	10	17	24	
S	4	11	18	25	

OCTOBER

M		3	10	17	24	31
T		4	11	18	25	
W		5	12	19	26	
T		6	13	20	27	
F		7	14	21	28	
S	1	8	15	22	29	
S	2	9	16	23	30	

NOVEMBER

M		7	14	21	28
T	1	8	15	22	29
W	2	9	16	23	30
T	3	10	17	24	
F	4	11	18	25	
S	5	12	19	26	
S	6	13	20	27	

DECEMBER

M		5	12	19	26
T		6	13	20	27
W		7	14	21	28
T	1	8	15	22	29
F	2	9	16	23	30
S	3	10	17	24	31
S	4	11	18	25	

PUBLIC HOLIDAYS

Good Friday .... *Friday April 1*
Easter Monday .... *Monday April 4*
Christmas Day .... *Sunday December 25*

UNITED KINGDOM

New Year's Day .... *Saturday January 1*
Bank Holiday .... *Monday January 3*
Bank Holiday (Scotland) .... *Tuesday January 4*
May Day Holiday .... *Monday May 2*
Spring Bank Holiday .... *Monday May 30*
Orangeman's Day (Northern Ireland) .... *Tuesday July 12*
Summer Bank Holiday (Scotland) .... *Monday August 1*
Summer Bank Holiday (England, Wales and Northern Ireland) .... *Monday August 29*
Boxing Day Holiday .... *Monday December 26*

REPUBLIC OF IRELAND

St Patrick's Day .... *Thursday March 17*
St Stephen's Day .... *Monday December 26*
Bank Holiday .... *Tuesday December 27*

UNITED STATES OF AMERICA

Martin Luther King Day .... *Monday January 17*
Washington's Birthday Holiday .... *Monday February 23*
Memorial Day .... *Monday May 30*
Independence Day Holiday .... *Monday July 4*
Labor Day .... *Monday September 5*
Columbus Day .... *Monday October 10*
Veteran's Day .... *Friday November 11*
Thanksgiving Day .... *Thursday November 24*
New Year Holiday .... *Friday December 31*

CANADA

New Year's Day Holiday .... *Monday January 3*
Victoria Day .... *Monday May 23*
Canada Day .... *Friday July 1*
Labour Day .... *Monday September 5*
Thanksgiving Day .... *Monday October 10*
Remembrance Day .... *Friday November 11*
Christmas Day Holiday .... *Monday December 26*
Boxing Day Holiday .... *Tuesday December 27*

AUSTRALIA AND NEW ZEALAND

New Year's Day Holiday .... *Monday January 3*
Australia Day (Australia) .... *Monday January 31*
Anzac Day .... *Monday April 25*
Labour Day (New Zealand) .... *Monday October 24*
Christmas Day Holiday .... *Monday December 26*
Boxing Day Holiday .... *Tuesday December 27*

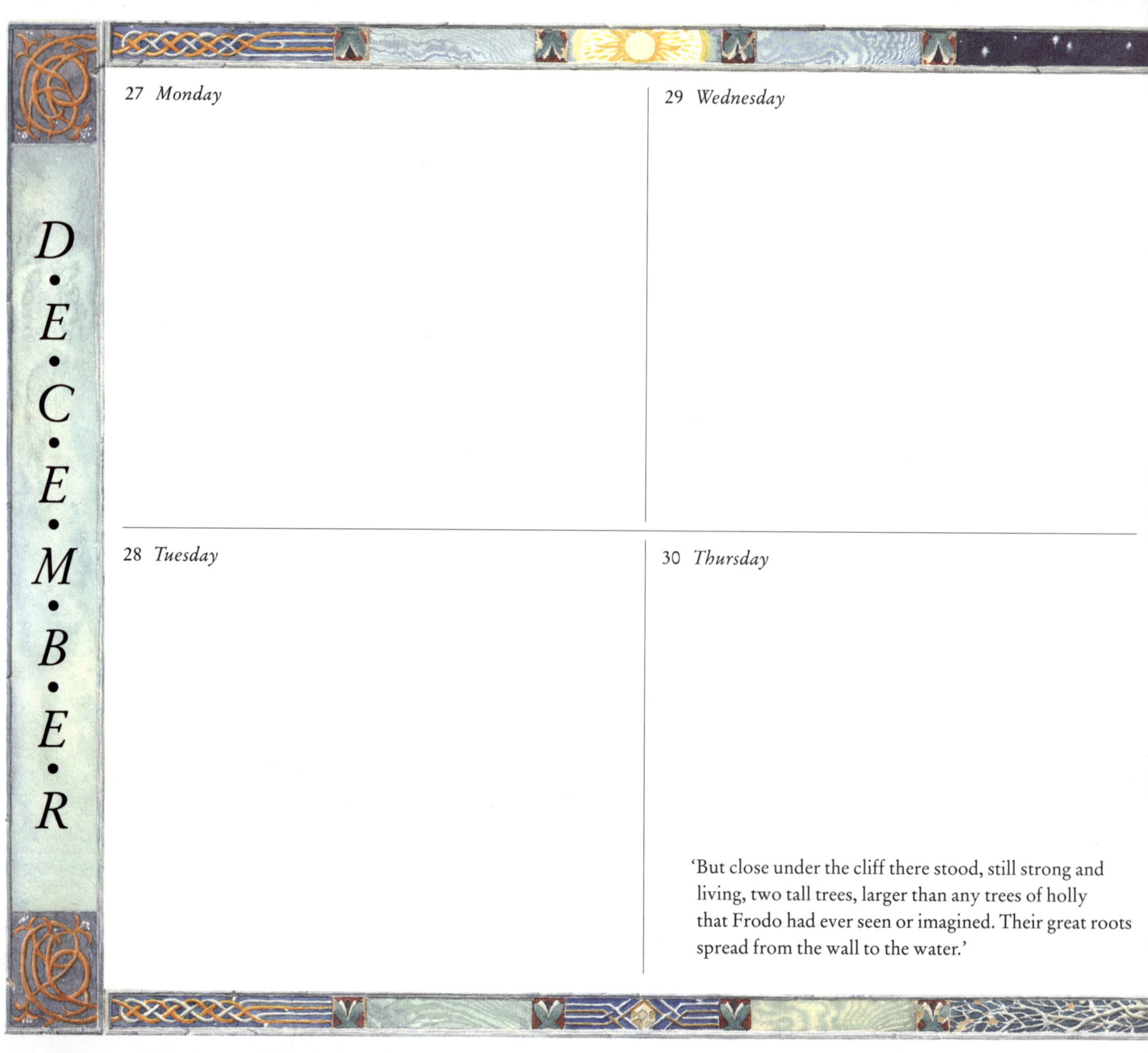

D·E·C·E·M·B·E·R

27 *Monday*

28 *Tuesday*

29 *Wednesday*

30 *Thursday*

'But close under the cliff there stood, still strong and living, two tall trees, larger than any trees of holly that Frodo had ever seen or imagined. Their great roots spread from the wall to the water.'

D•E•C•E•M•B•E•R

31 *Friday*

2 *Sunday*

1 *Saturday*

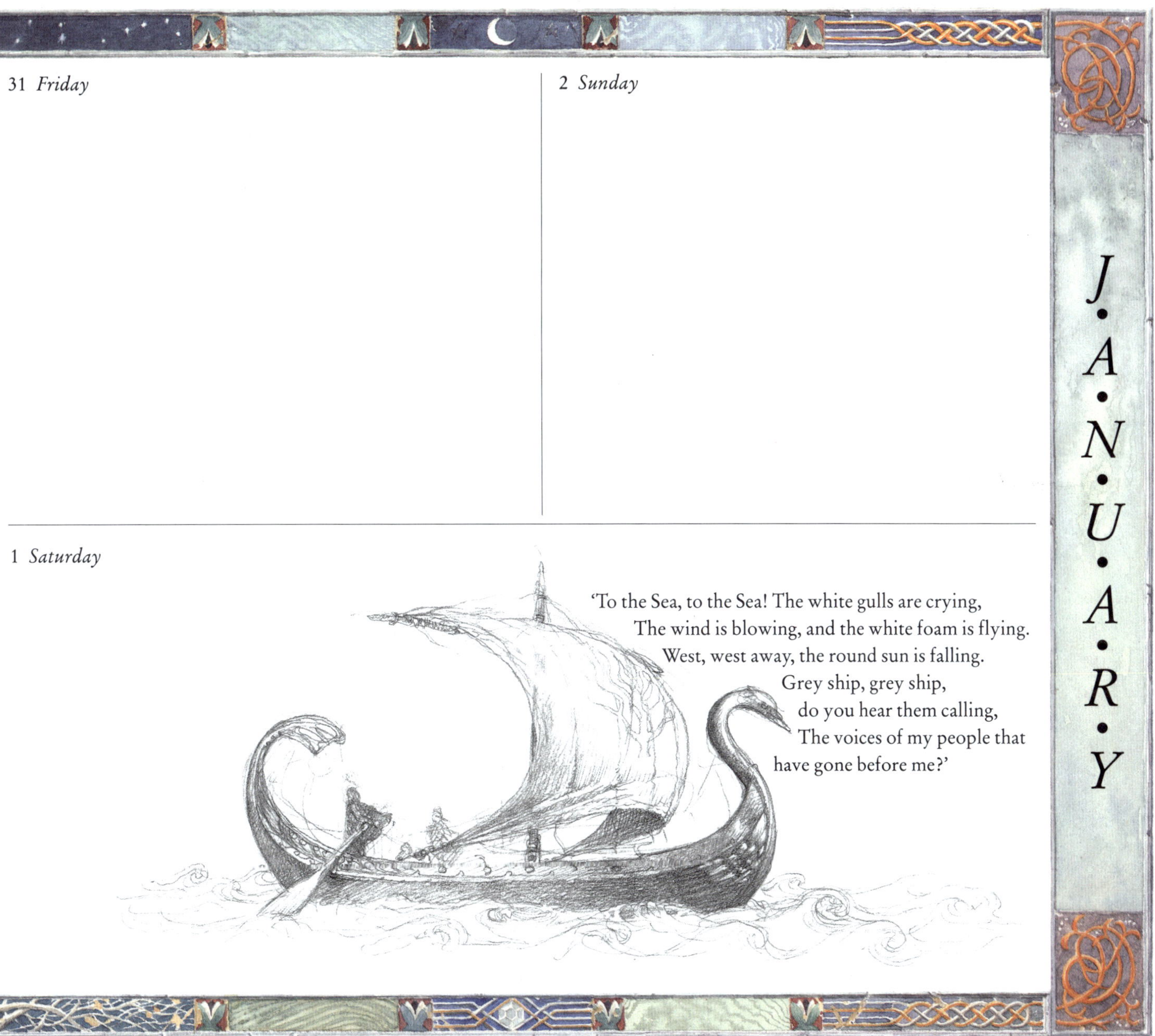

'To the Sea, to the Sea! The white gulls are crying,
The wind is blowing, and the white foam is flying.
West, west away, the round sun is falling.
Grey ship, grey ship,
do you hear them calling,
The voices of my people that
have gone before me?'

J•A•N•U•A•R•Y

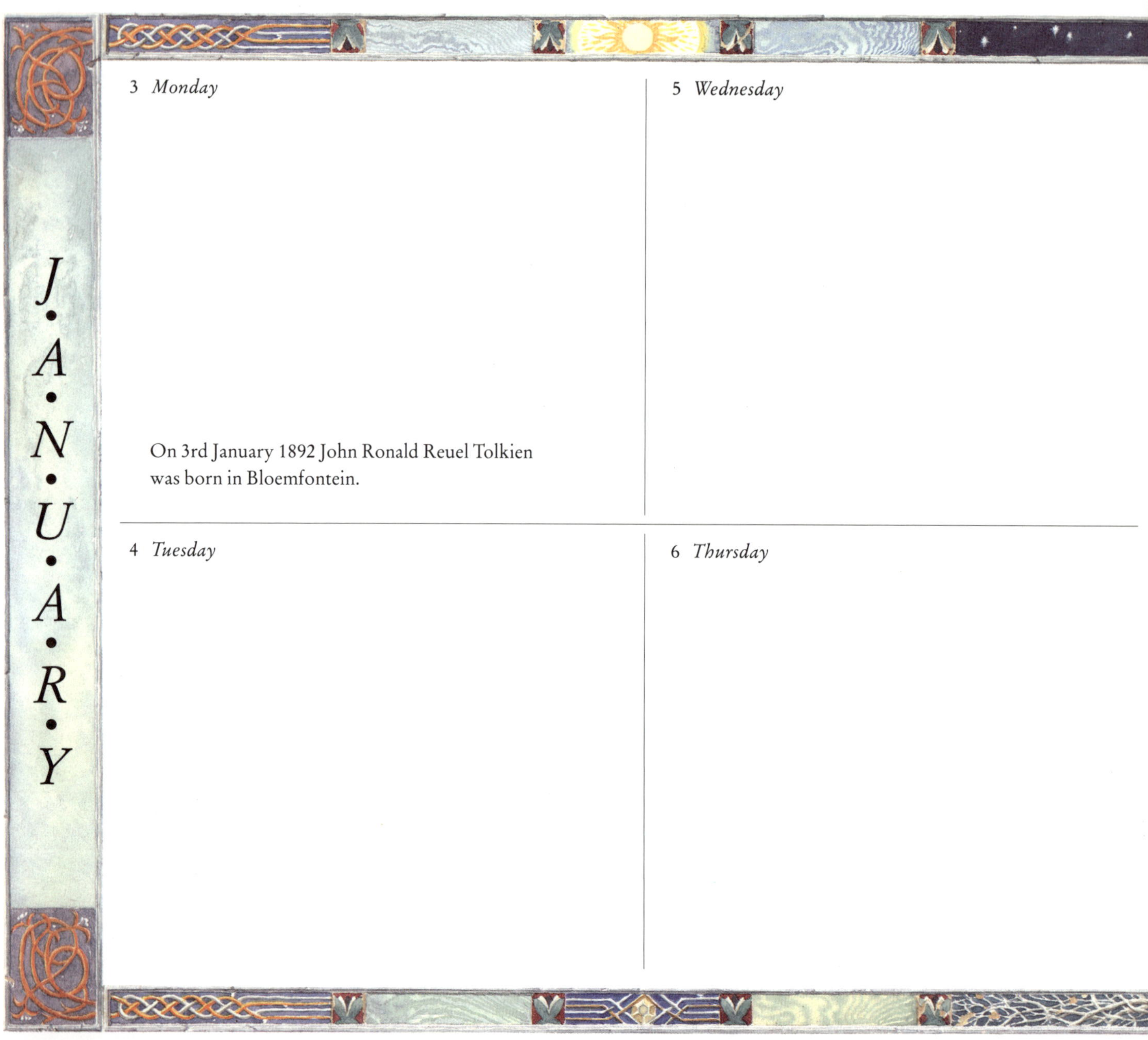

3 *Monday*

On 3rd January 1892 John Ronald Reuel Tolkien was born in Bloemfontein.

4 *Tuesday*

5 *Wednesday*

6 *Thursday*

7 *Friday*

9 *Sunday*

8 *Saturday*

J•A•N•U•A•R•Y

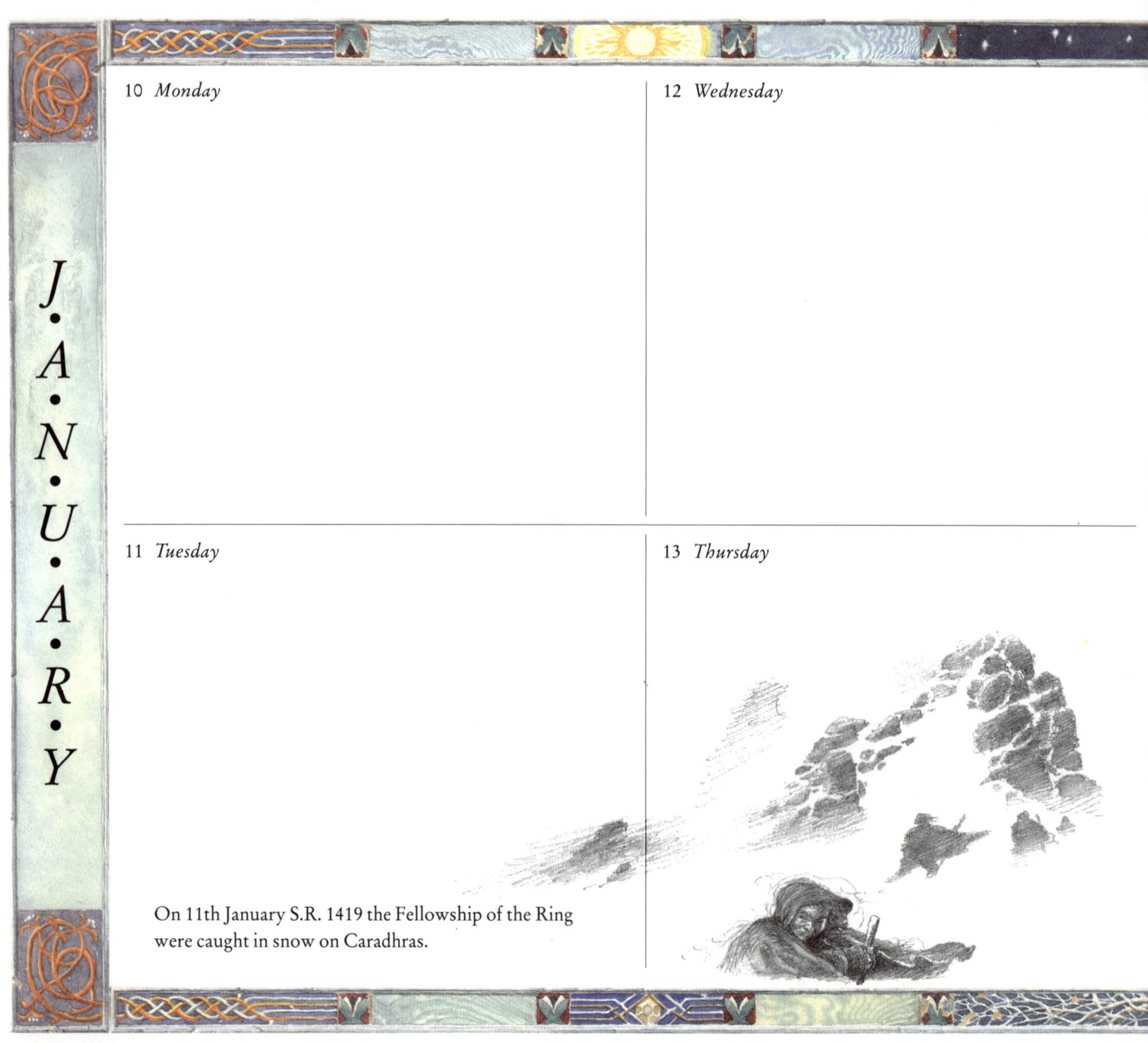

J•A•N•U•A•R•Y

10 *Monday*

11 *Tuesday*

On 11th January S.R. 1419 the Fellowship of the Ring were caught in snow on Caradhras.

12 *Wednesday*

13 *Thursday*

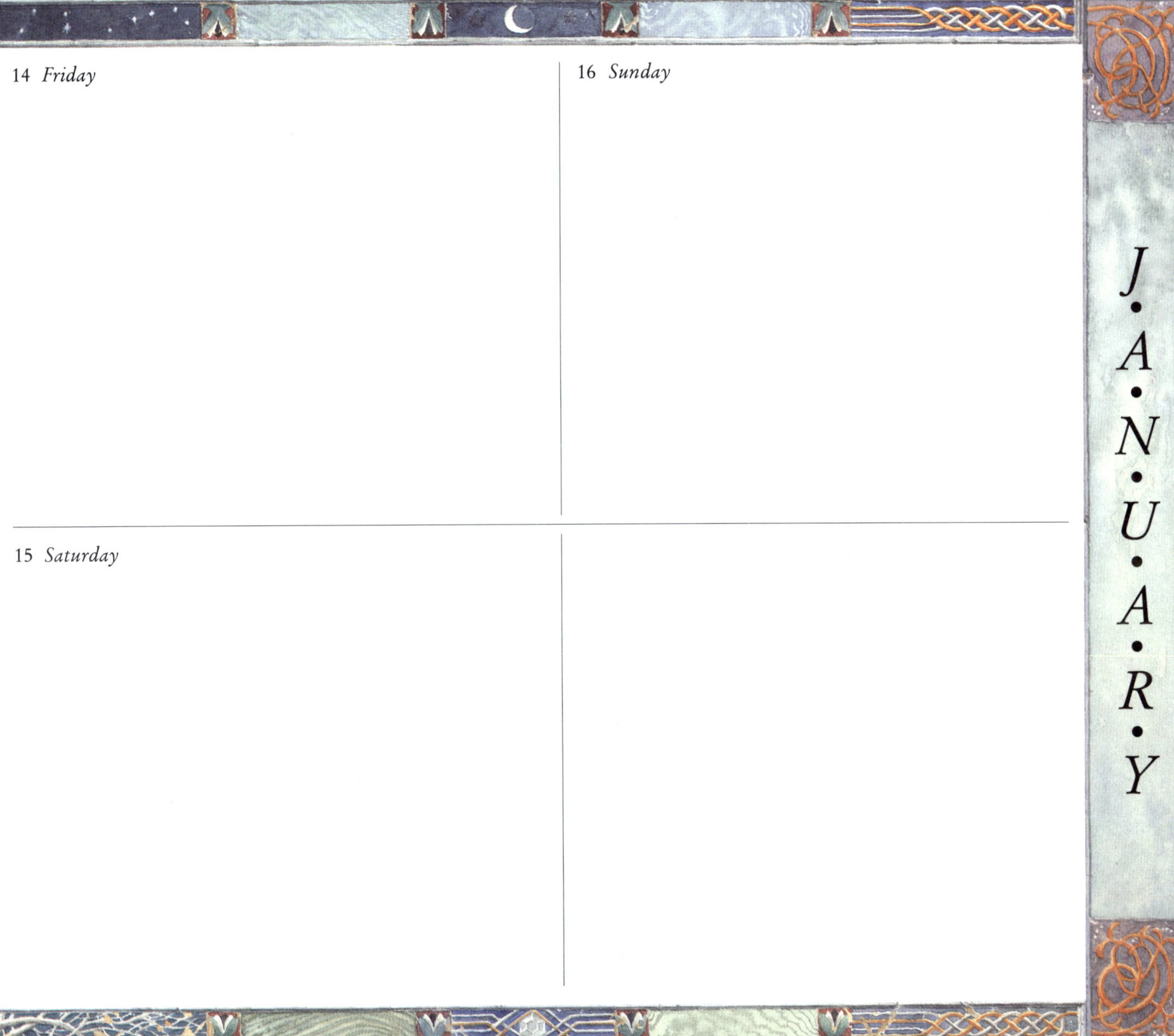

14 *Friday*

16 *Sunday*

15 *Saturday*

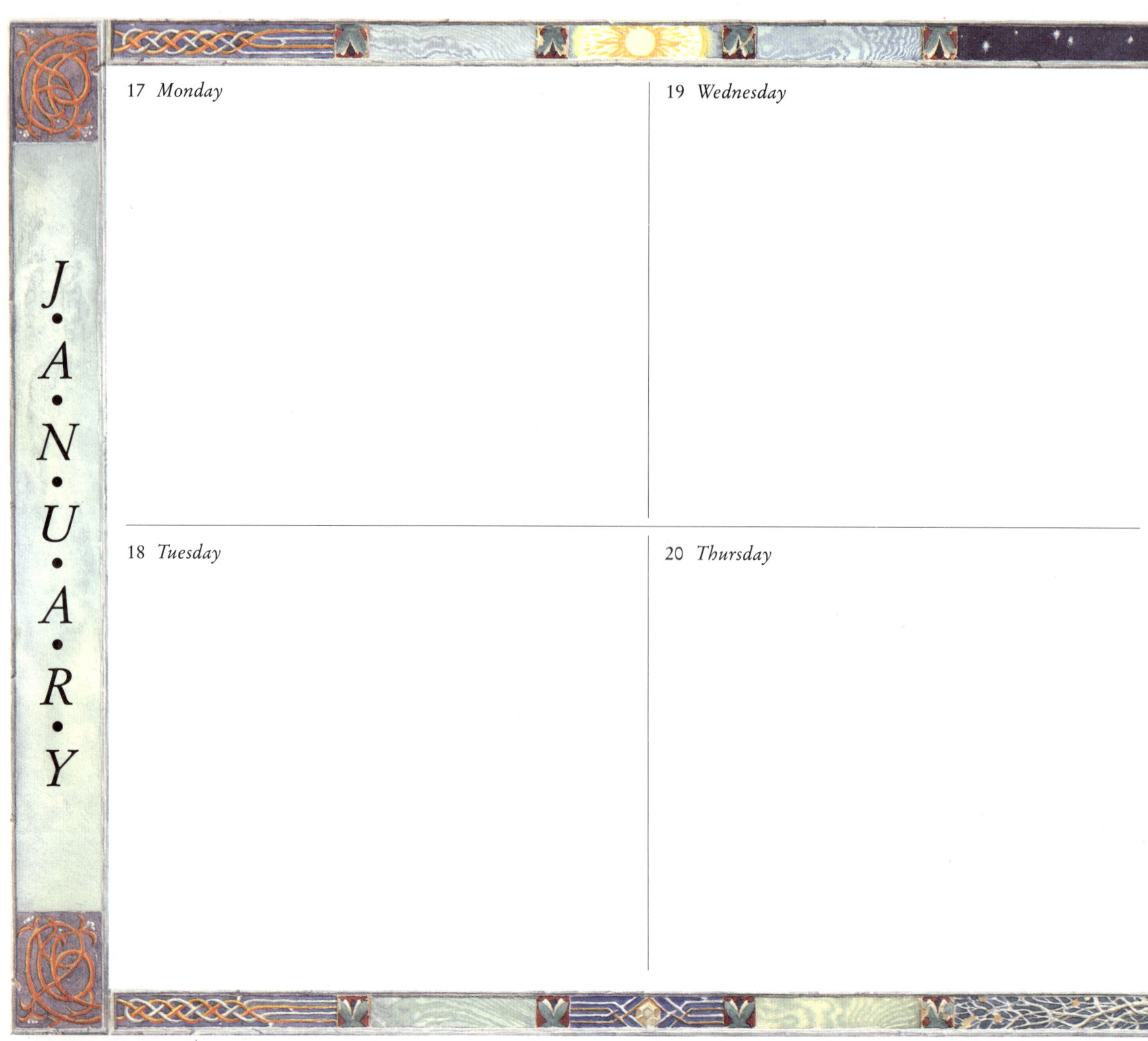

17 *Monday*

18 *Tuesday*

19 *Wednesday*

20 *Thursday*

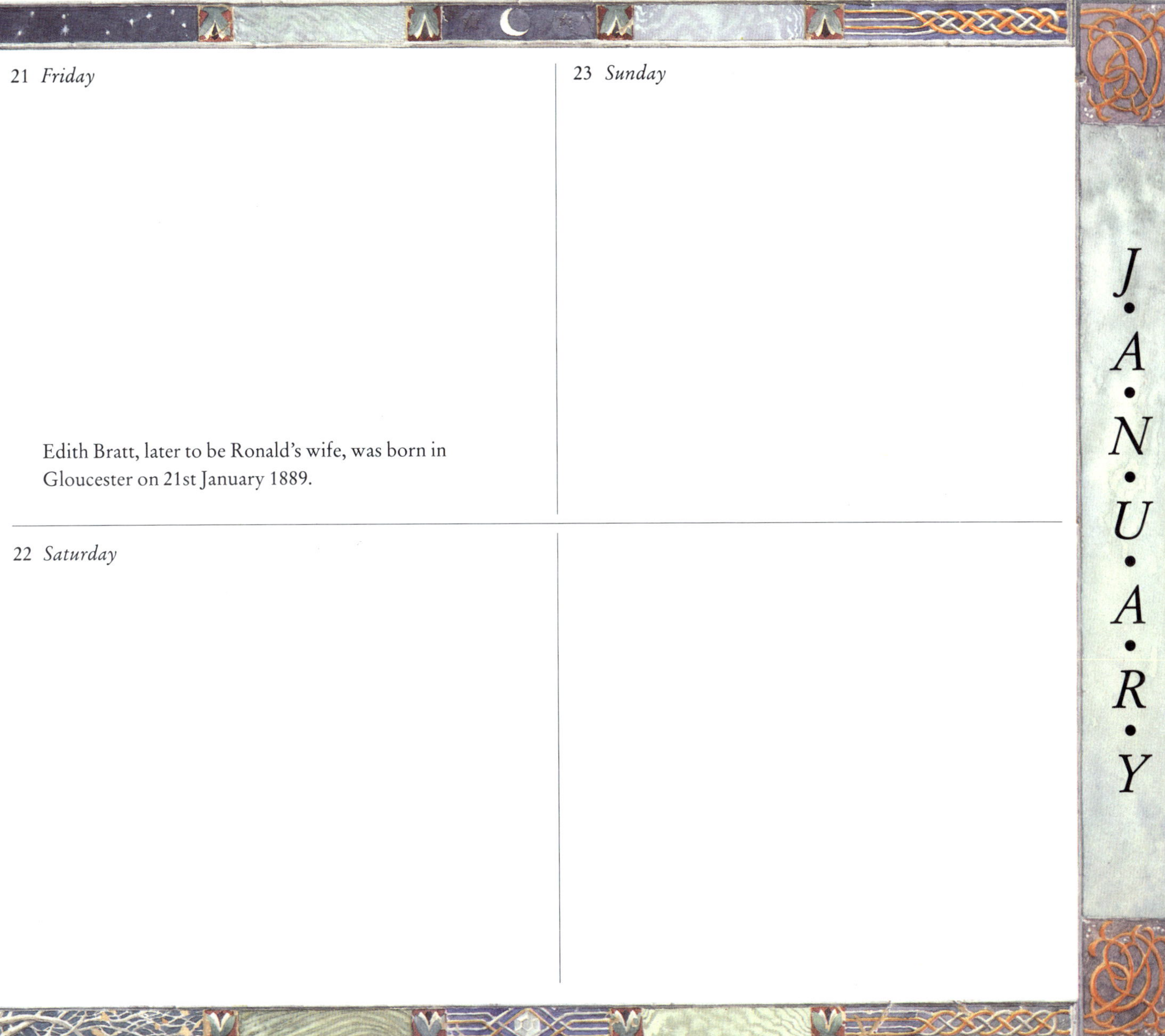

21 *Friday*

Edith Bratt, later to be Ronald's wife, was born in Gloucester on 21st January 1889.

22 *Saturday*

23 *Sunday*

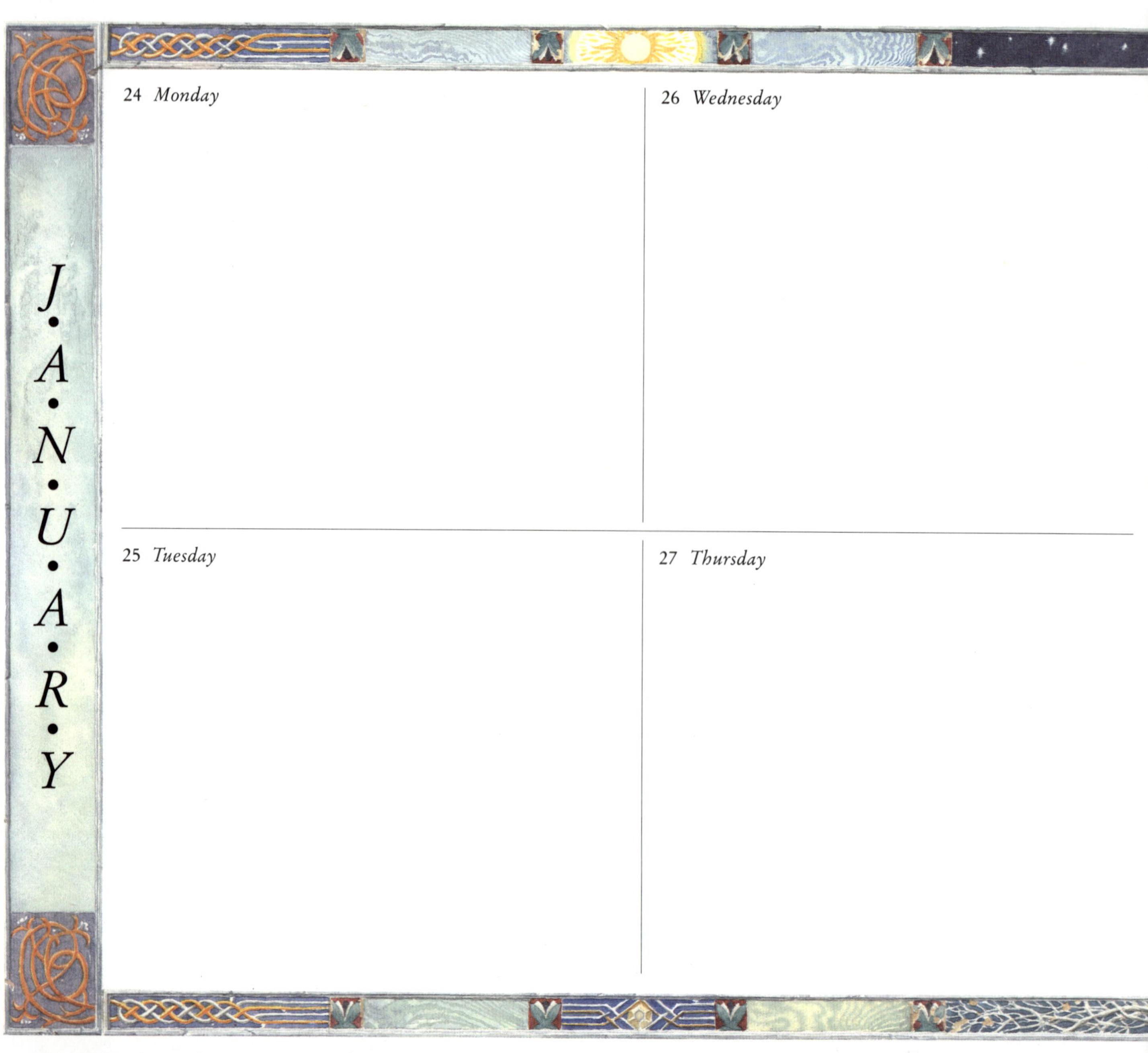

JANUARY

24 *Monday*

26 *Wednesday*

25 *Tuesday*

27 *Thursday*

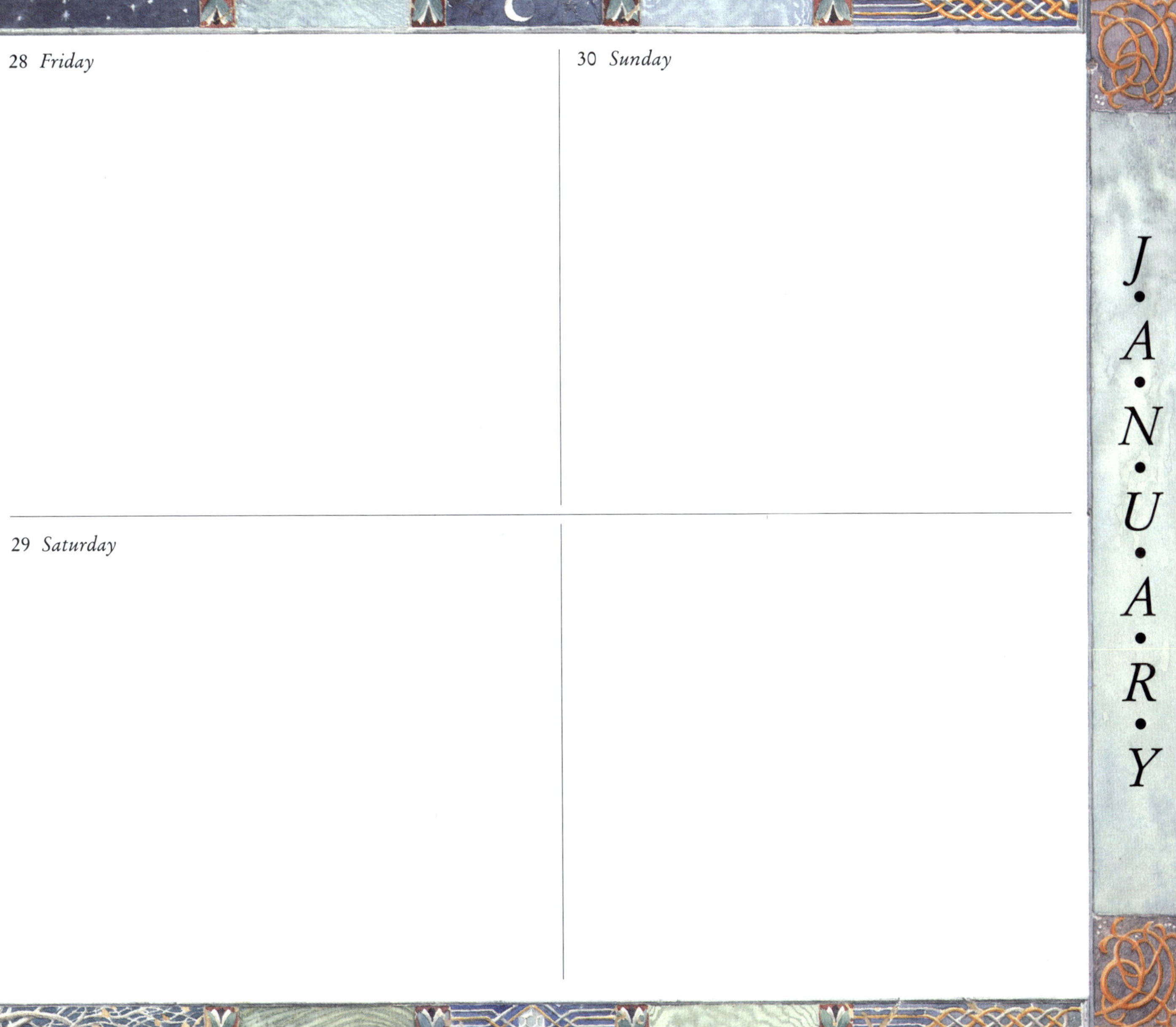
28 Friday
30 Sunday
29 Saturday
J•A•N•U•A•R•Y

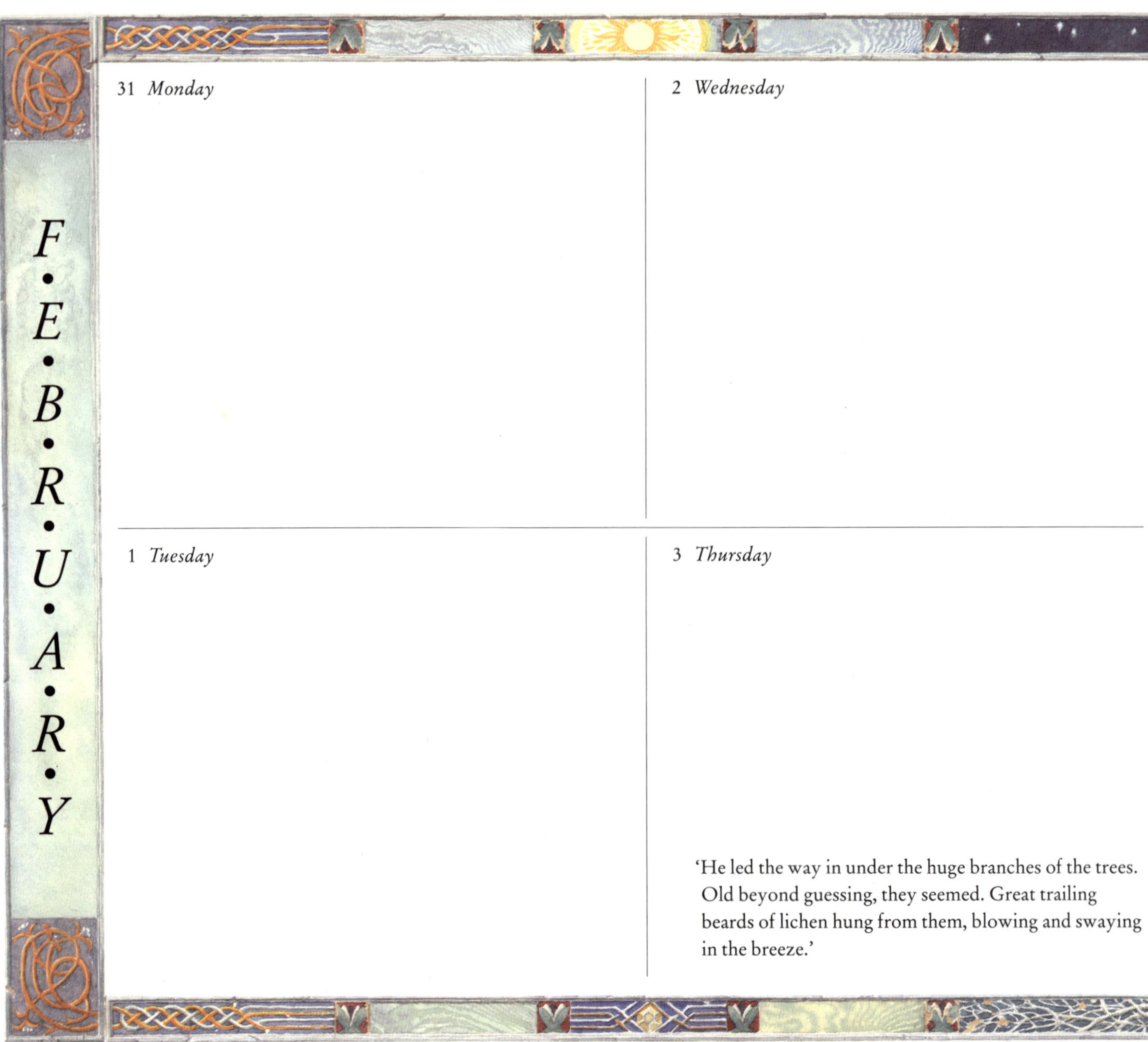

F • E • B • R • U • A • R • Y

31 *Monday*

1 *Tuesday*

2 *Wednesday*

3 *Thursday*

'He led the way in under the huge branches of the trees. Old beyond guessing, they seemed. Great trailing beards of lichen hung from them, blowing and swaying in the breeze.'

F•E•B•R•U•A•R•Y

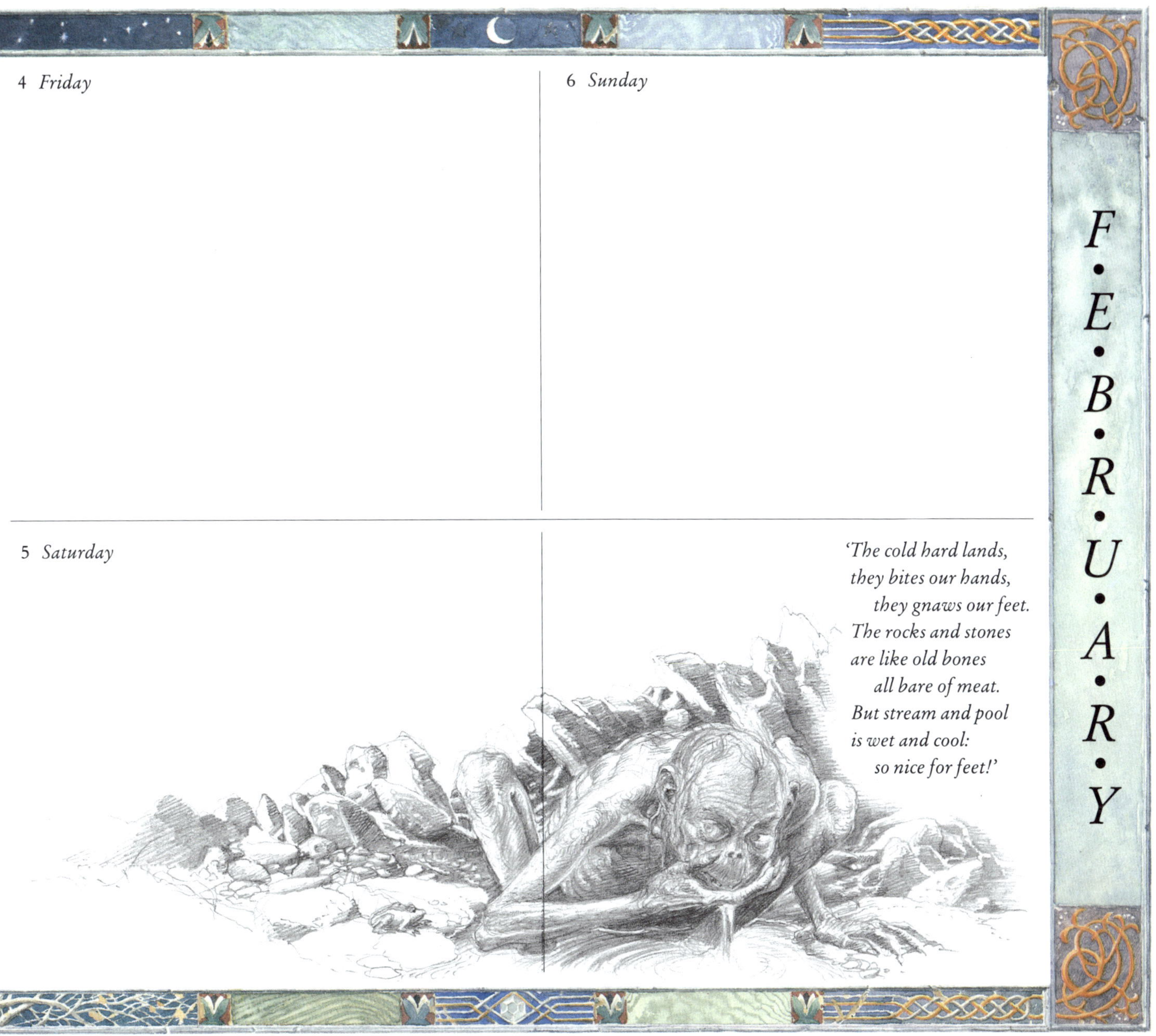

4 *Friday*

5 *Saturday*

6 *Sunday*

'The cold hard lands,
they bites our hands,
they gnaws our feet.
The rocks and stones
are like old bones
all bare of meat.
But stream and pool
is wet and cool:
so nice for feet!'

F • E • B • R • U • A • R • Y

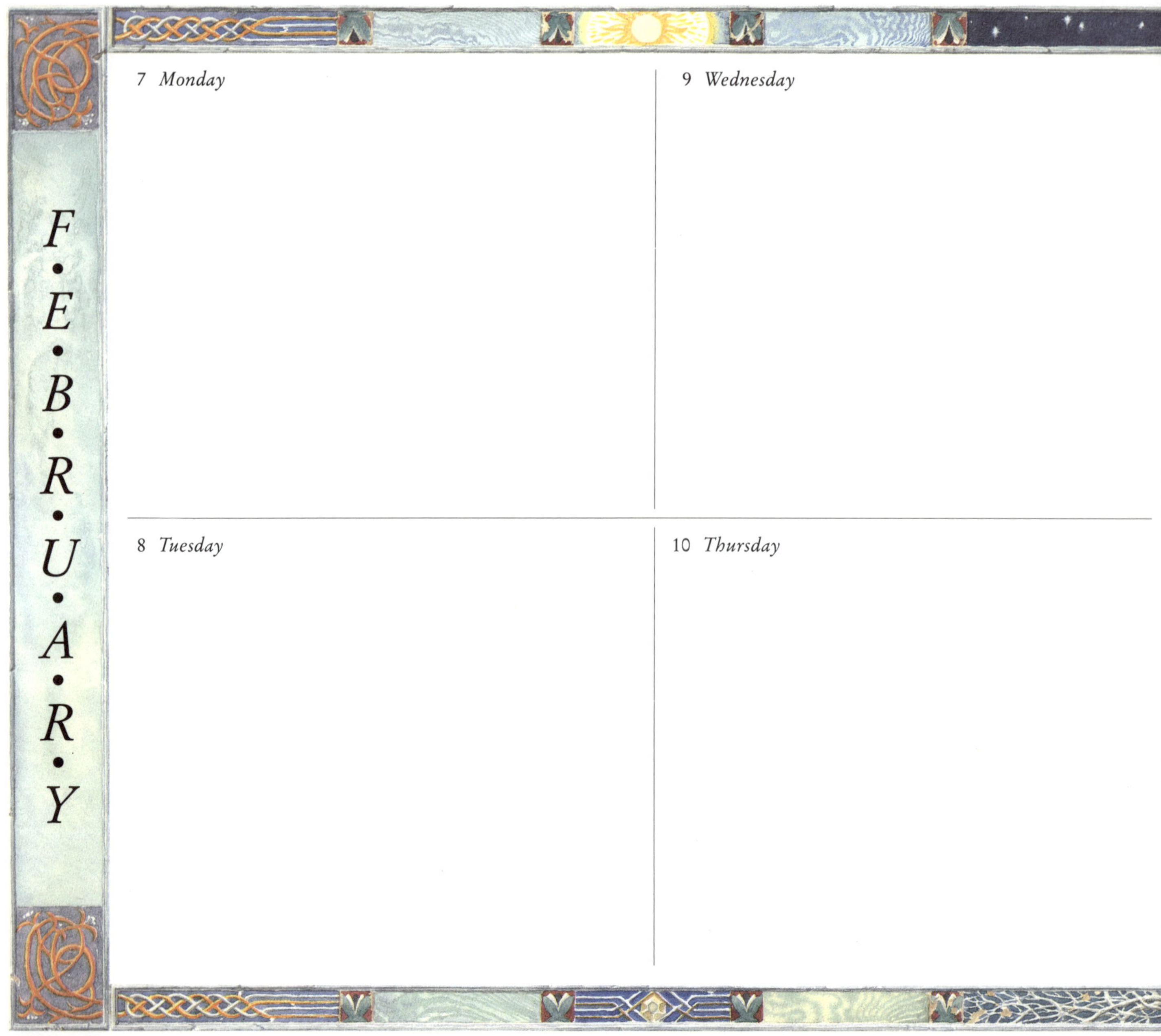

F•E•B•R•U•A•R•Y

7 *Monday*

8 *Tuesday*

9 *Wednesday*

10 *Thursday*

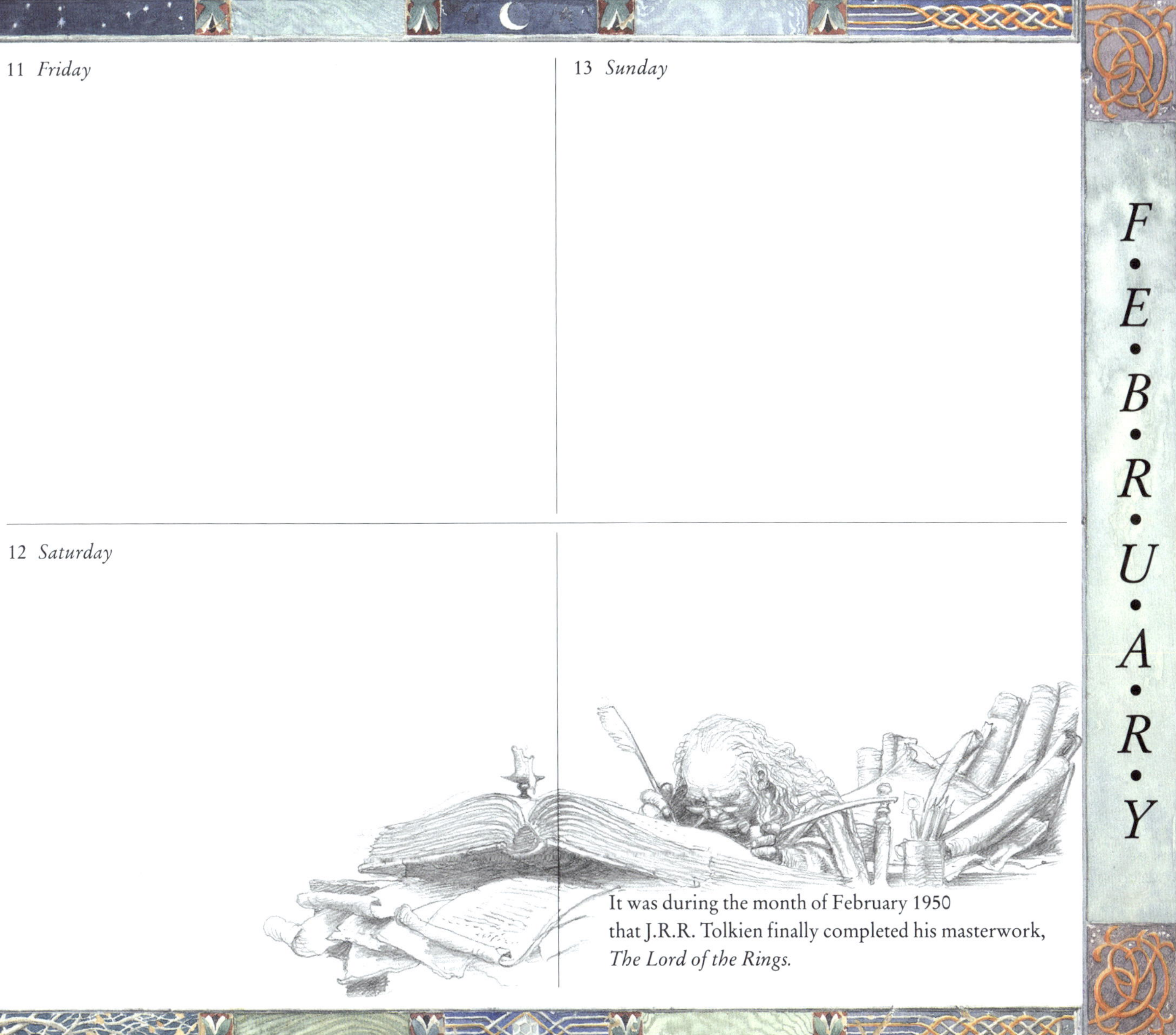

11 *Friday*

13 *Sunday*

12 *Saturday*

It was during the month of February 1950 that J.R.R. Tolkien finally completed his masterwork, *The Lord of the Rings.*

F•E•B•R•U•A•R•Y

14 *Monday*

16 *Wednesday*

15 *Tuesday*

17 *Thursday*

On 17th February S.R. 1419 Gwaihir bore Gandalf to Lórien.

18 *Friday*

20 *Sunday*

19 *Saturday*

F • E • B • R • U • A • R • Y

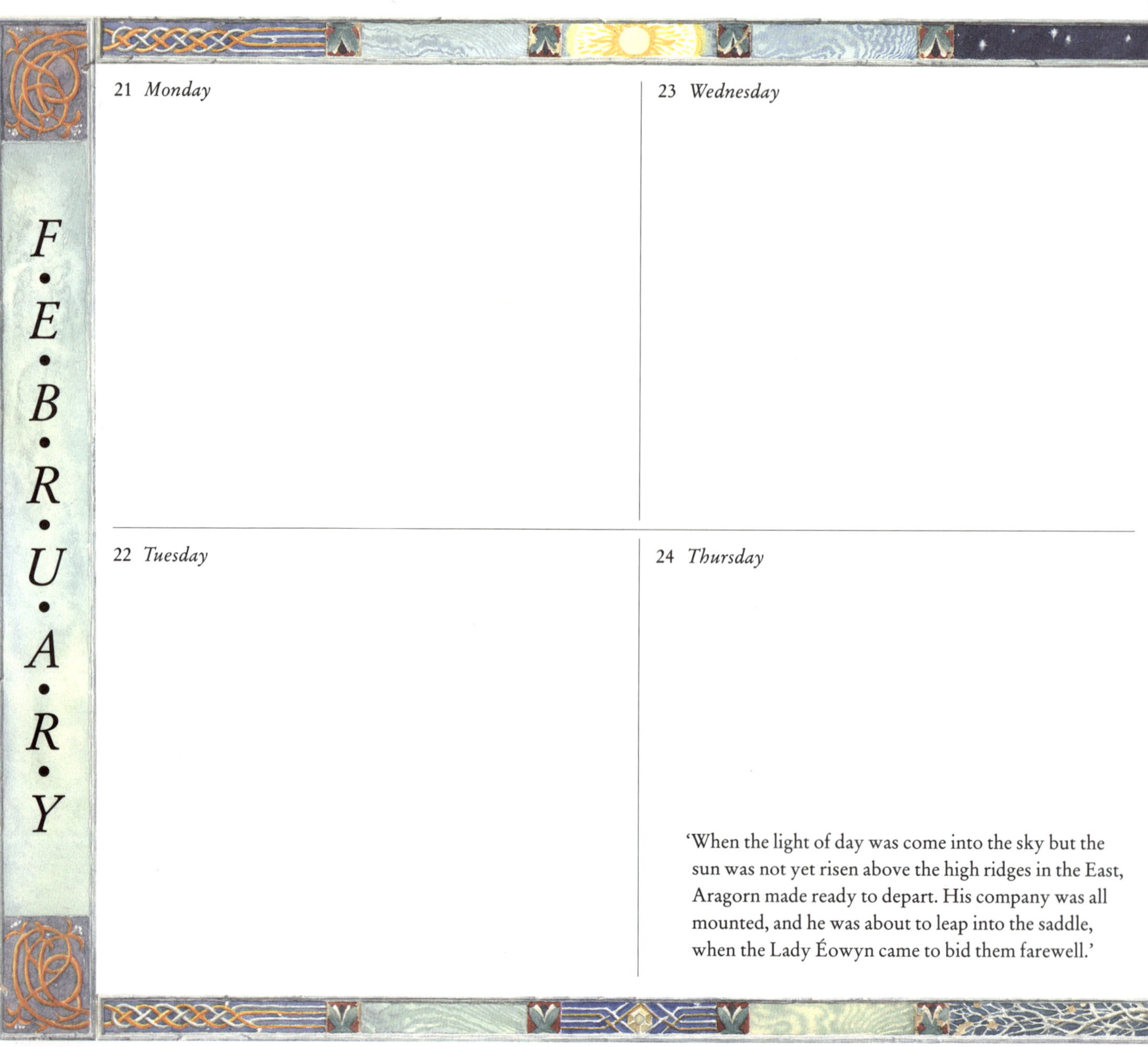

F·E·B·R·U·A·R·Y

21 *Monday*

22 *Tuesday*

23 *Wednesday*

24 *Thursday*

'When the light of day was come into the sky but the sun was not yet risen above the high ridges in the East, Aragorn made ready to depart. His company was all mounted, and he was about to leap into the saddle, when the Lady Éowyn came to bid them farewell.'

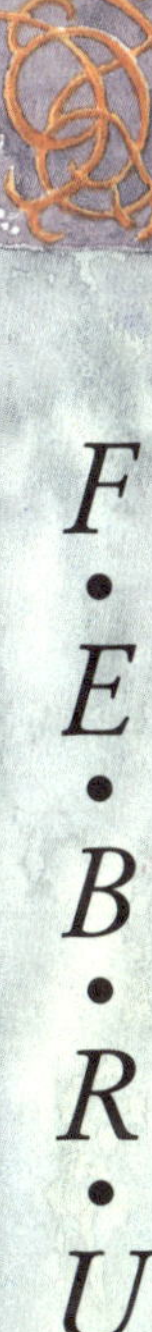
F•E•B•R•U•A•R•Y

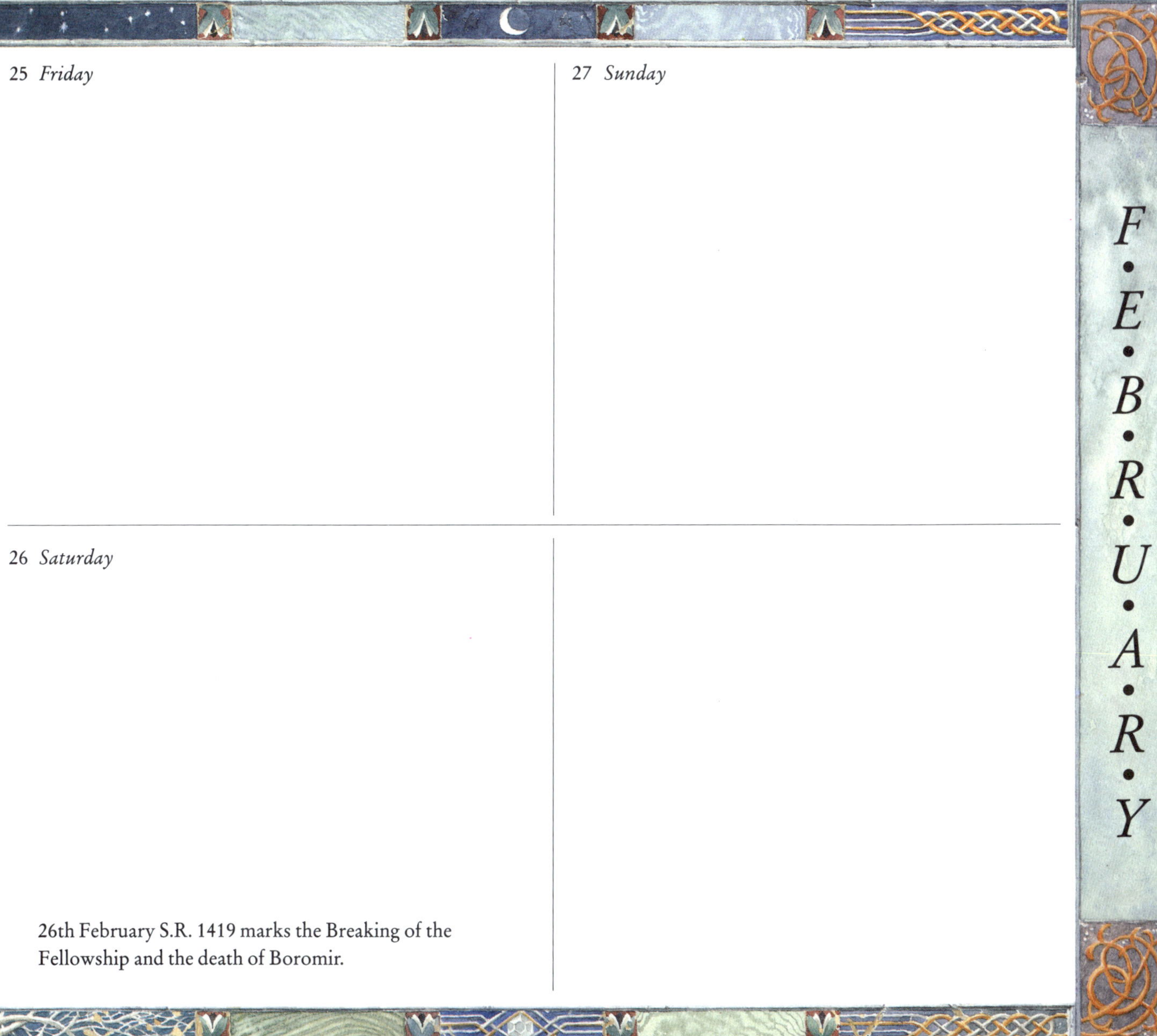

25 *Friday*

27 *Sunday*

26 *Saturday*

26th February S.R. 1419 marks the Breaking of the Fellowship and the death of Boromir.

F • E • B • R • U • A • R • Y

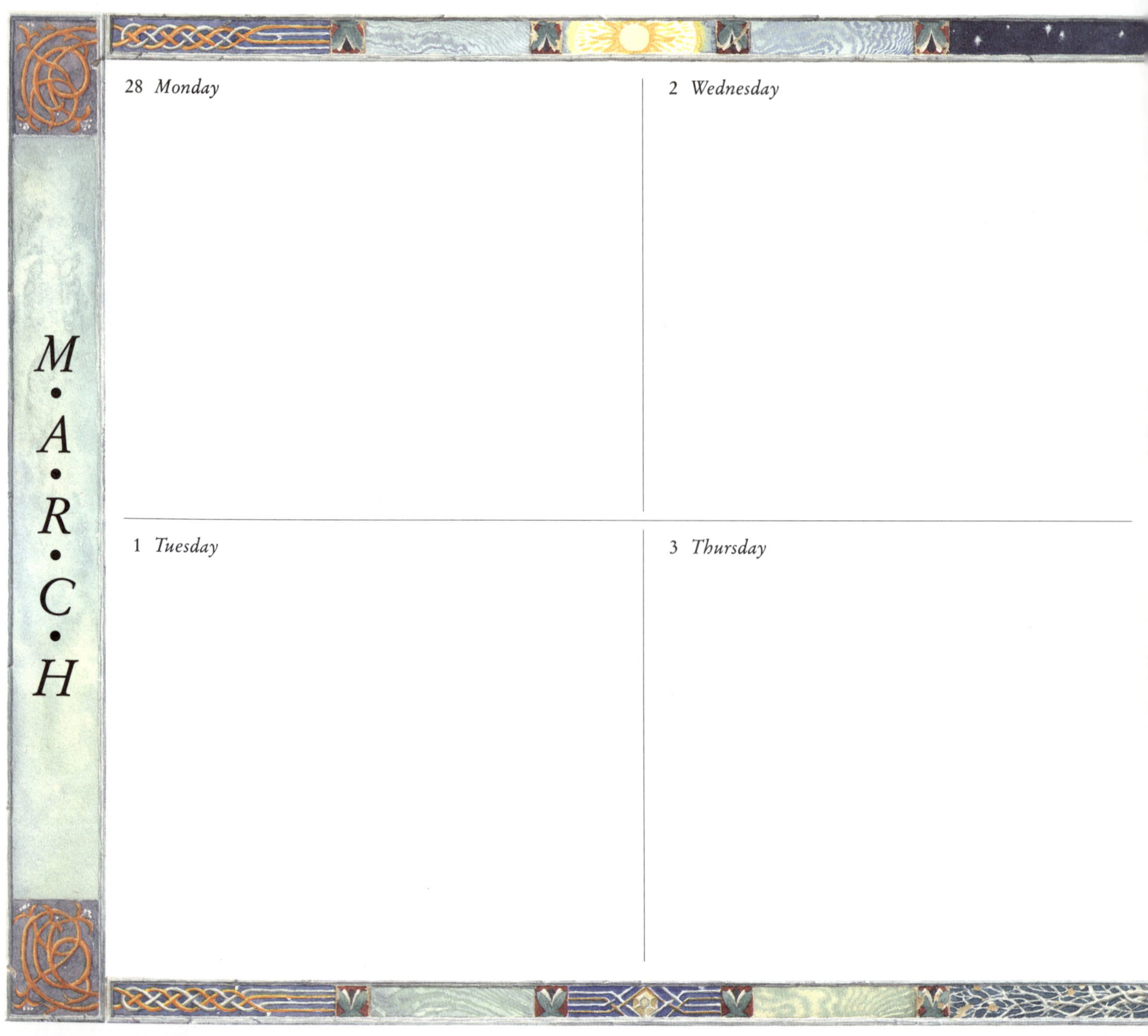

28 *Monday*

1 *Tuesday*

2 *Wednesday*

3 *Thursday*

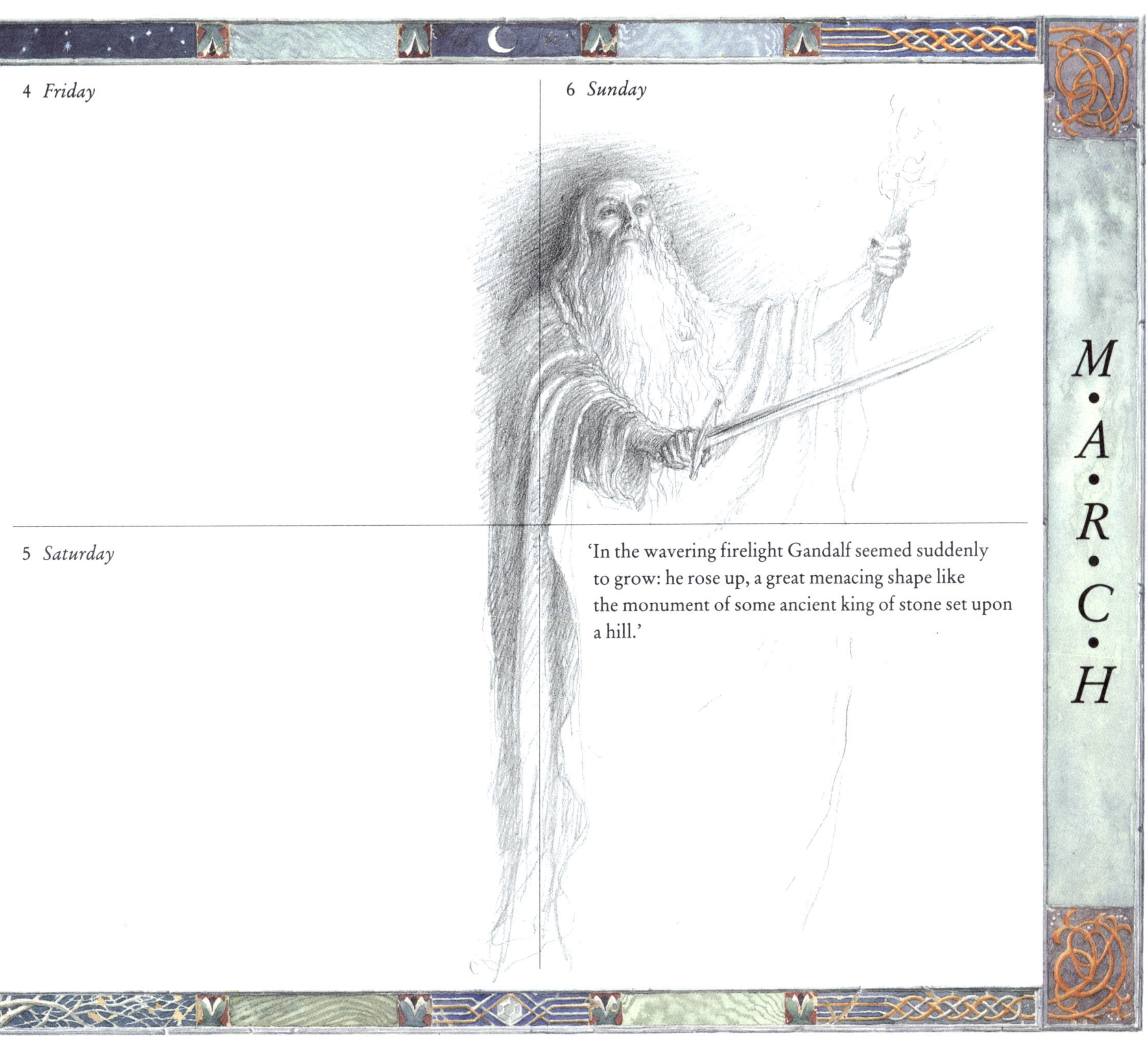

4 *Friday*

5 *Saturday*

6 *Sunday*

'In the wavering firelight Gandalf seemed suddenly to grow: he rose up, a great menacing shape like the monument of some ancient king of stone set upon a hill.'

M·A·R·C·H

M·A·R·C·H

7 *Monday*

8 *Tuesday*

9 *Wednesday*

10 *Thursday*

11 *Friday*

13 *Sunday*

12 *Saturday*

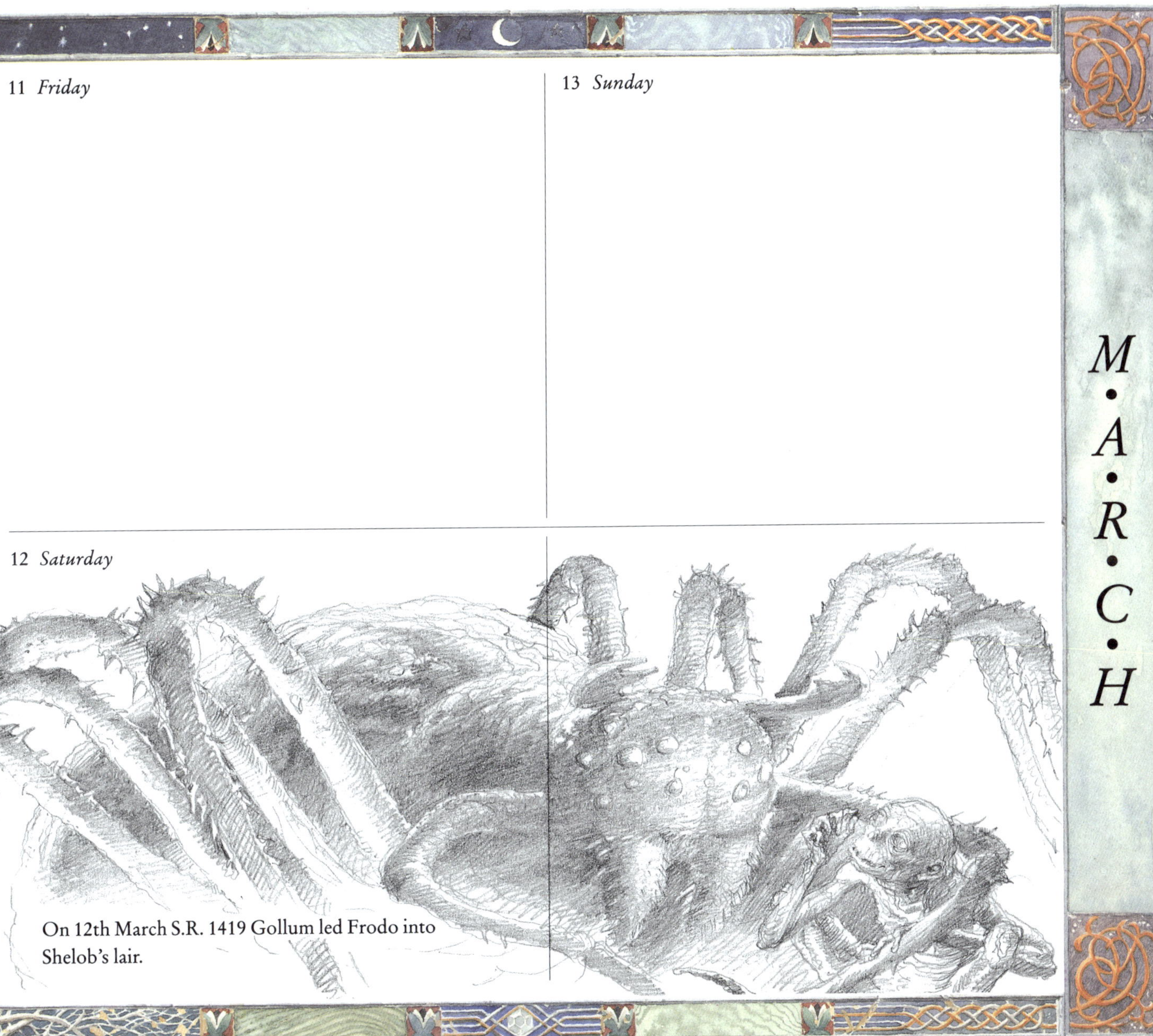

On 12th March S.R. 1419 Gollum led Frodo into Shelob's lair.

M•A•R•C•H

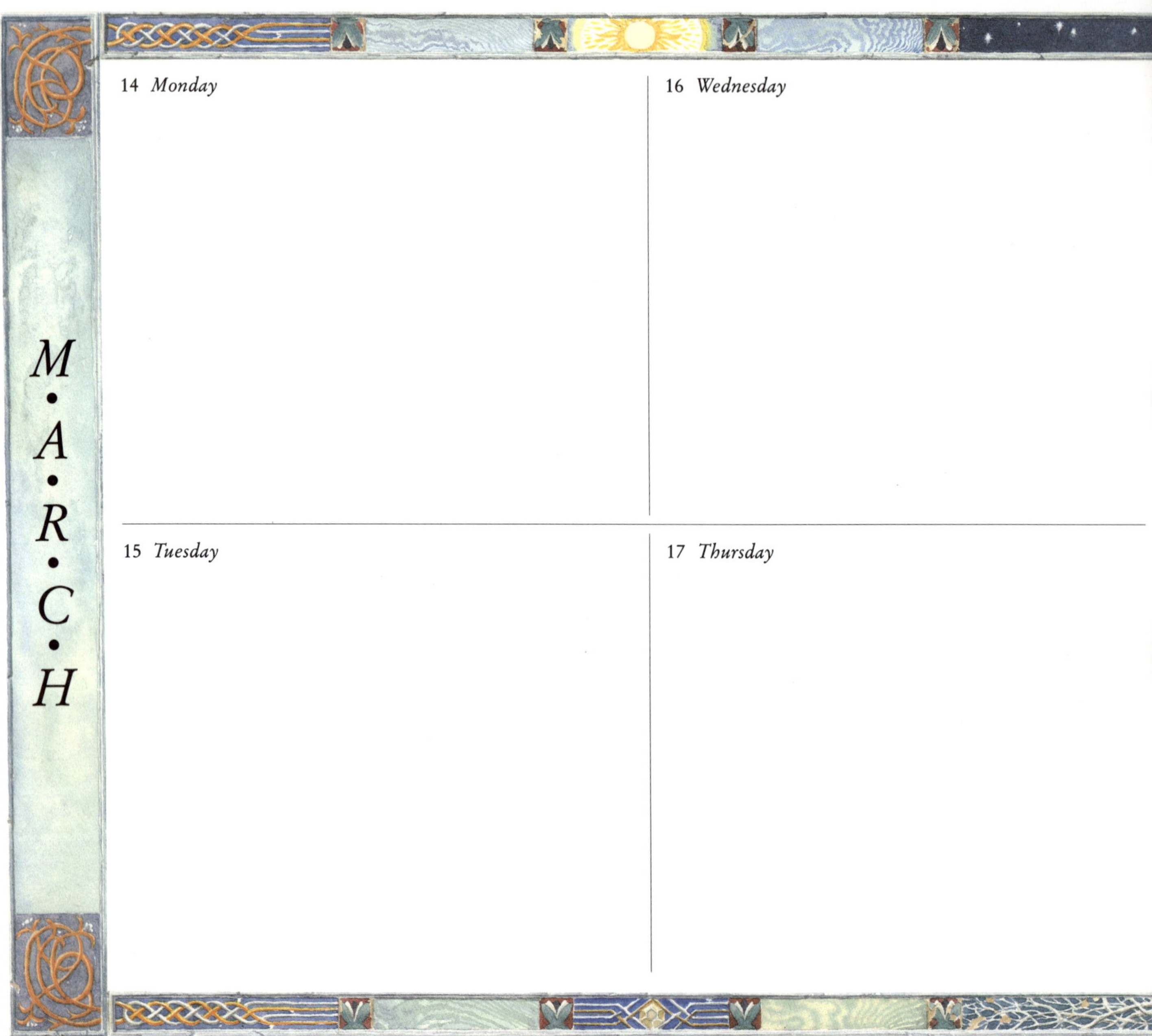

14 *Monday*

15 *Tuesday*

16 *Wednesday*

17 *Thursday*

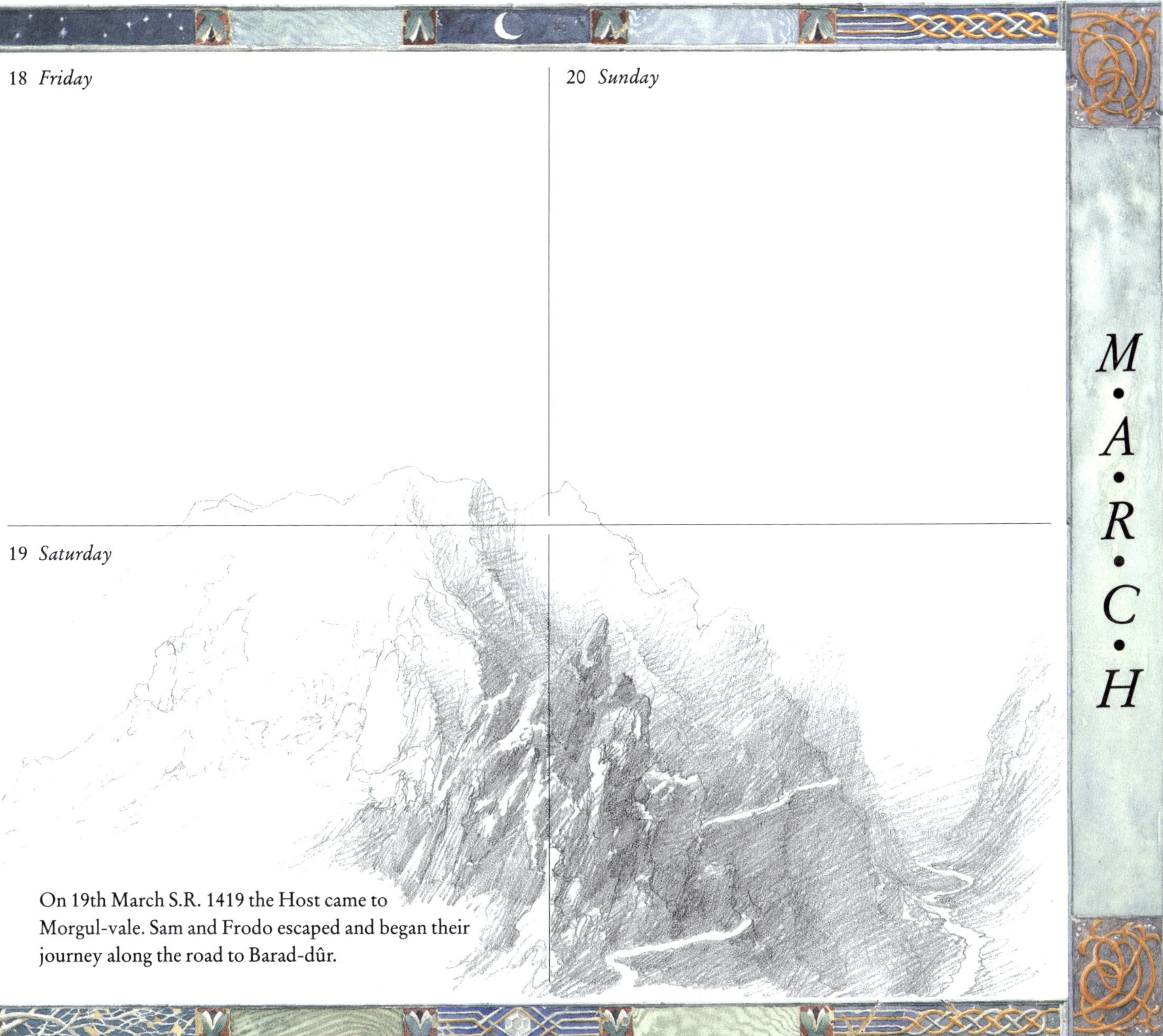

18 *Friday*

20 *Sunday*

19 *Saturday*

On 19th March S.R. 1419 the Host came to Morgul-vale. Sam and Frodo escaped and began their journey along the road to Barad-dûr.

M·A·R·C·H

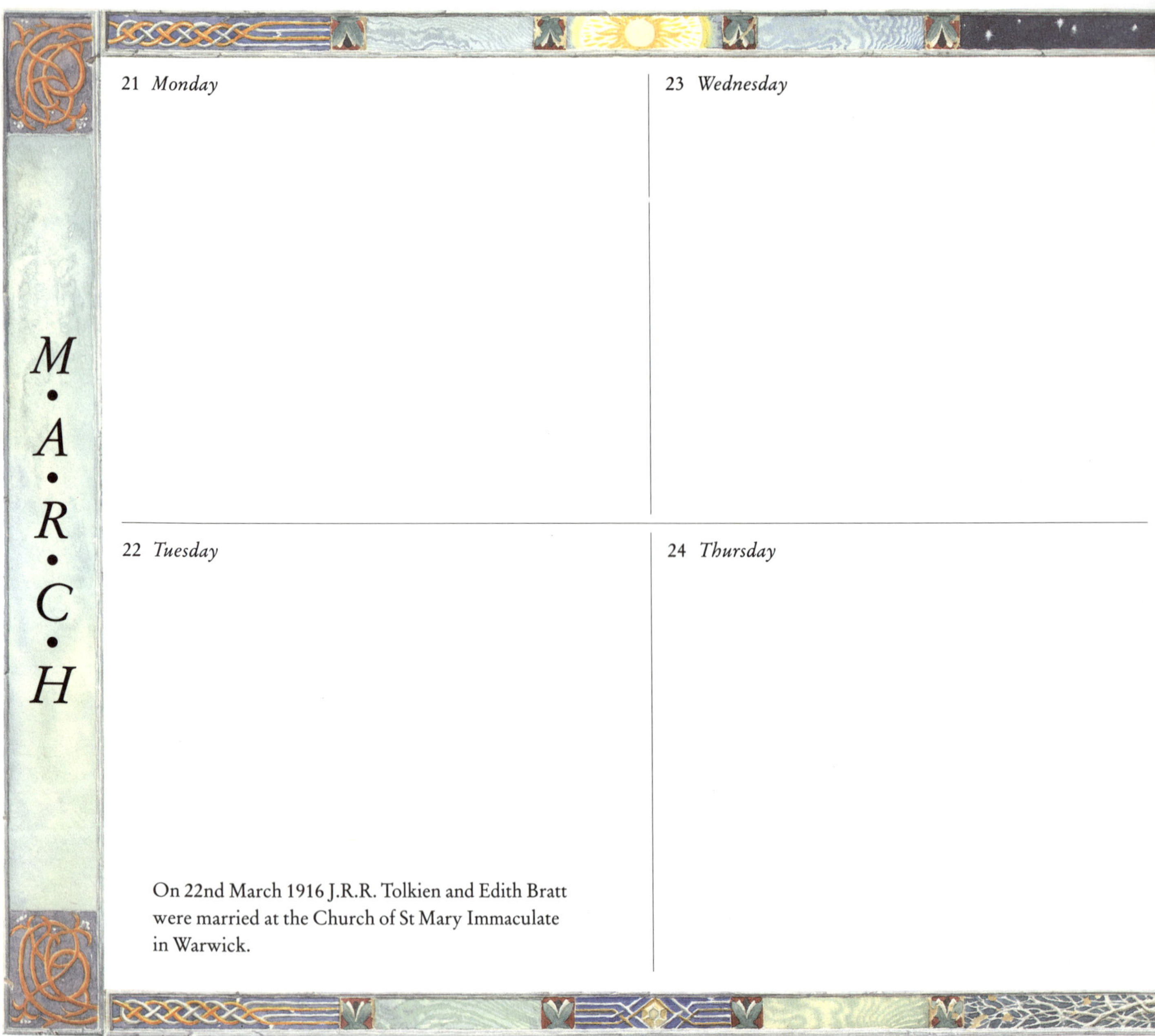

M·A·R·C·H

21 *Monday*

22 *Tuesday*

On 22nd March 1916 J.R.R. Tolkien and Edith Bratt were married at the Church of St Mary Immaculate in Warwick.

23 *Wednesday*

24 *Thursday*

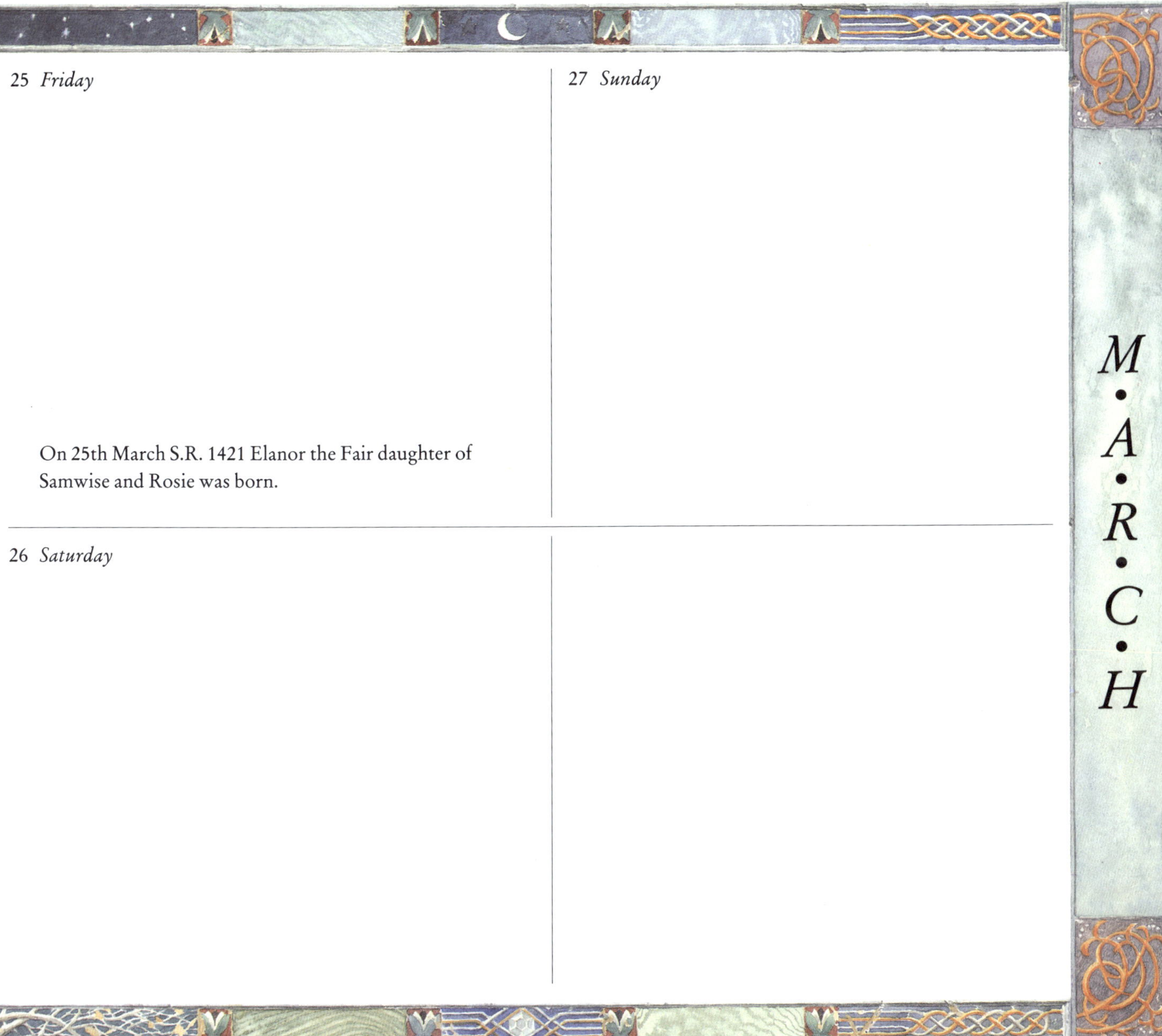

25 *Friday*

On 25th March S.R. 1421 Elanor the Fair daughter of Samwise and Rosie was born.

27 *Sunday*

26 *Saturday*

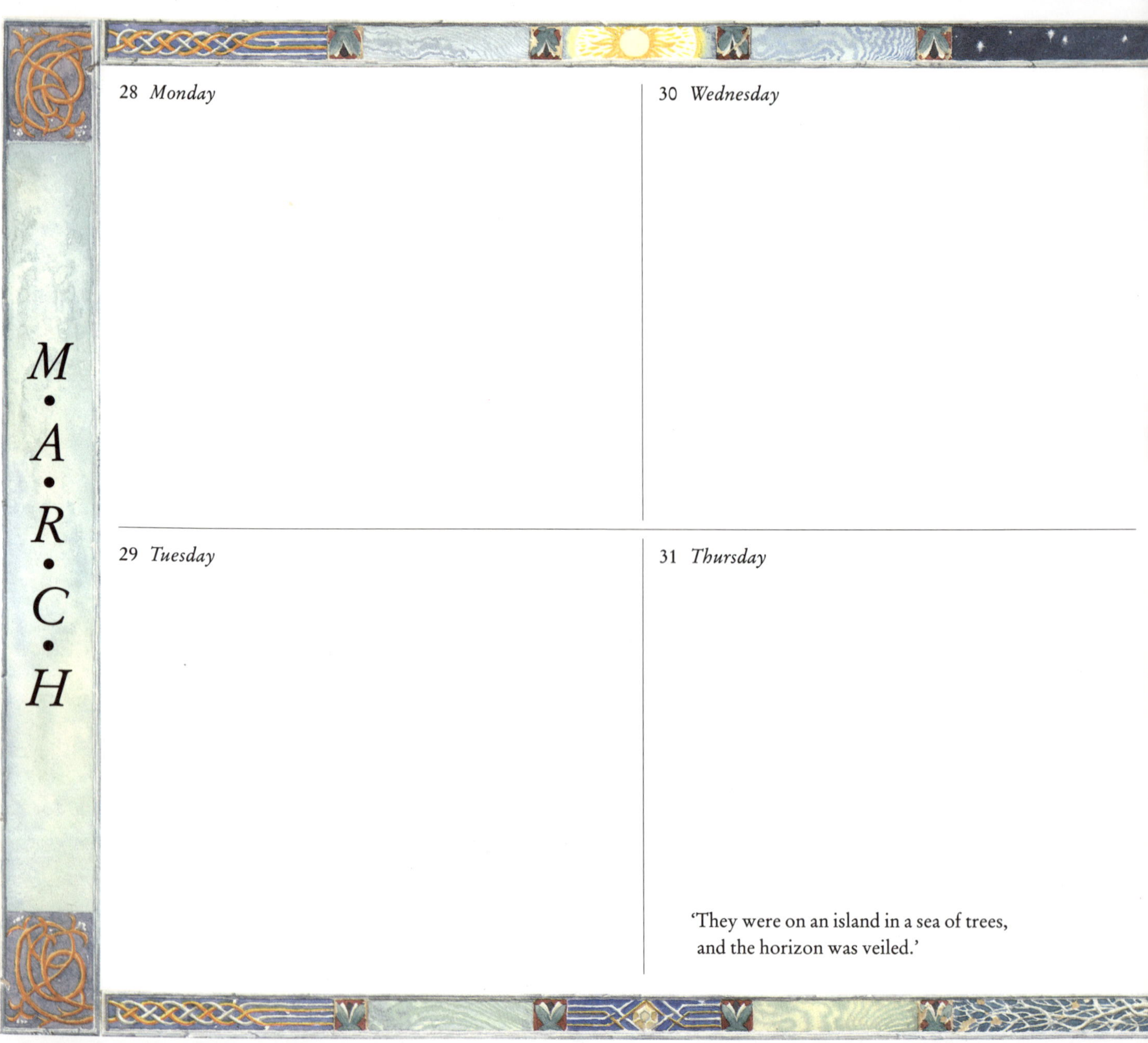

28 *Monday*

30 *Wednesday*

29 *Tuesday*

31 *Thursday*

'They were on an island in a sea of trees, and the horizon was veiled.'

M·A·R·C·H

1 *Friday*

3 *Sunday*

2 *Saturday*

A • P • R • I • L

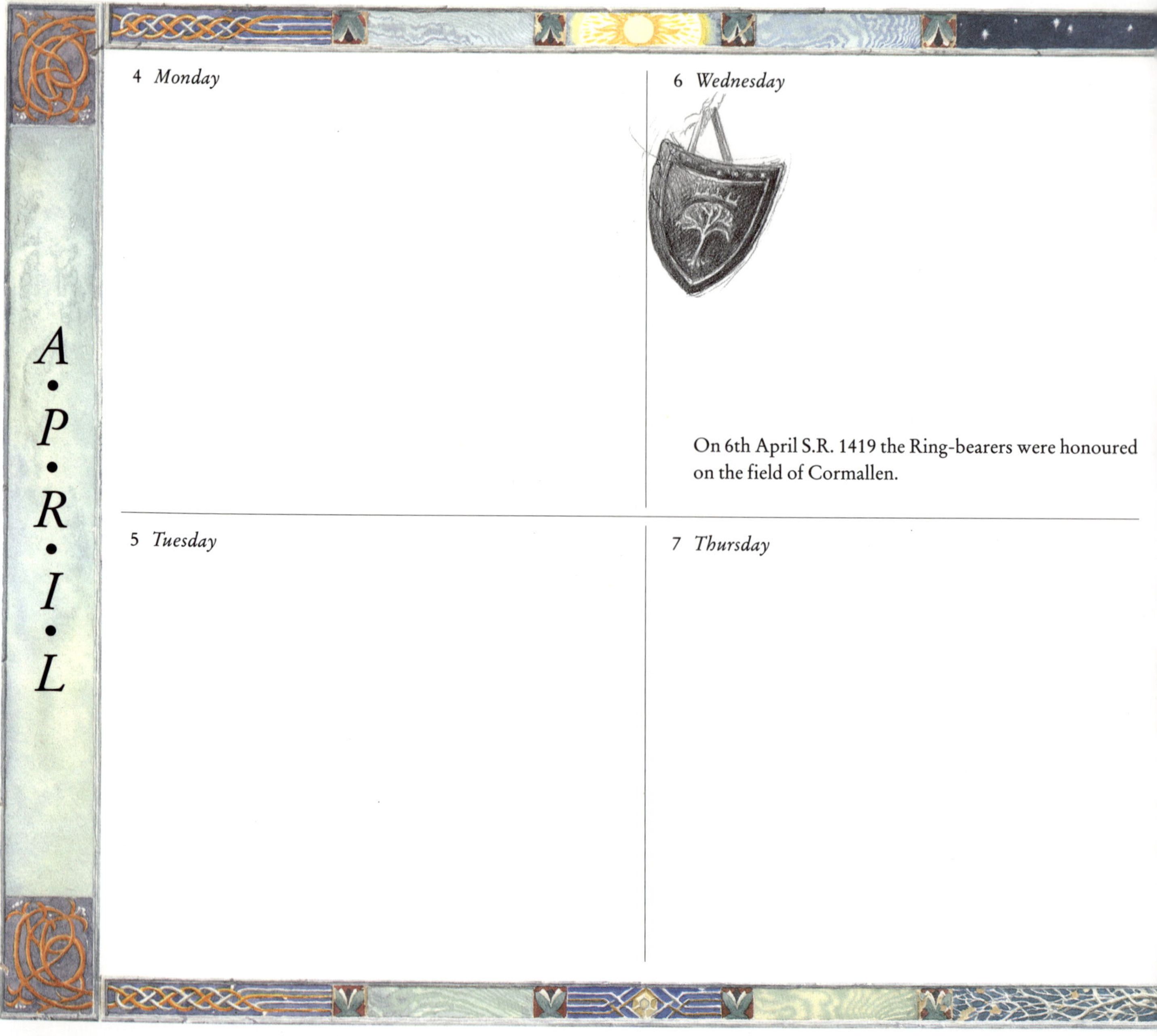

A·P·R·I·L

4 *Monday*

5 *Tuesday*

6 *Wednesday*

On 6th April S.R. 1419 the Ring-bearers were honoured on the field of Cormallen.

7 *Thursday*

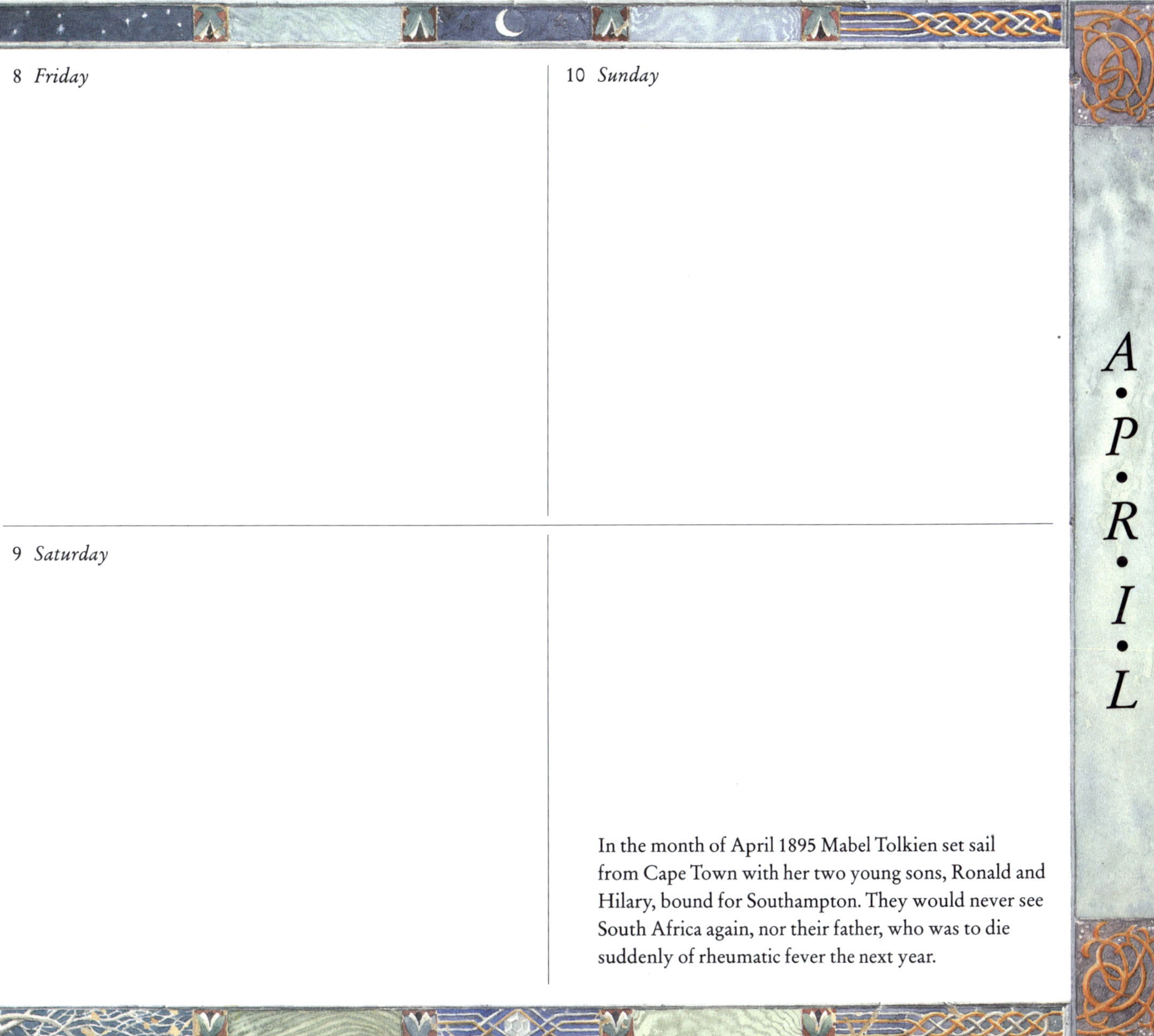

8 *Friday*

9 *Saturday*

10 *Sunday*

In the month of April 1895 Mabel Tolkien set sail from Cape Town with her two young sons, Ronald and Hilary, bound for Southampton. They would never see South Africa again, nor their father, who was to die suddenly of rheumatic fever the next year.

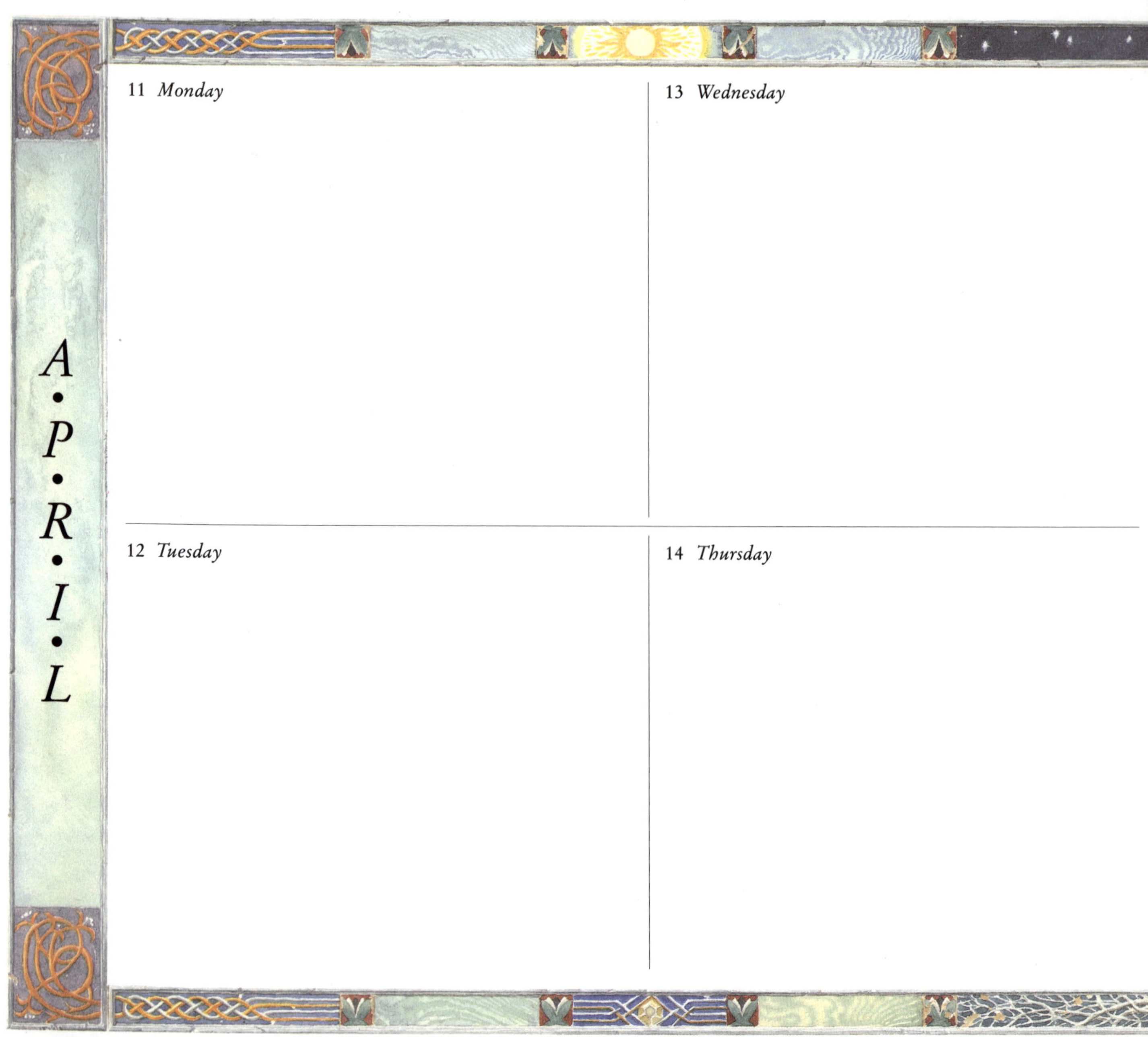

11 *Monday*

12 *Tuesday*

13 *Wednesday*

14 *Thursday*

15 *Friday*

17 *Sunday*

16 *Saturday*

A • P • R • I • L

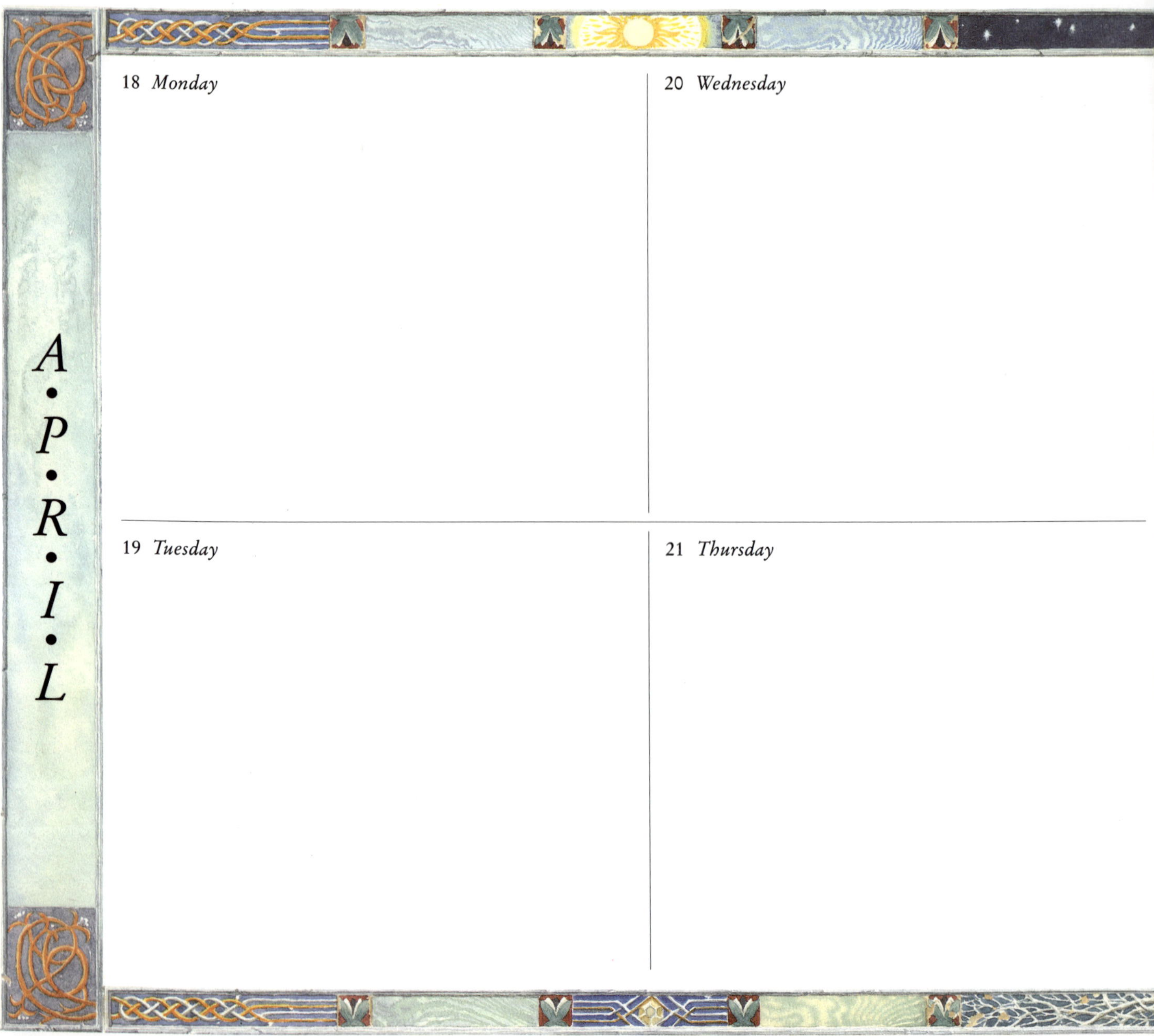

A • P • R • I • L

18 *Monday*

20 *Wednesday*

19 *Tuesday*

21 *Thursday*

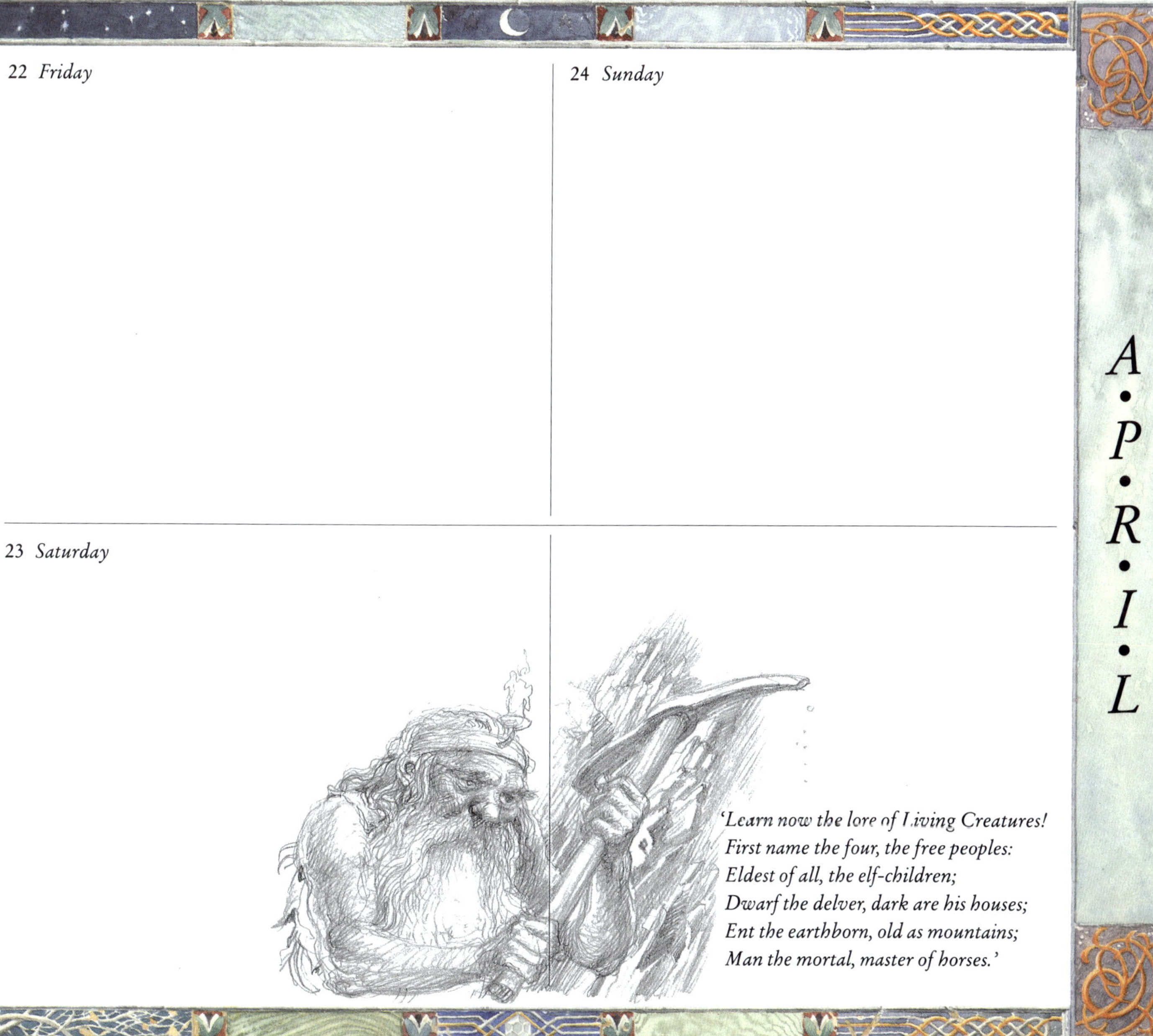

22 *Friday*

24 *Sunday*

23 *Saturday*

'Learn now the lore of Living Creatures!
First name the four, the free peoples:
Eldest of all, the elf-children;
Dwarf the delver, dark are his houses;
Ent the earthborn, old as mountains;
Man the mortal, master of horses.'

A·P·R·I·L

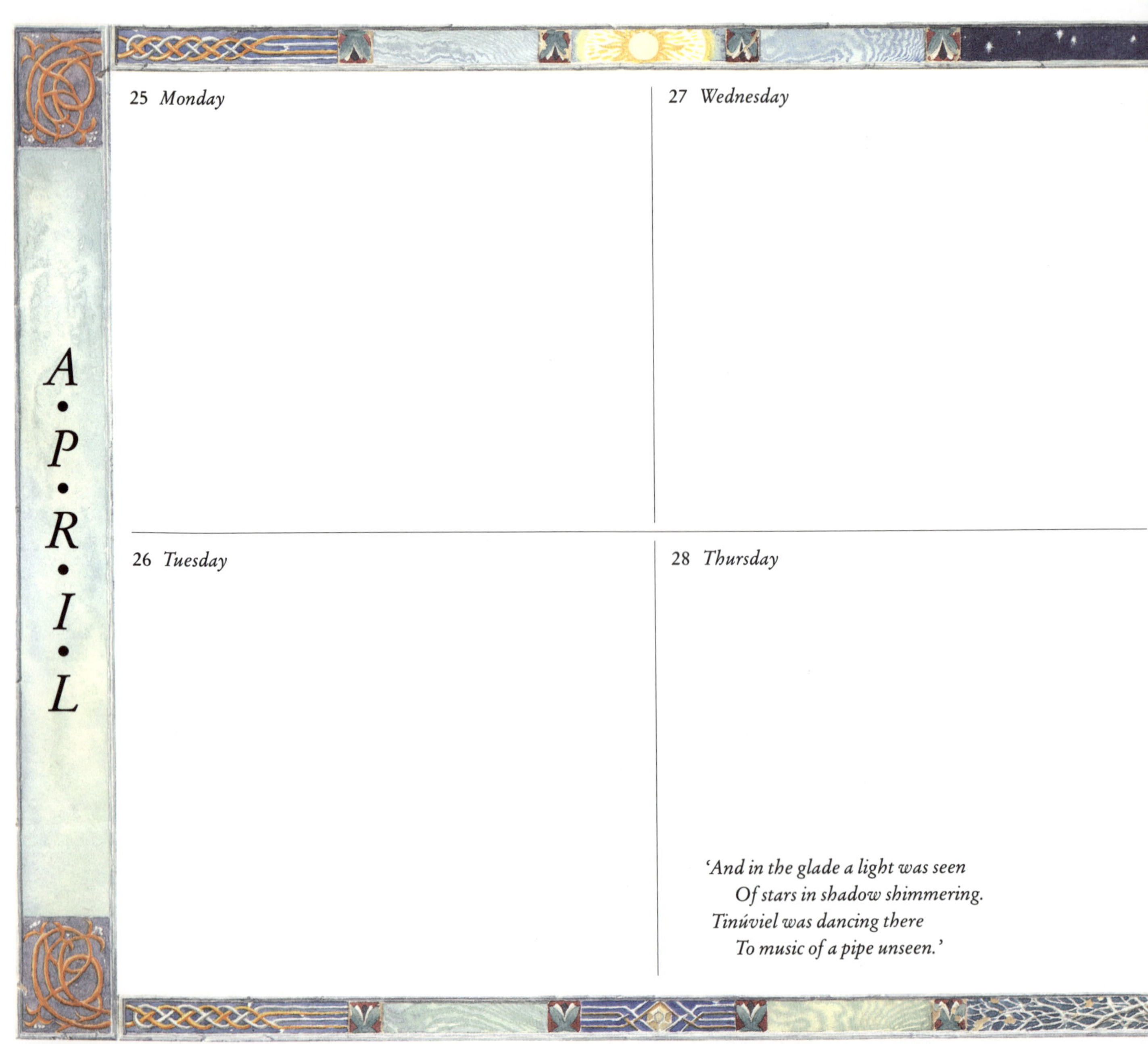

A•P•R•I•L

25 *Monday*

26 *Tuesday*

27 *Wednesday*

28 *Thursday*

'And in the glade a light was seen
Of stars in shadow shimmering.
Tinúviel was dancing there
To music of a pipe unseen.'

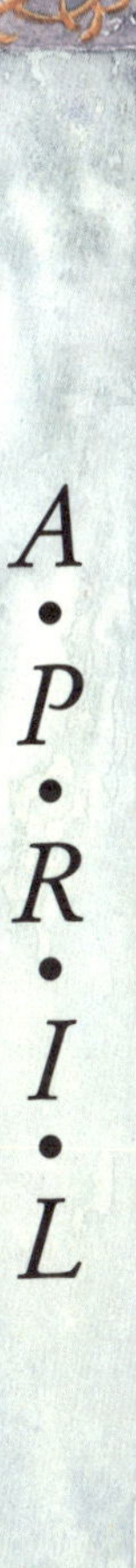
A • P • R • I • L

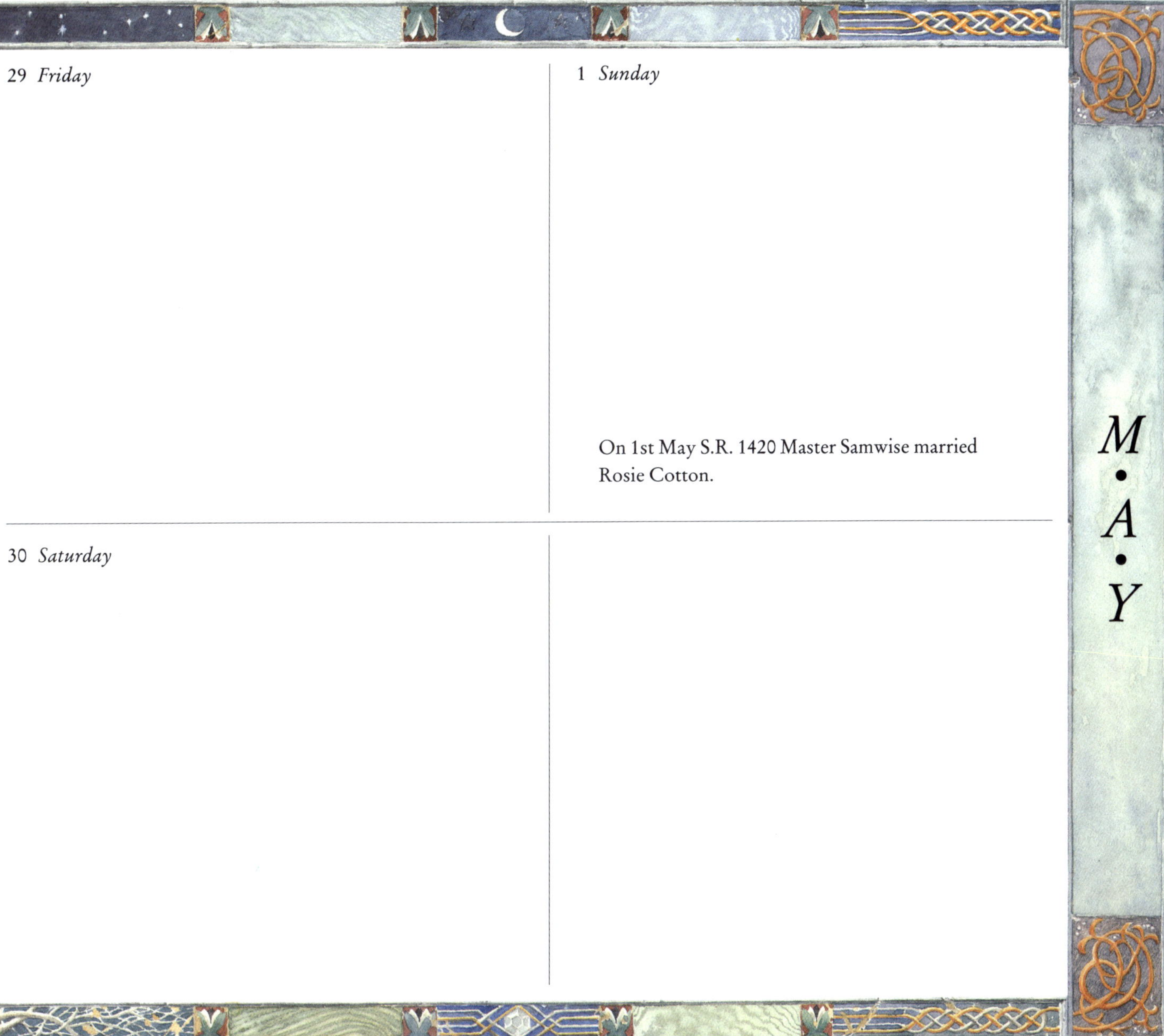

29 *Friday*

1 *Sunday*

On 1st May S.R. 1420 Master Samwise married Rosie Cotton.

30 *Saturday*

M • A • Y

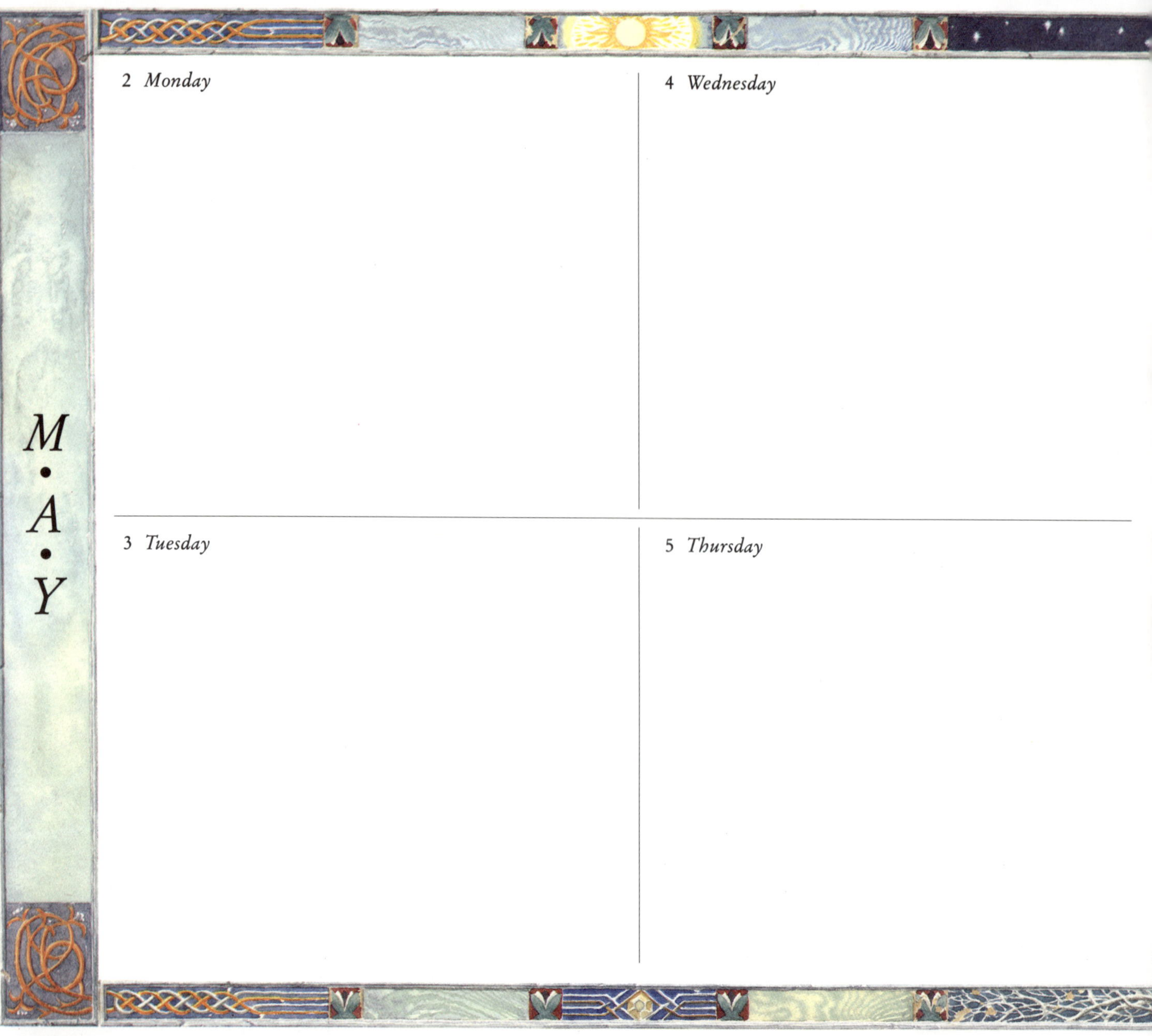

M·A·Y

2 *Monday*

3 *Tuesday*

4 *Wednesday*

5 *Thursday*

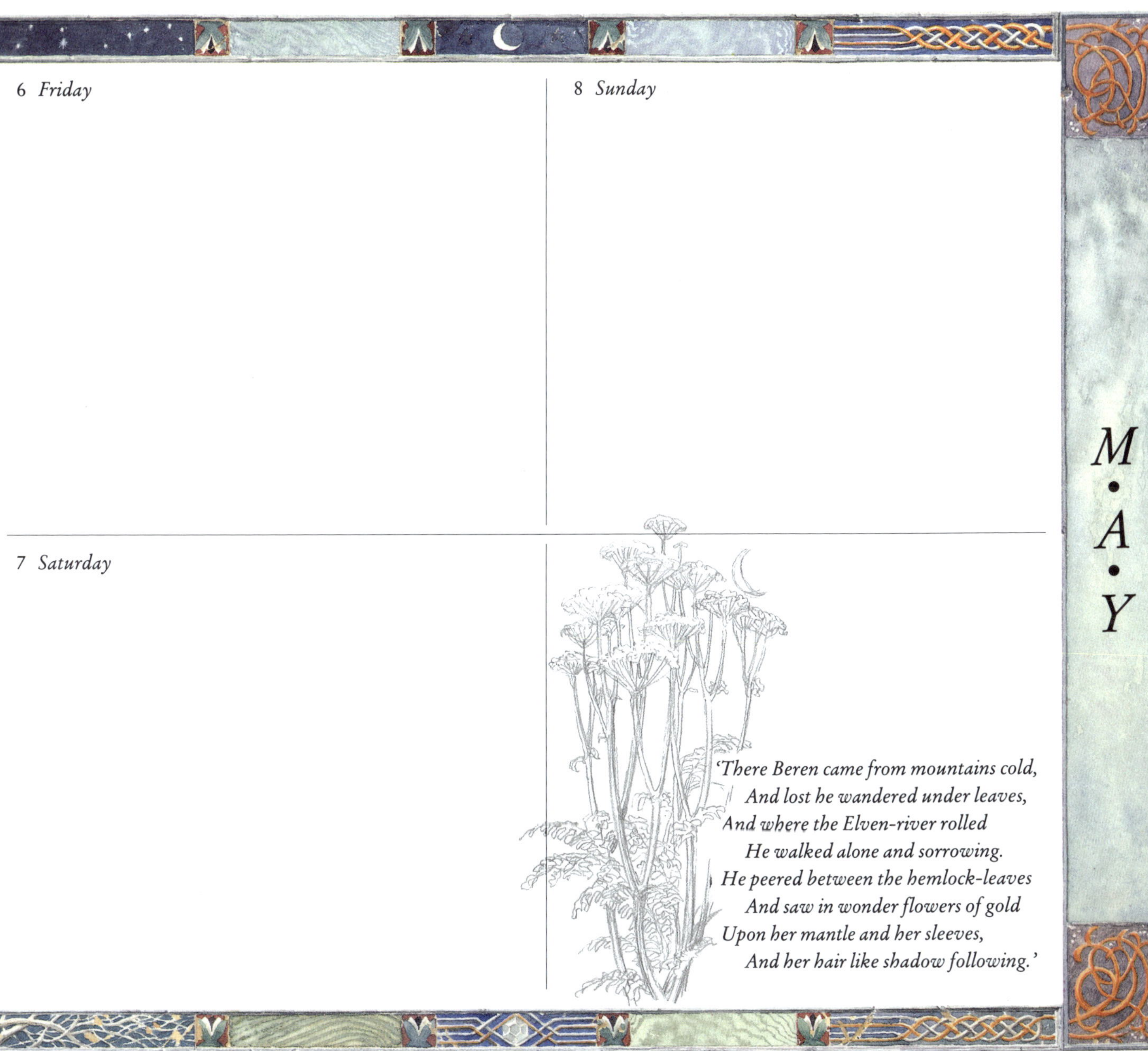

6 *Friday*

8 *Sunday*

7 *Saturday*

'There Beren came from mountains cold,
And lost he wandered under leaves,
And where the Elven-river rolled
He walked alone and sorrowing.
He peered between the hemlock-leaves
And saw in wonder flowers of gold
Upon her mantle and her sleeves,
And her hair like shadow following.'

M·A·Y

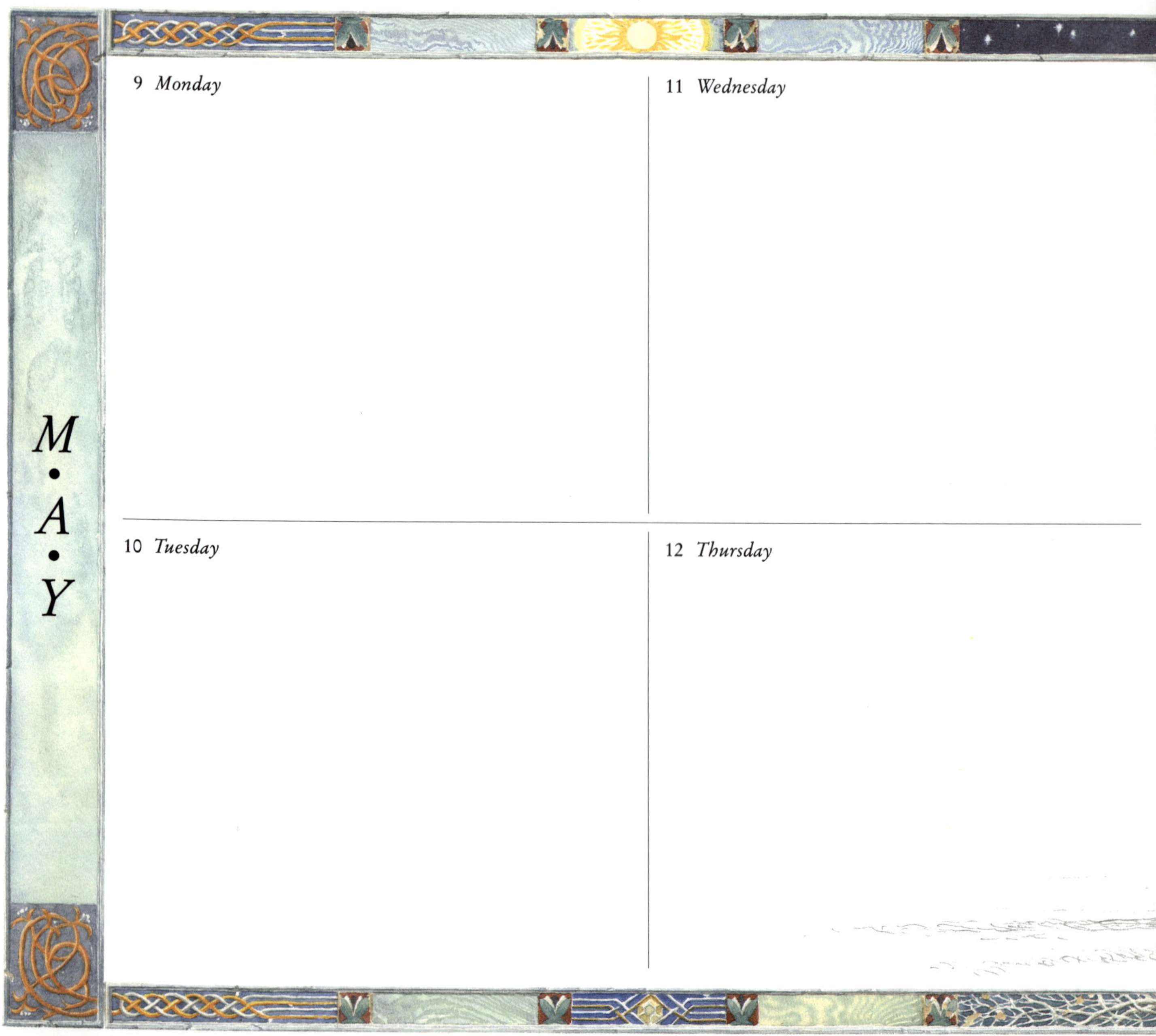

M·A·Y

9 *Monday*

10 *Tuesday*

11 *Wednesday*

12 *Thursday*

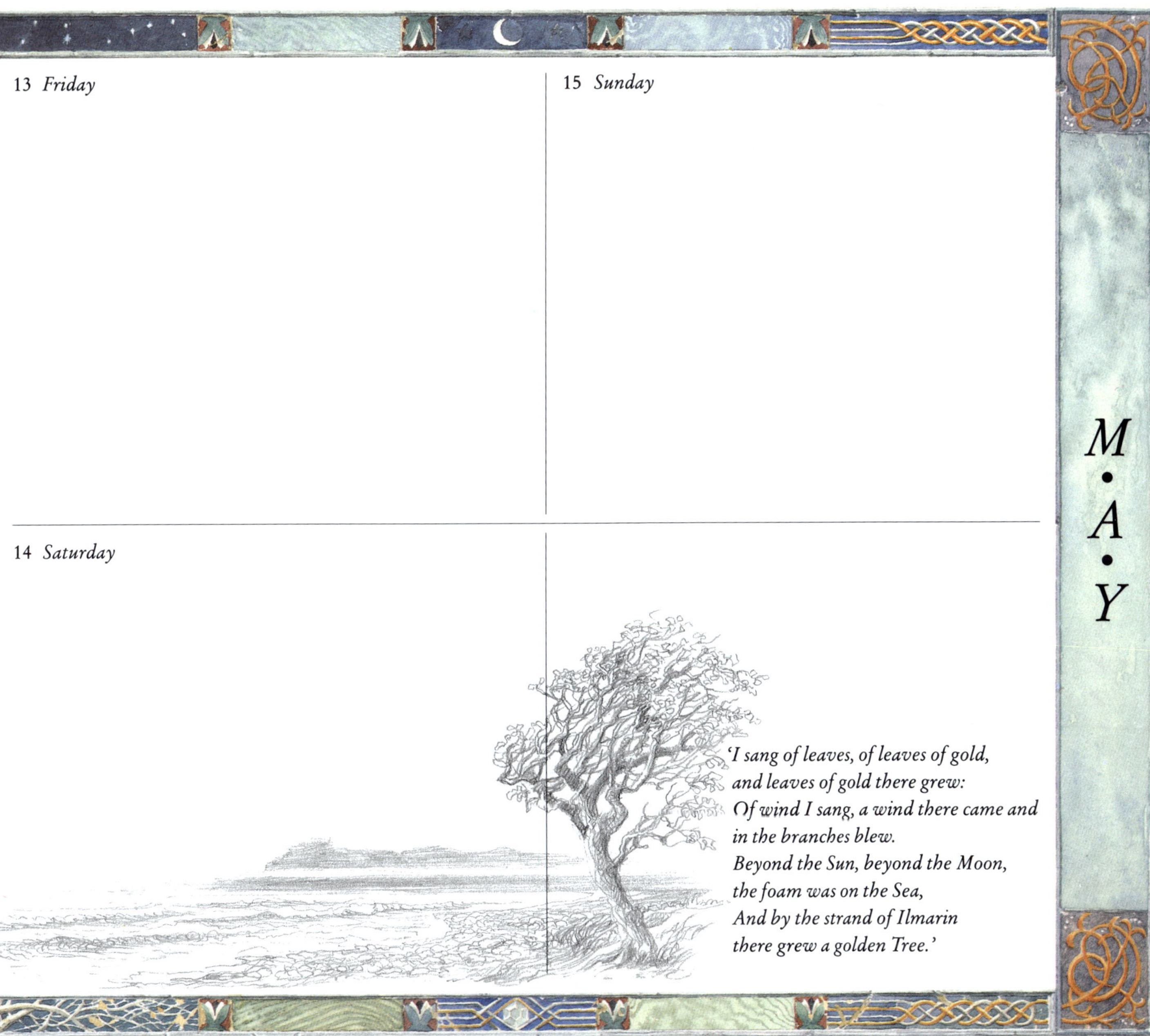

13 *Friday*

15 *Sunday*

14 *Saturday*

'I sang of leaves, of leaves of gold,
and leaves of gold there grew:
Of wind I sang, a wind there came and
in the branches blew.
Beyond the Sun, beyond the Moon,
the foam was on the Sea,
And by the strand of Ilmarin
there grew a golden Tree.'

M·A·Y

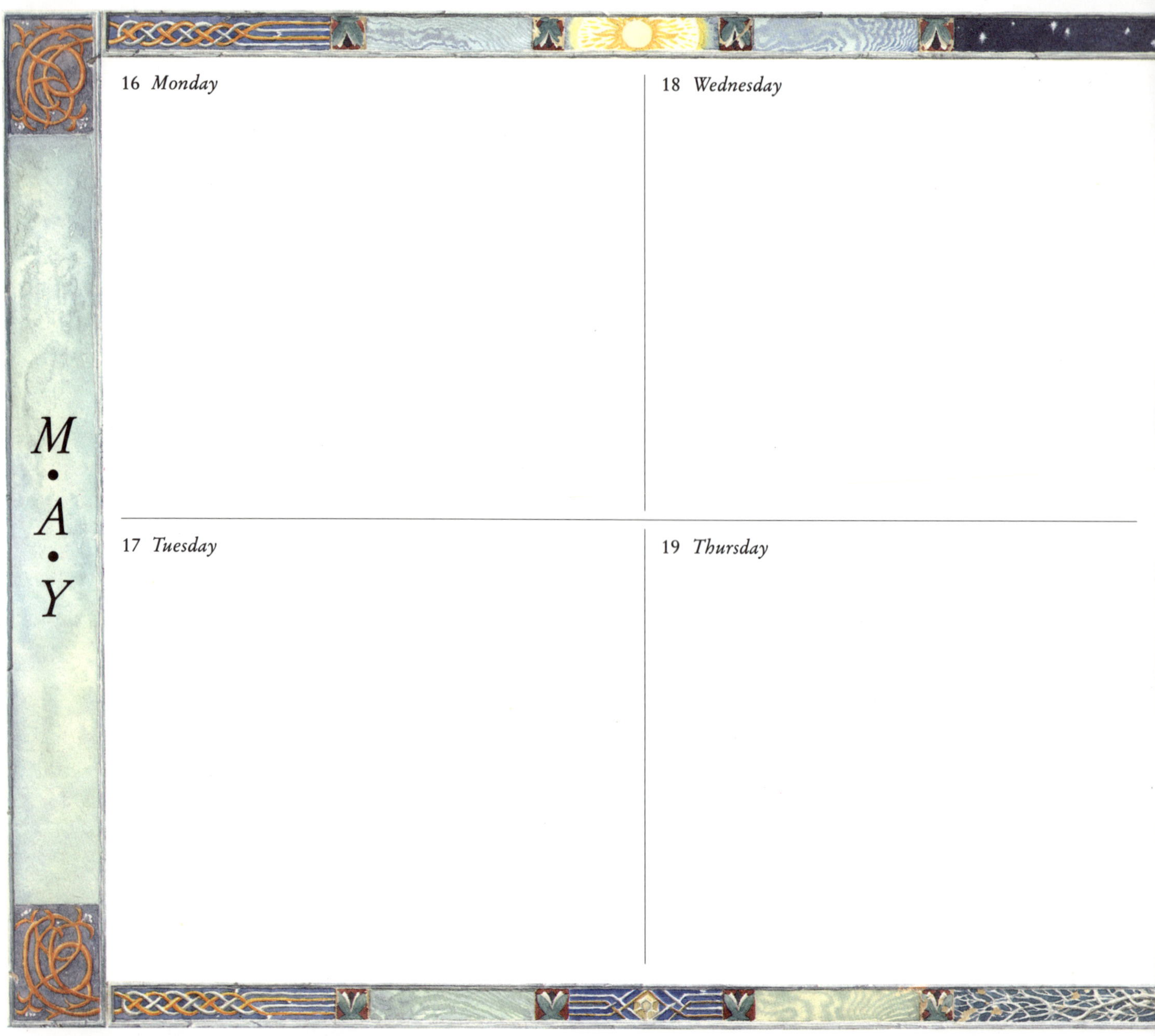

M • A • Y

16 *Monday*

17 *Tuesday*

18 *Wednesday*

19 *Thursday*

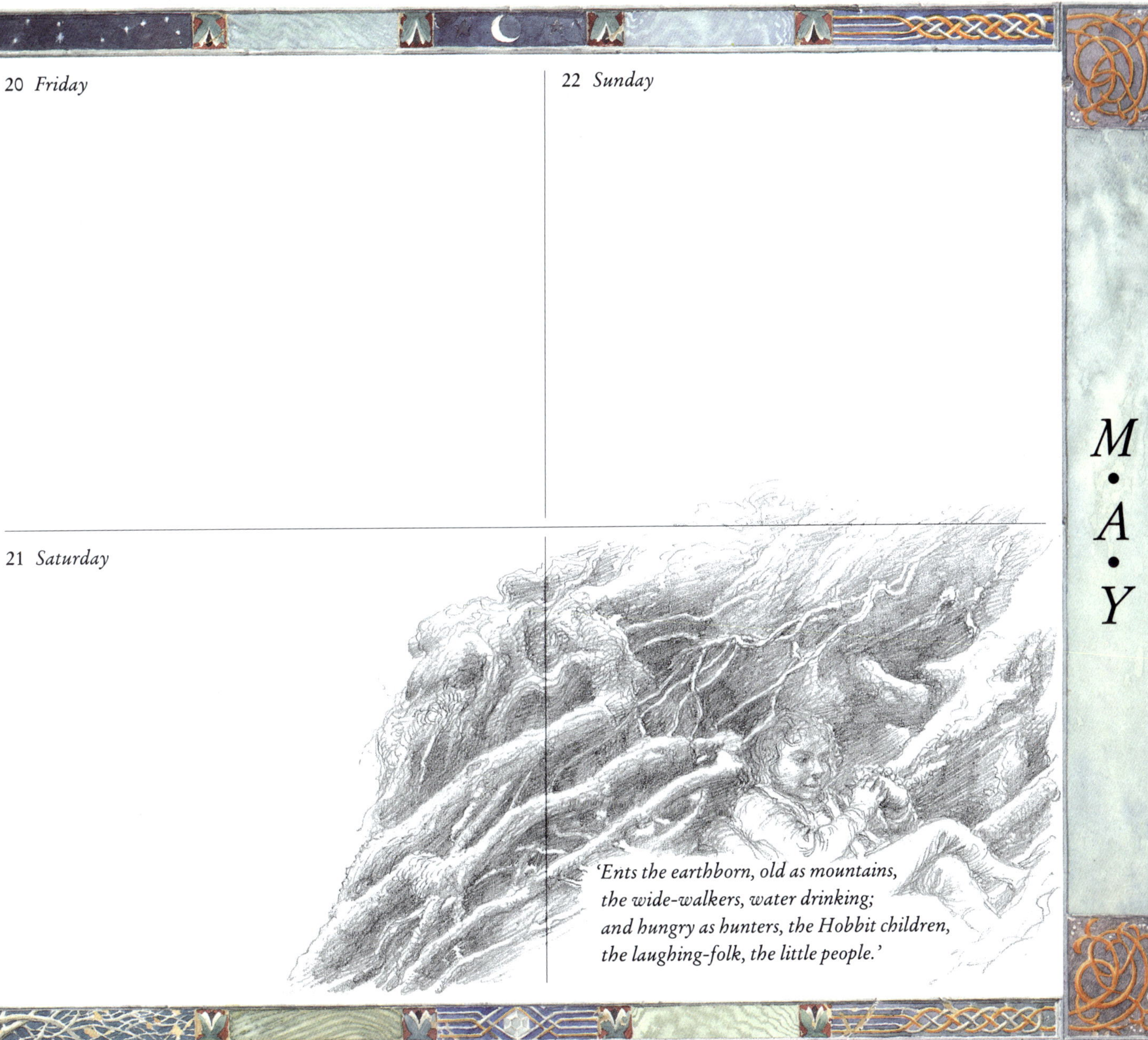

20 *Friday*

22 *Sunday*

21 *Saturday*

'Ents the earthborn, old as mountains,
the wide-walkers, water drinking;
and hungry as hunters, the Hobbit children,
the laughing-folk, the little people.'

M • A • Y

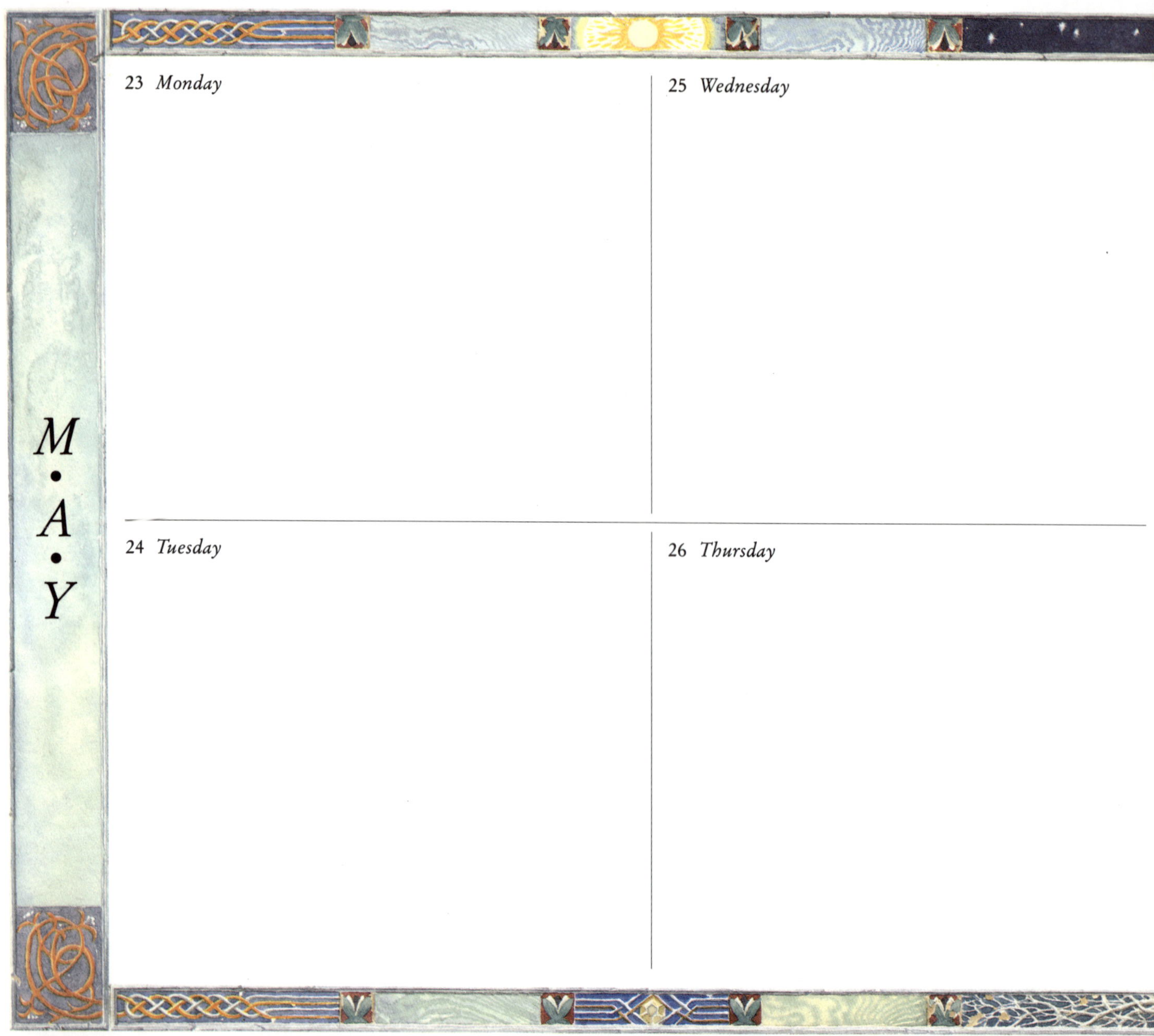

23 *Monday*

24 *Tuesday*

25 *Wednesday*

26 *Thursday*

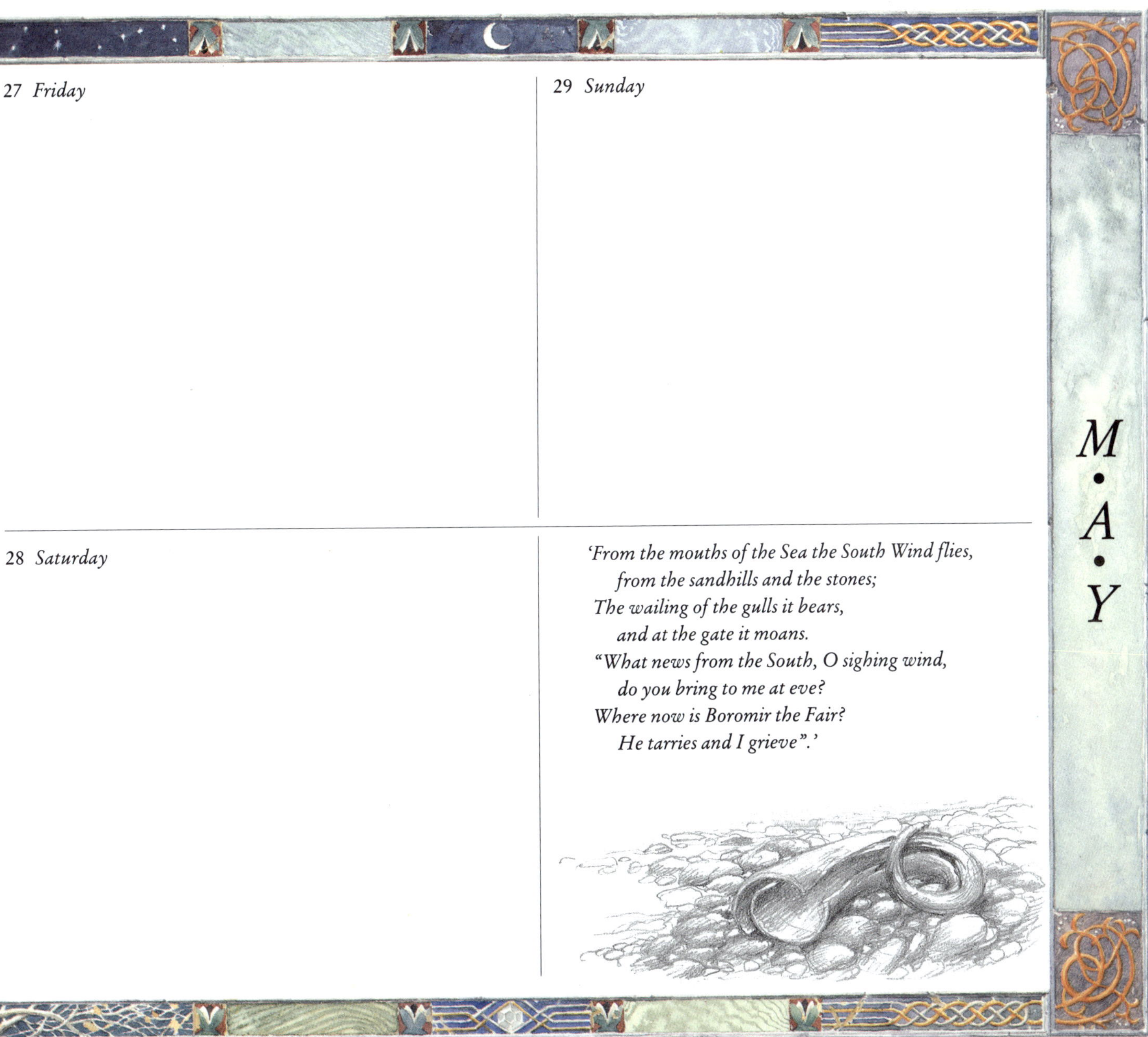

27 *Friday*

29 *Sunday*

28 *Saturday*

'From the mouths of the Sea the South Wind flies,
from the sandhills and the stones;
The wailing of the gulls it bears,
and at the gate it moans.
"What news from the South, O sighing wind,
do you bring to me at eve?
Where now is Boromir the Fair?
He tarries and I grieve".'

M·A·Y

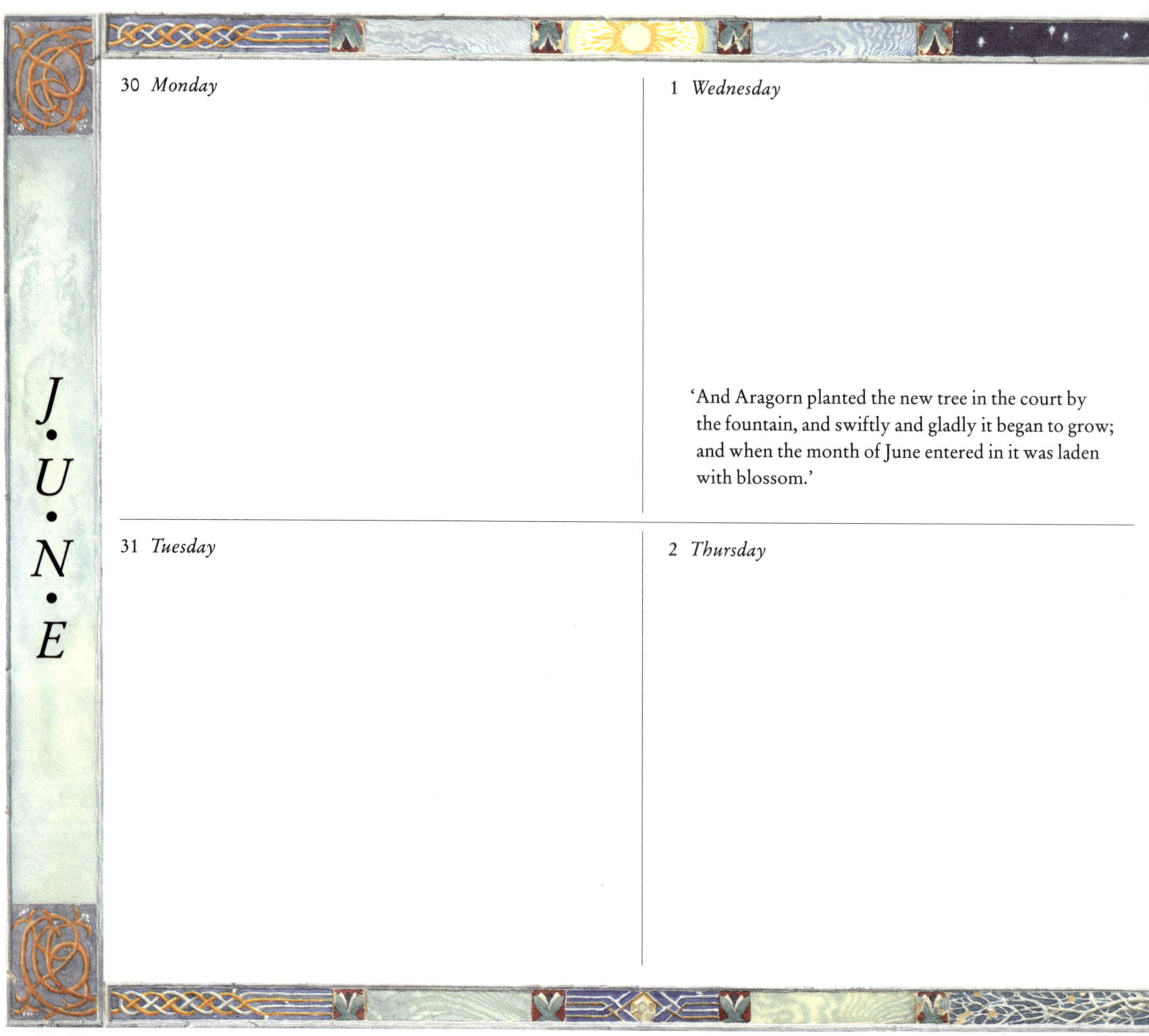

J•U•N•E

30 *Monday*

31 *Tuesday*

1 *Wednesday*

'And Aragorn planted the new tree in the court by the fountain, and swiftly and gladly it began to grow; and when the month of June entered in it was laden with blossom.'

2 *Thursday*

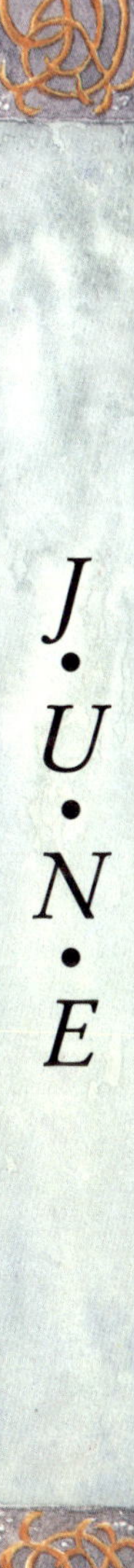
J•U•N•E

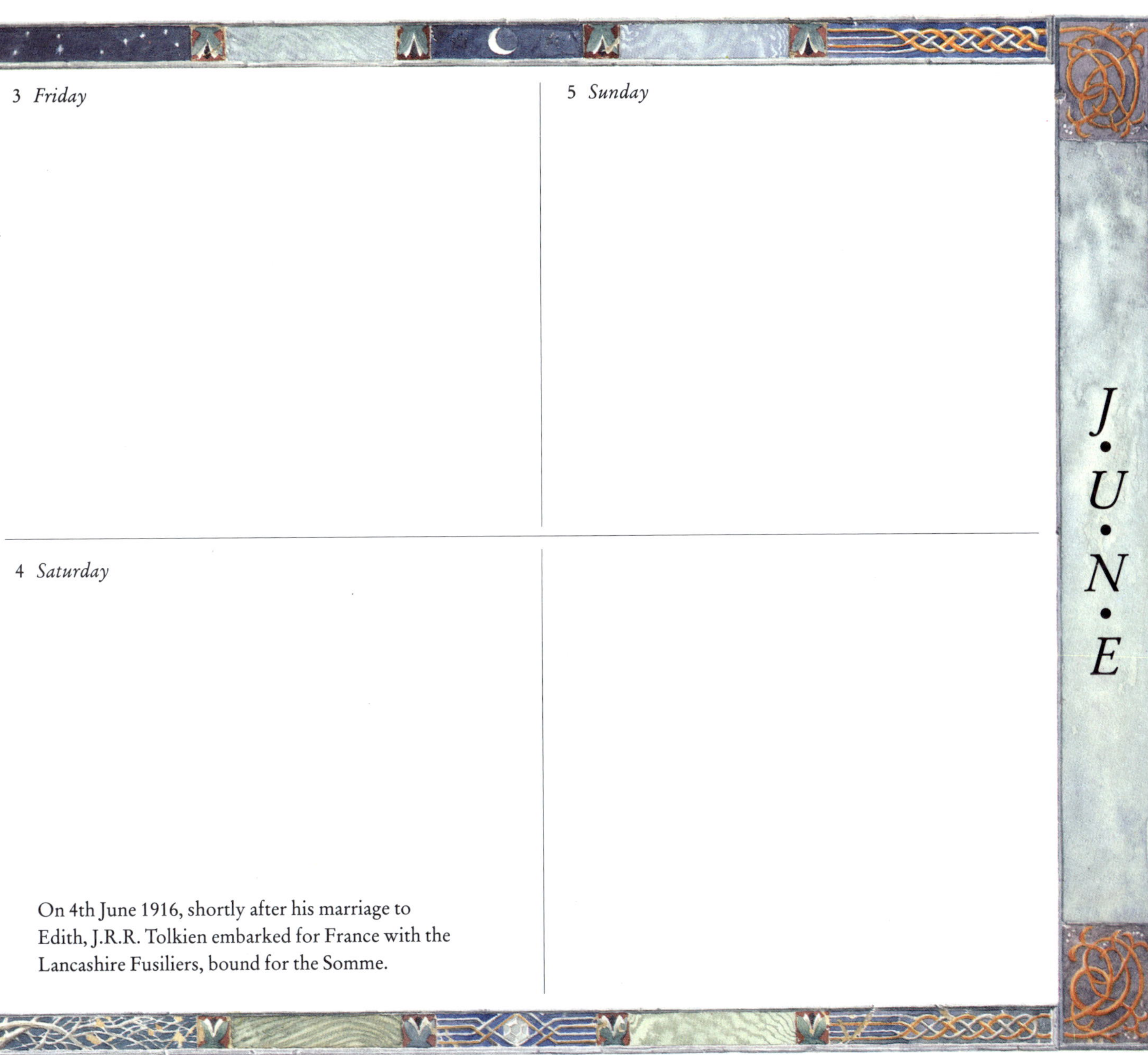

3 *Friday*

5 *Sunday*

4 *Saturday*

On 4th June 1916, shortly after his marriage to Edith, J.R.R. Tolkien embarked for France with the Lancashire Fusiliers, bound for the Somme.

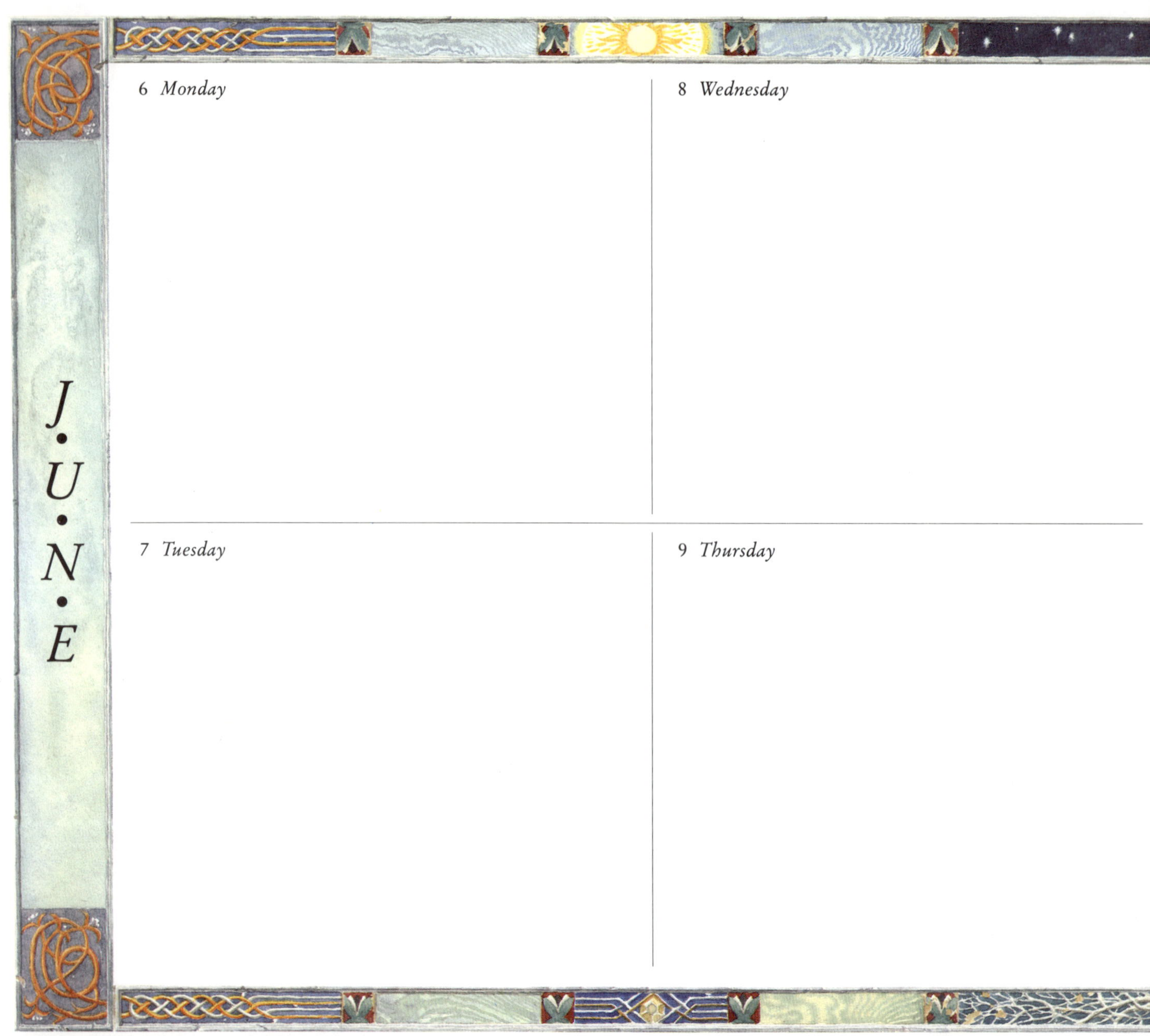

J•U•N•E

6 *Monday*

7 *Tuesday*

8 *Wednesday*

9 *Thursday*

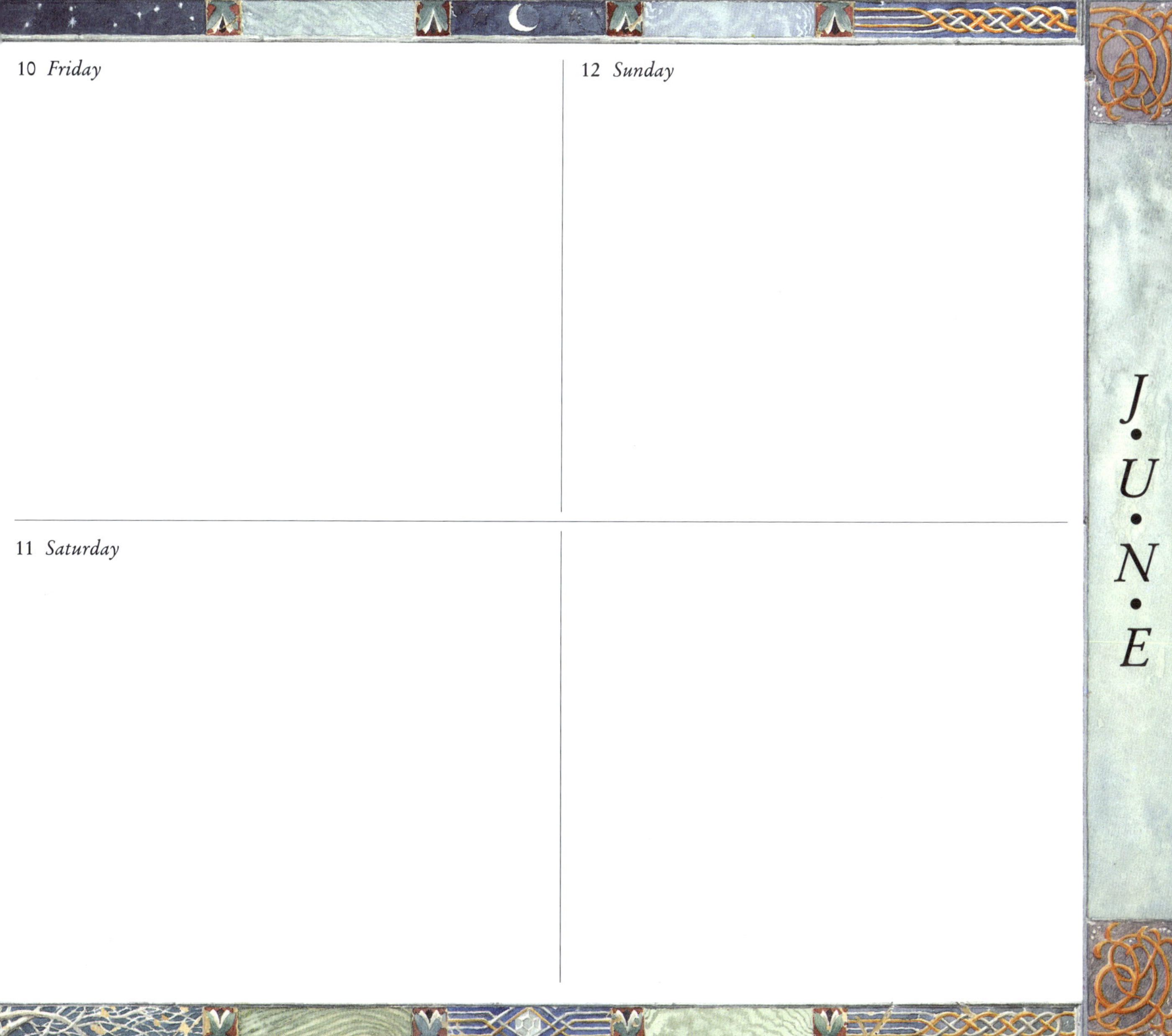

10 *Friday*

12 *Sunday*

11 *Saturday*

J•U•N•E

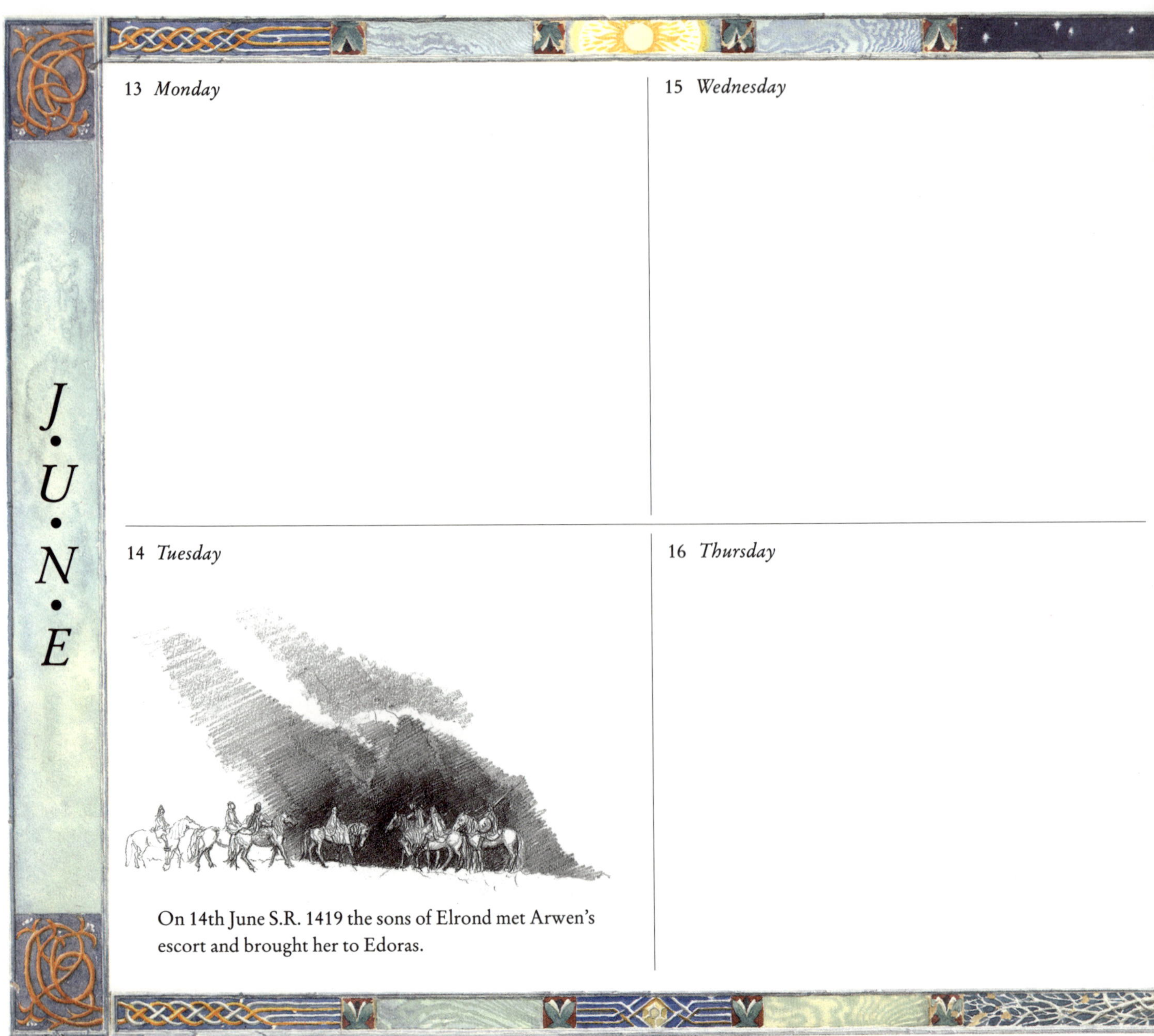

J • U • N • E

13 *Monday*

15 *Wednesday*

14 *Tuesday*

On 14th June S.R. 1419 the sons of Elrond met Arwen's escort and brought her to Edoras.

16 *Thursday*

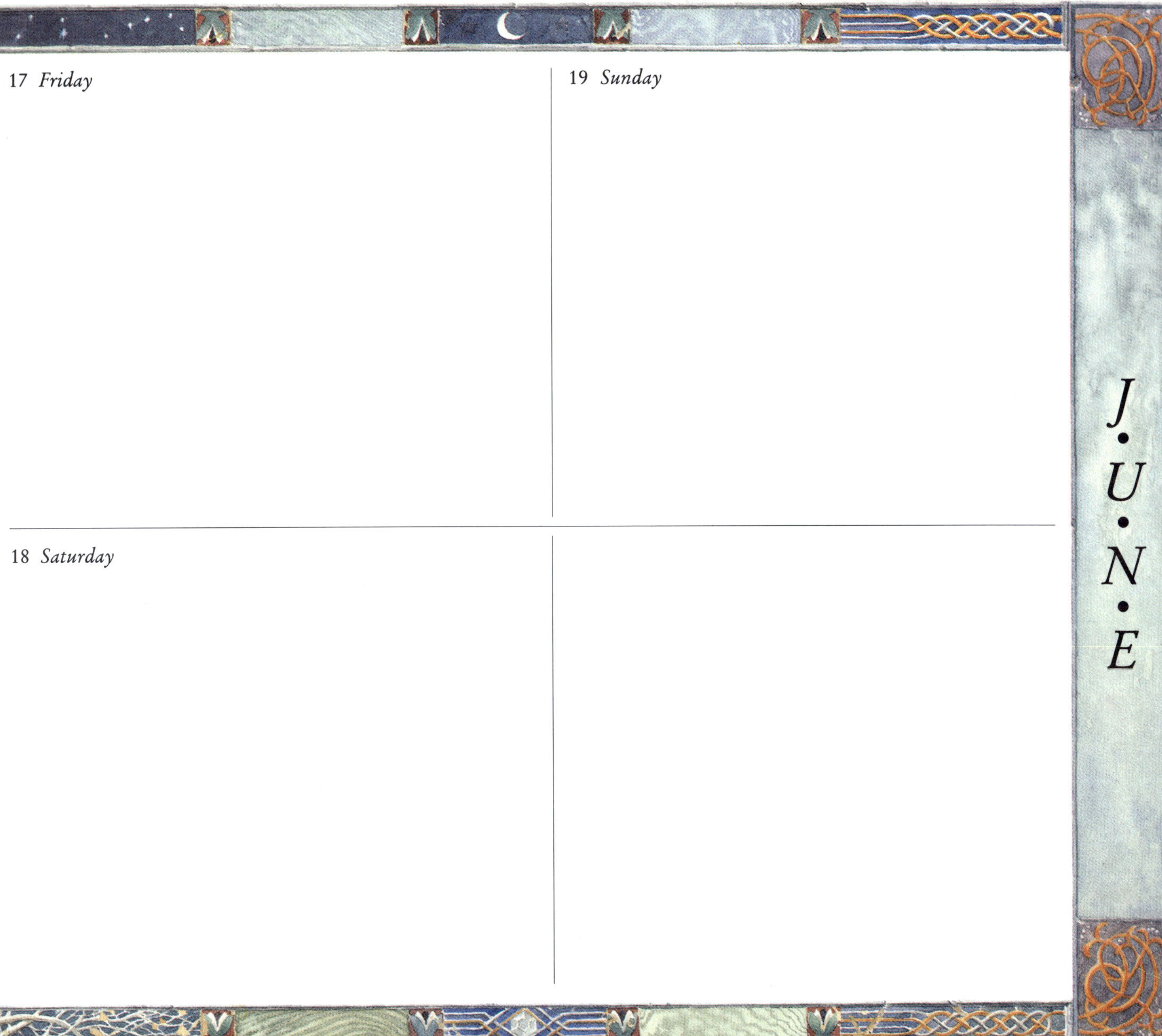

17 *Friday*

19 *Sunday*

18 *Saturday*

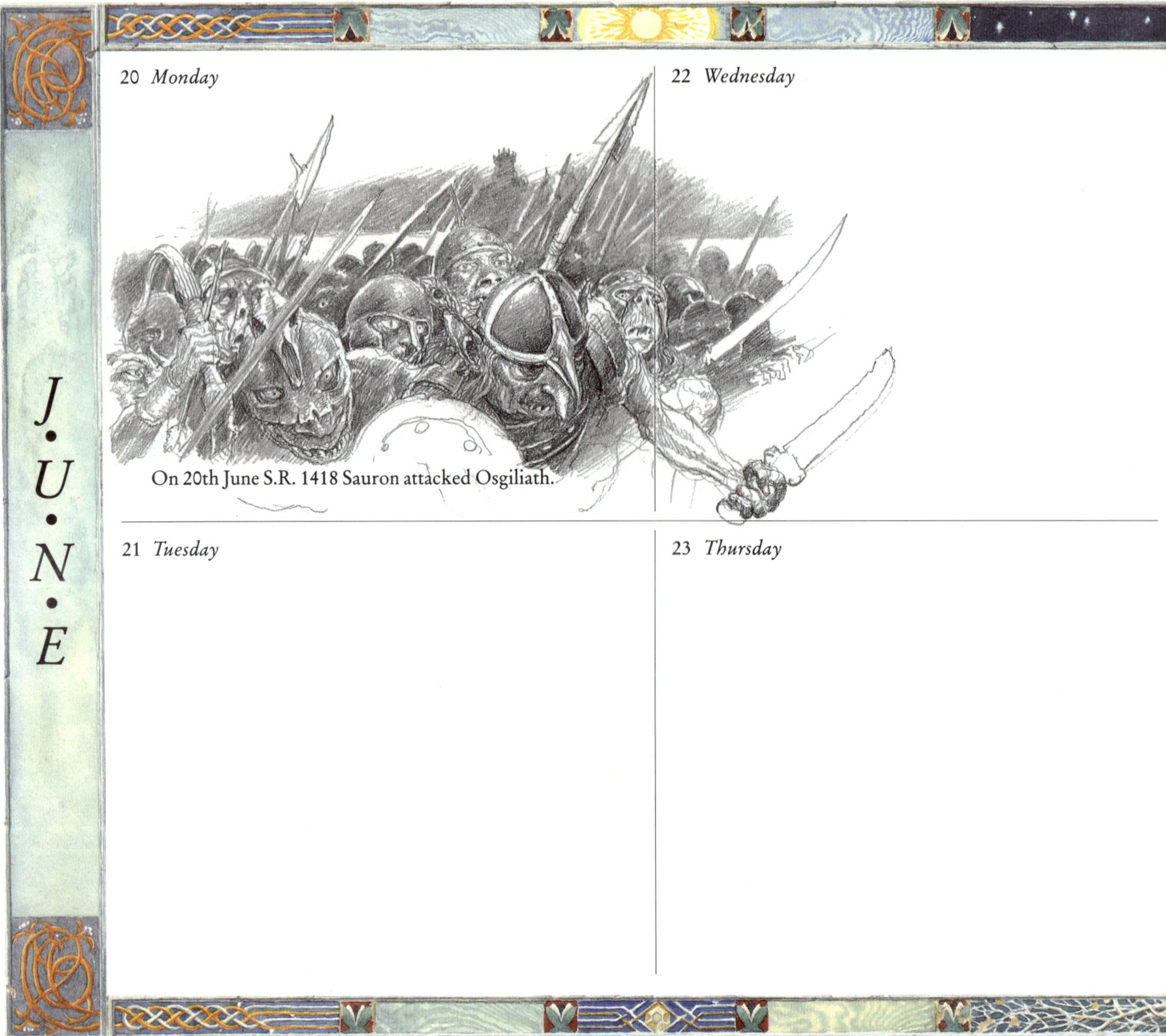

J•U•N•E

20 *Monday*

On 20th June S.R. 1418 Sauron attacked Osgiliath.

21 *Tuesday*

22 *Wednesday*

23 *Thursday*

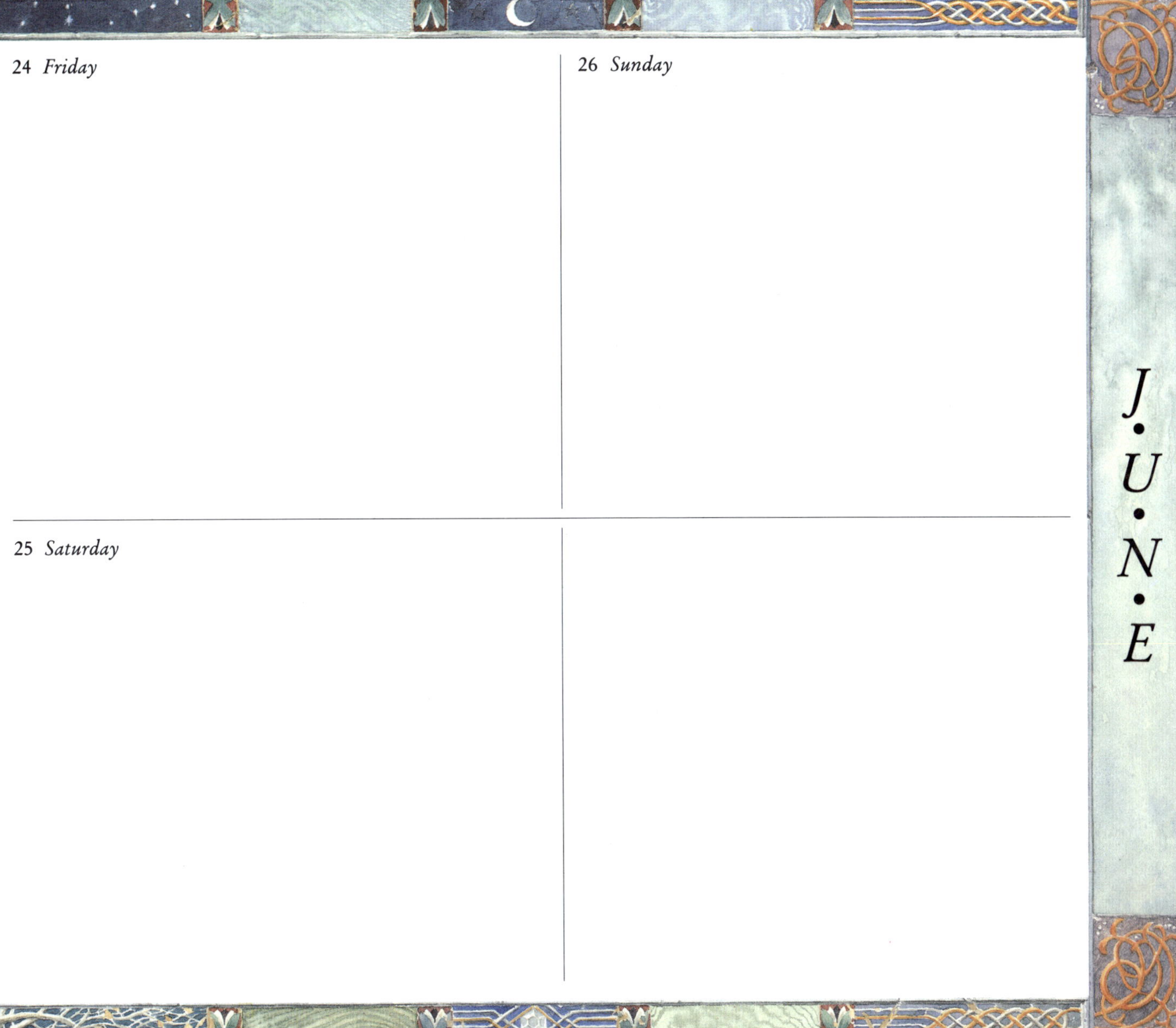

24 *Friday*

26 *Sunday*

25 *Saturday*

J•U•N•E

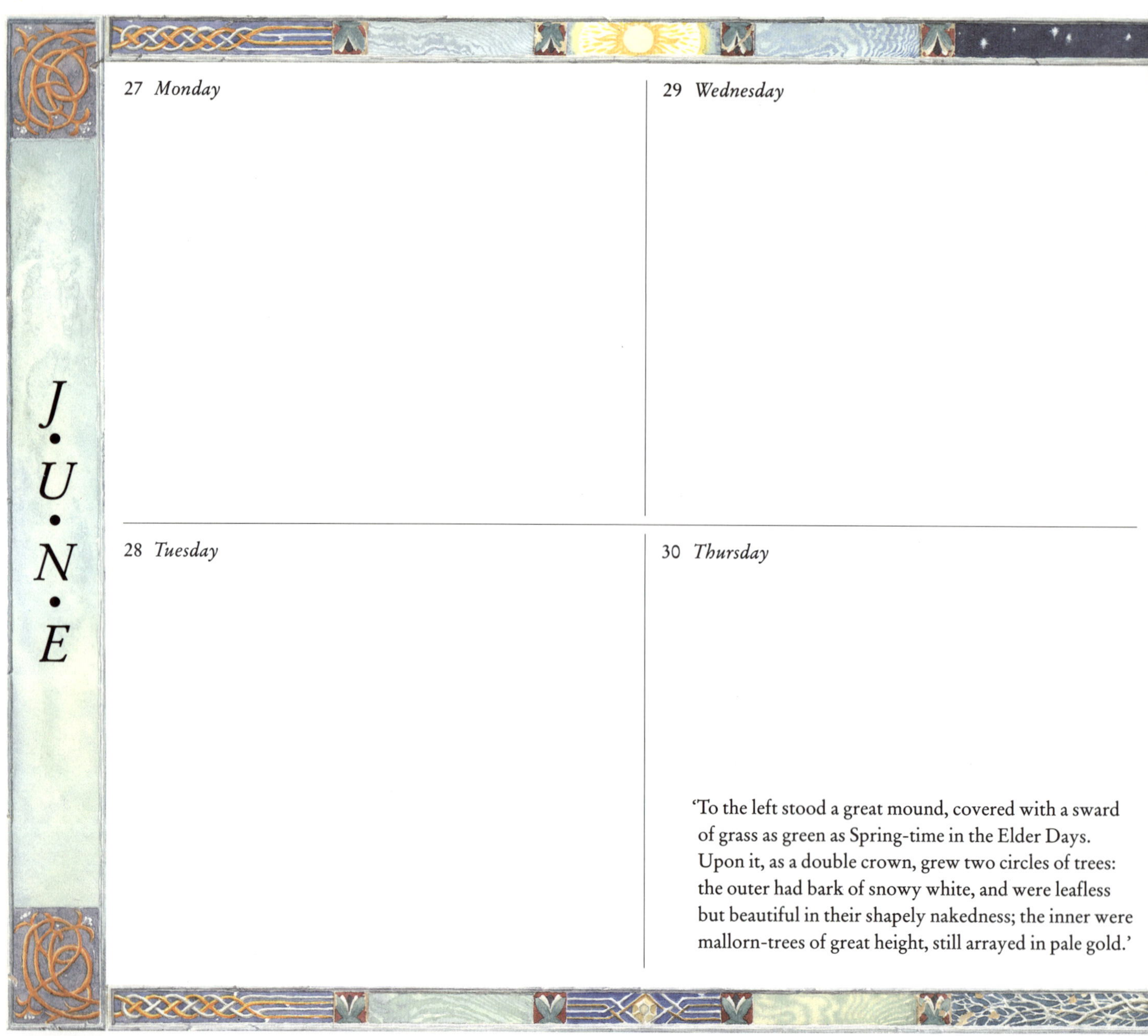

J•U•N•E

27 *Monday*

28 *Tuesday*

29 *Wednesday*

30 *Thursday*

'To the left stood a great mound, covered with a sward of grass as green as Spring-time in the Elder Days. Upon it, as a double crown, grew two circles of trees: the outer had bark of snowy white, and were leafless but beautiful in their shapely nakedness; the inner were mallorn-trees of great height, still arrayed in pale gold.'

J•U•N•E

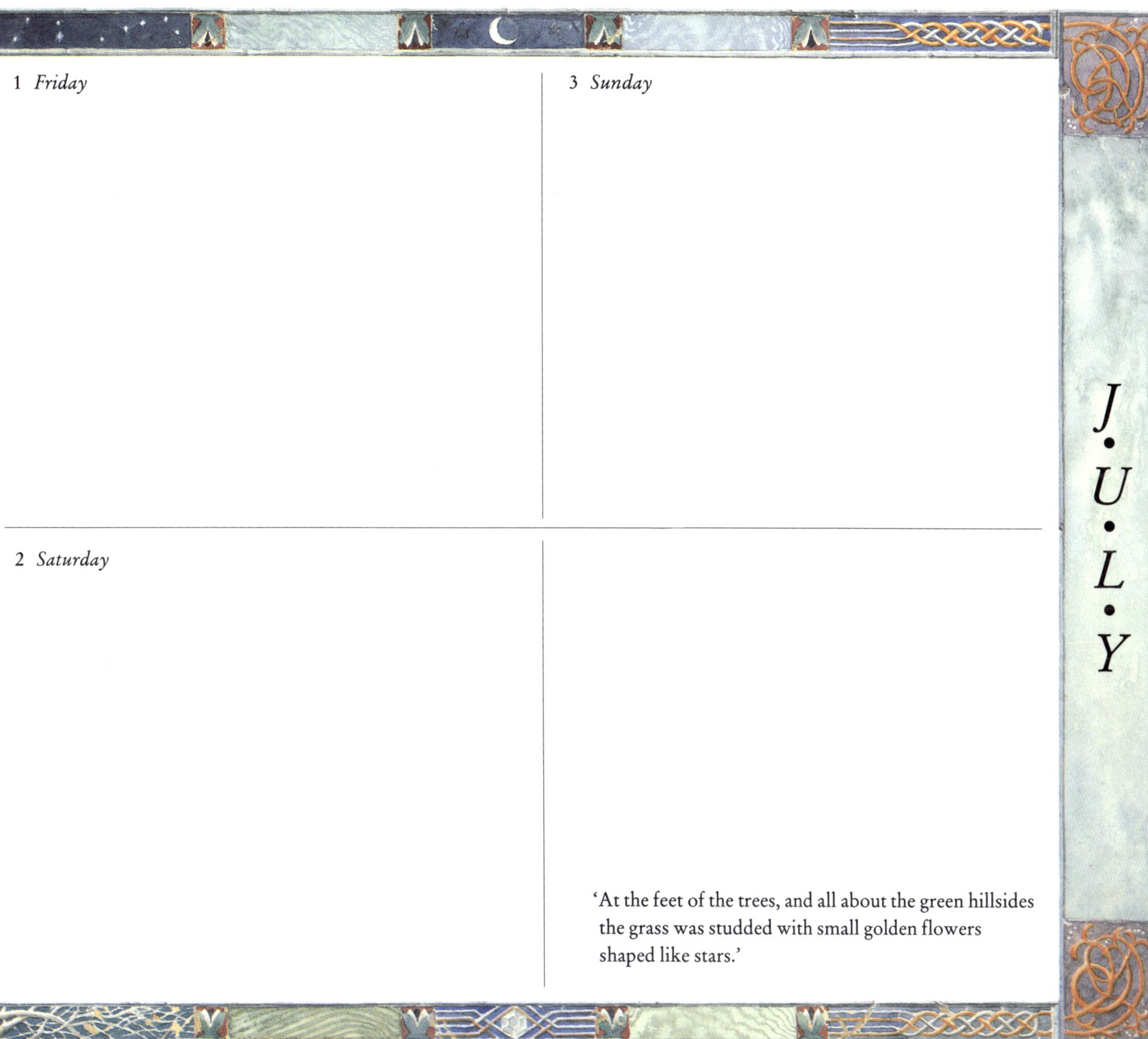

1 *Friday*

3 *Sunday*

2 *Saturday*

'At the feet of the trees, and all about the green hillsides the grass was studded with small golden flowers shaped like stars.'

J•U•L•Y

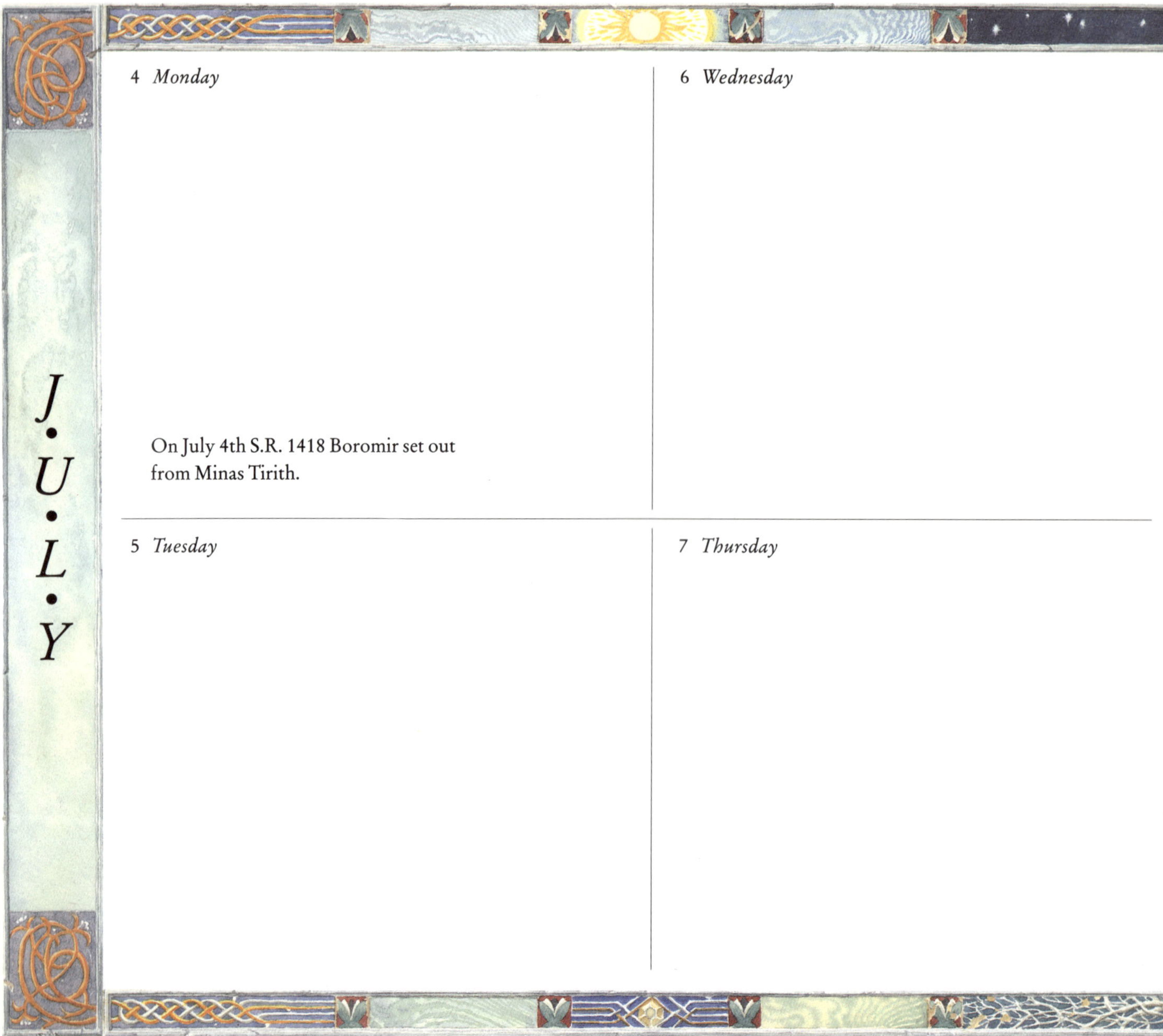

J • U • L • Y

4 *Monday*

On July 4th S.R. 1418 Boromir set out from Minas Tirith.

5 *Tuesday*

6 *Wednesday*

7 *Thursday*

8 *Friday*

10 *Sunday*

9 *Saturday*

J•U•L•Y

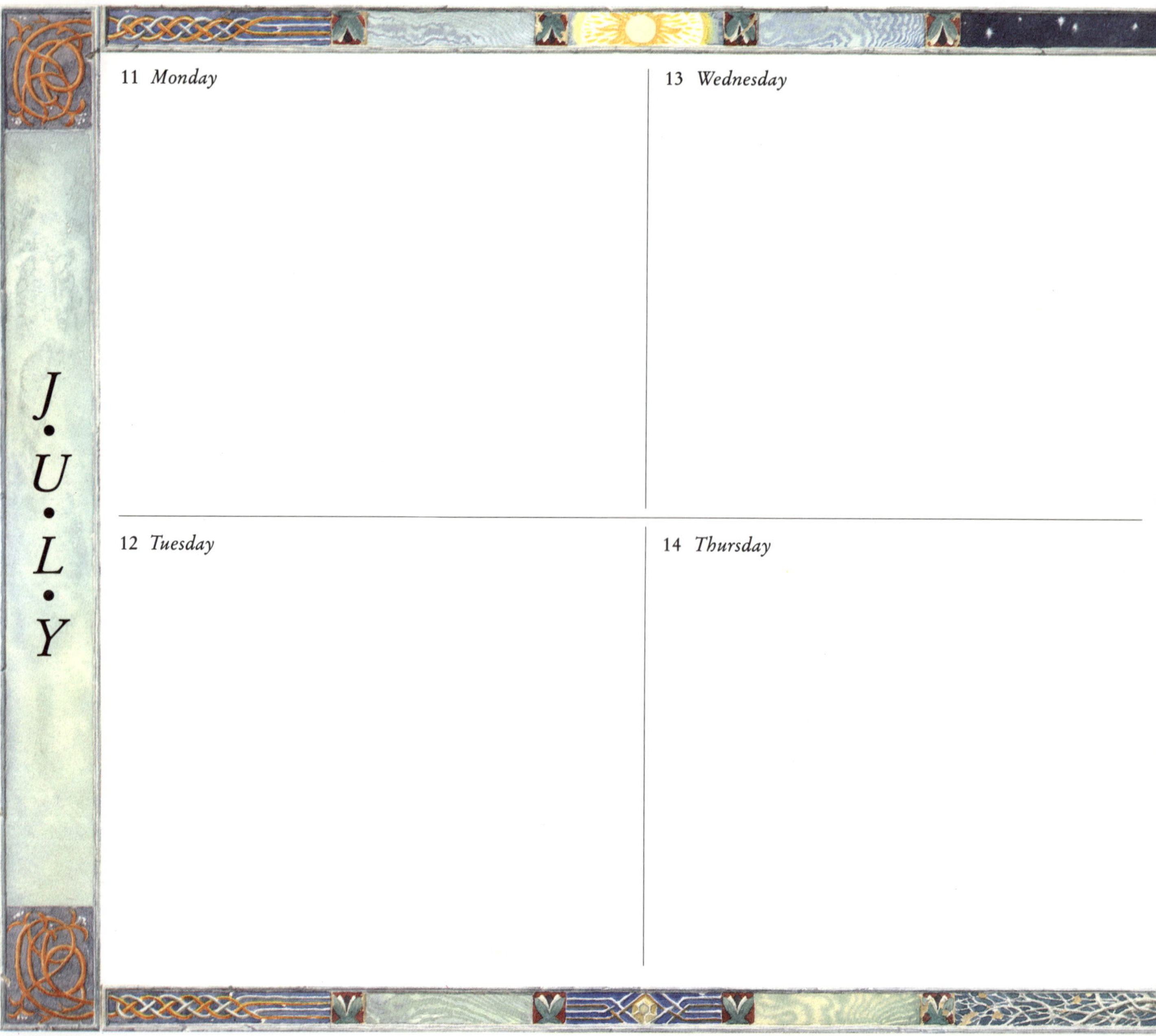

J•U•L•Y

11 *Monday*

13 *Wednesday*

12 *Tuesday*

14 *Thursday*

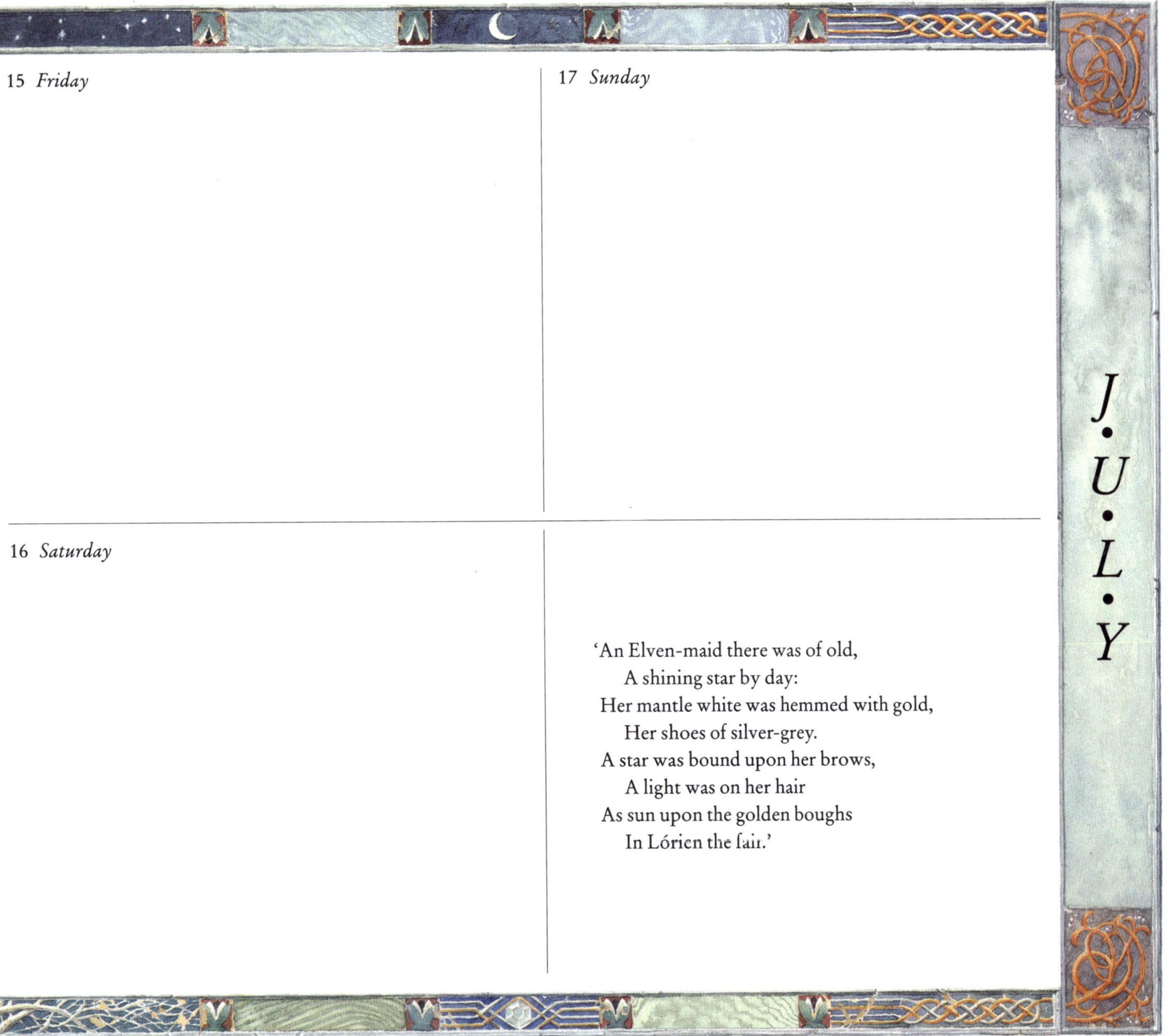

15 *Friday*

16 *Saturday*

17 *Sunday*

'An Elven-maid there was of old,
  A shining star by day:
Her mantle white was hemmed with gold,
  Her shoes of silver-grey.
A star was bound upon her brows,
  A light was on her hair
As sun upon the golden boughs
  In Lórien the fair.'

J•U•L•Y

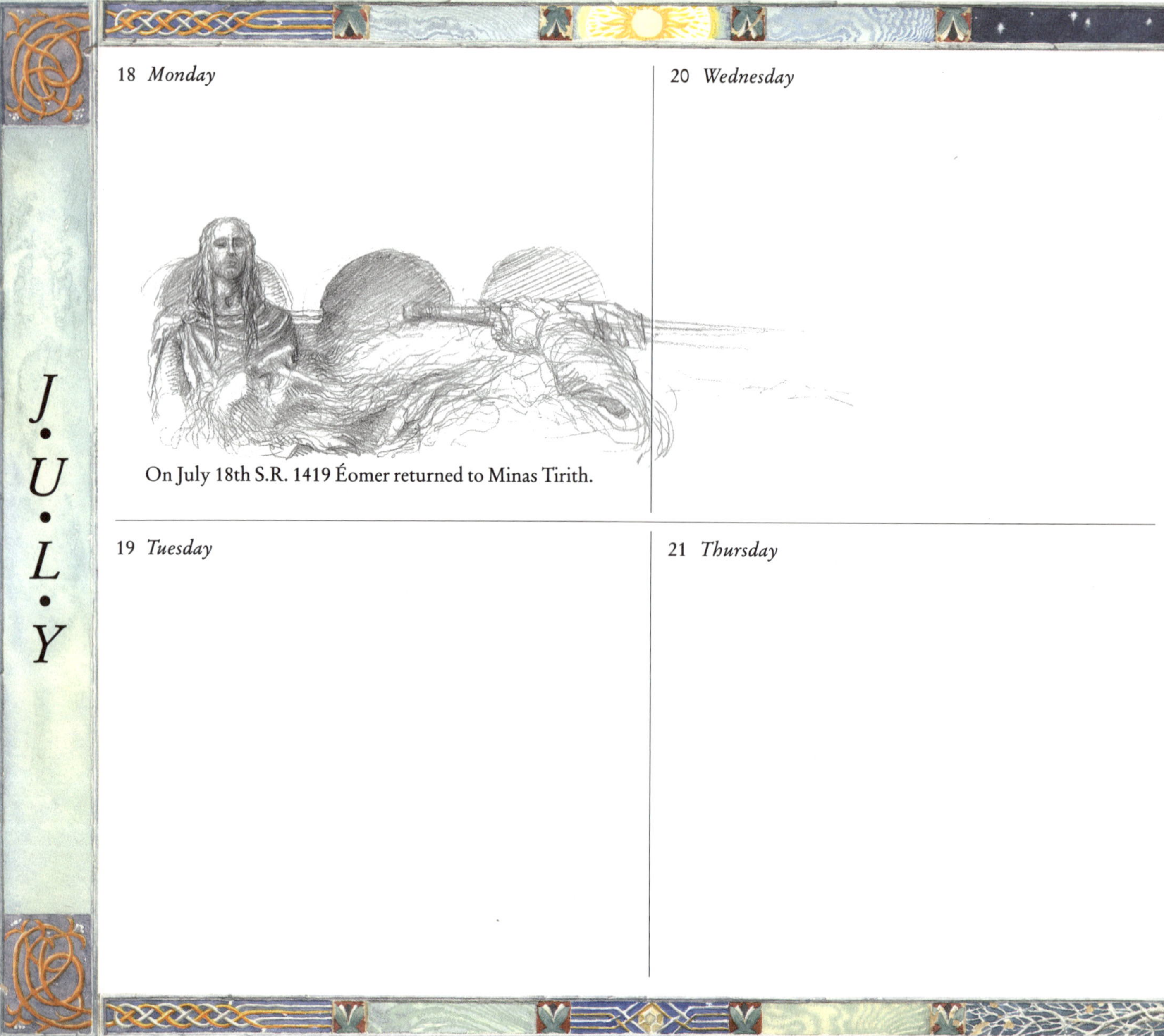

J•U•L•Y

18 *Monday*

On July 18th S.R. 1419 Éomer returned to Minas Tirith.

19 *Tuesday*

20 *Wednesday*

21 *Thursday*

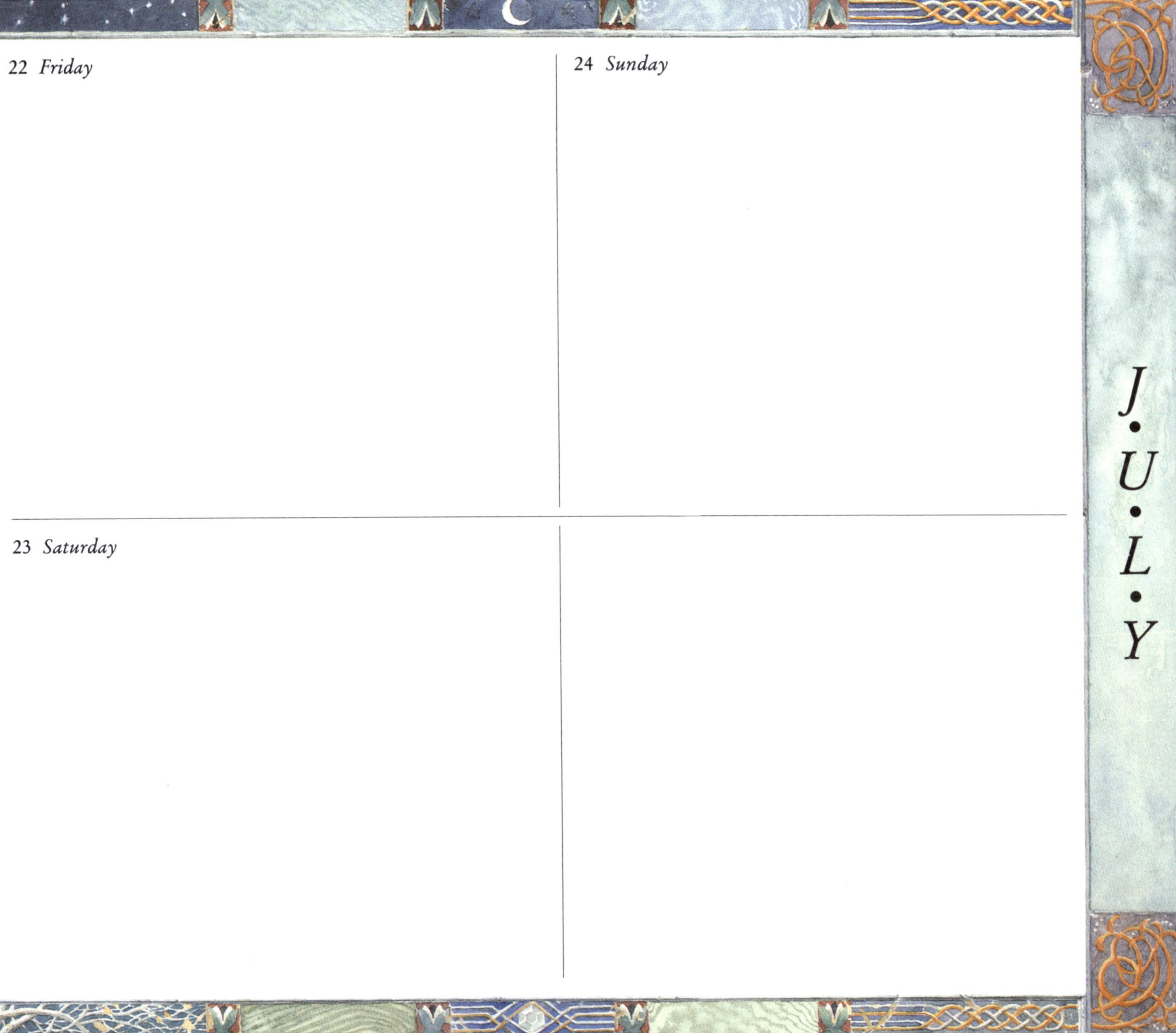

22 *Friday*

24 *Sunday*

23 *Saturday*

J·U·L·Y

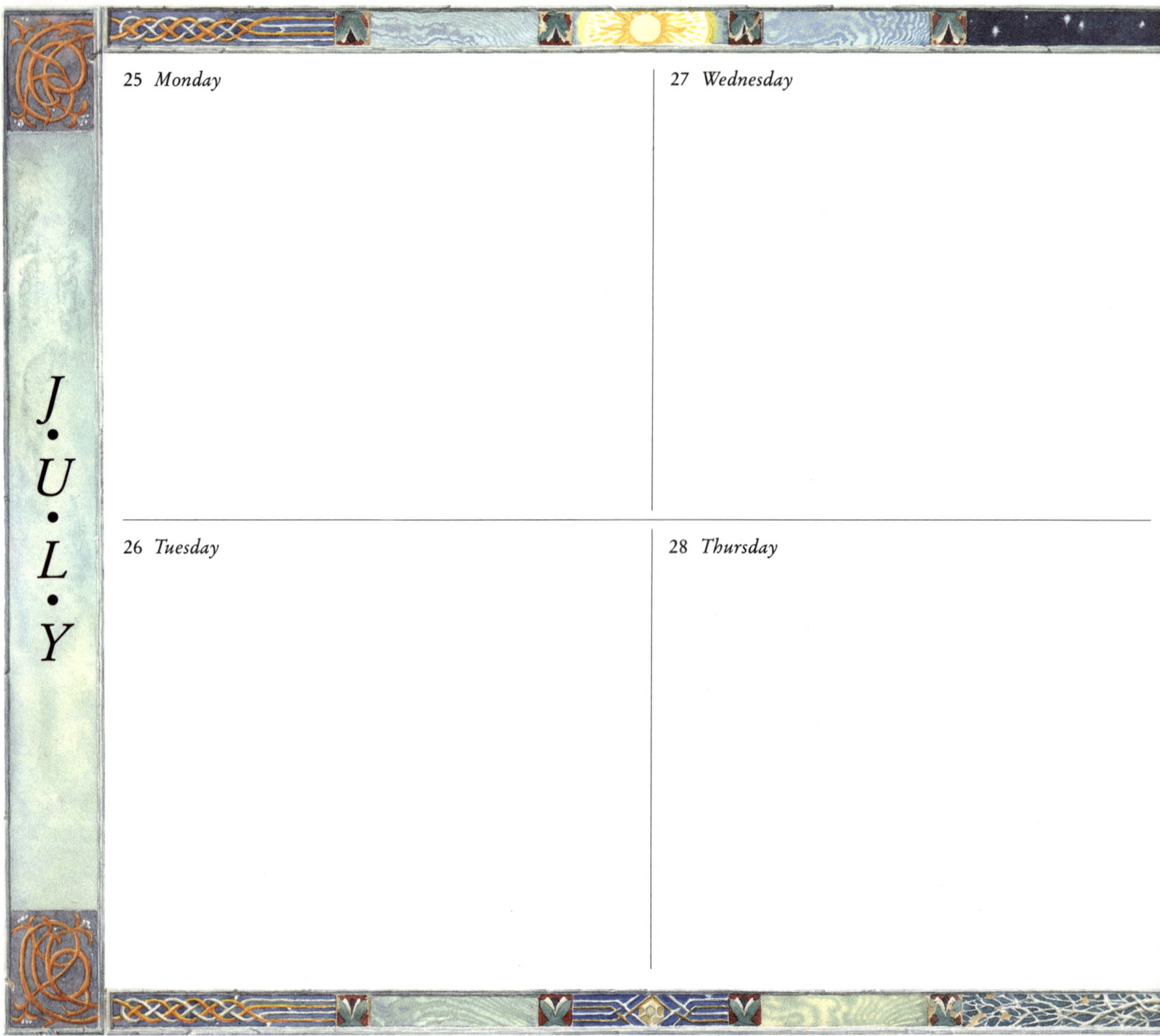

25 *Monday*

27 *Wednesday*

26 *Tuesday*

28 *Thursday*

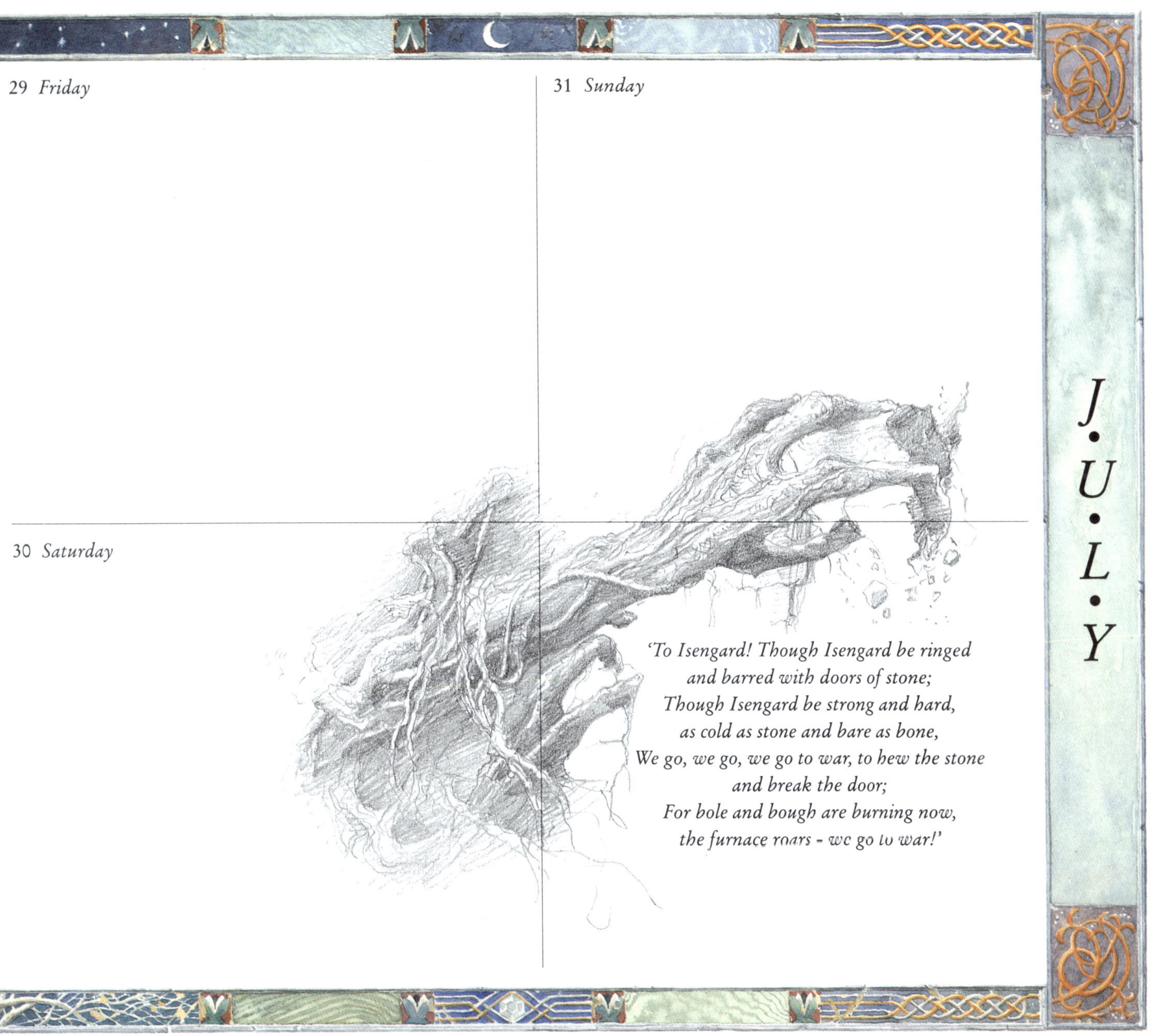

29 *Friday*

31 *Sunday*

30 *Saturday*

'To Isengard! Though Isengard be ringed
and barred with doors of stone;
Though Isengard be strong and hard,
as cold as stone and bare as bone,
We go, we go, we go to war, to hew the stone
and break the door;
For bole and bough are burning now,
the furnace roars - we go to war!'

J • U • L • Y

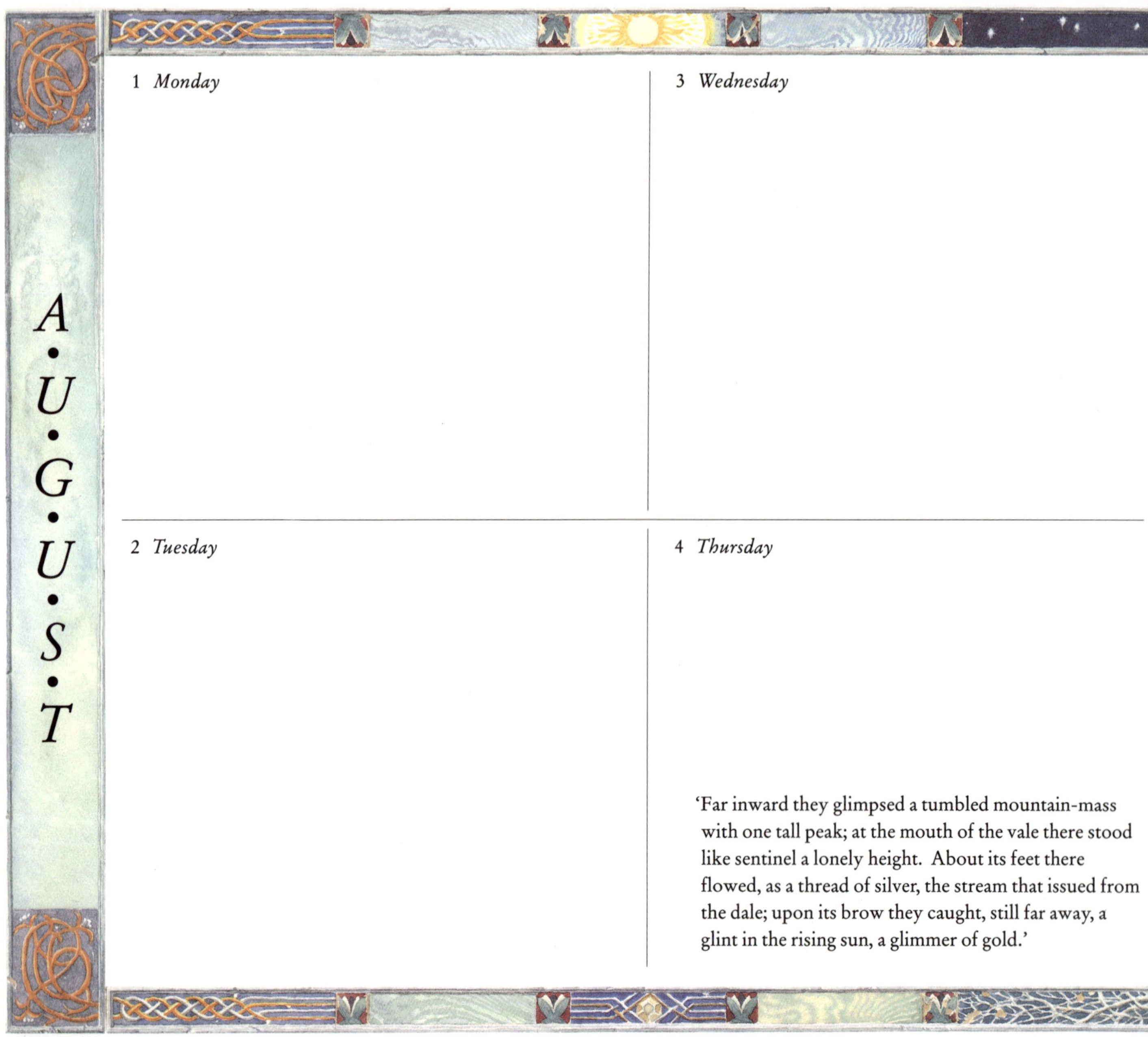

1 *Monday*

2 *Tuesday*

3 *Wednesday*

4 *Thursday*

'Far inward they glimpsed a tumbled mountain-mass with one tall peak; at the mouth of the vale there stood like sentinel a lonely height. About its feet there flowed, as a thread of silver, the stream that issued from the dale; upon its brow they caught, still far away, a glint in the rising sun, a glimmer of gold.'

A•U•G•U•S•T

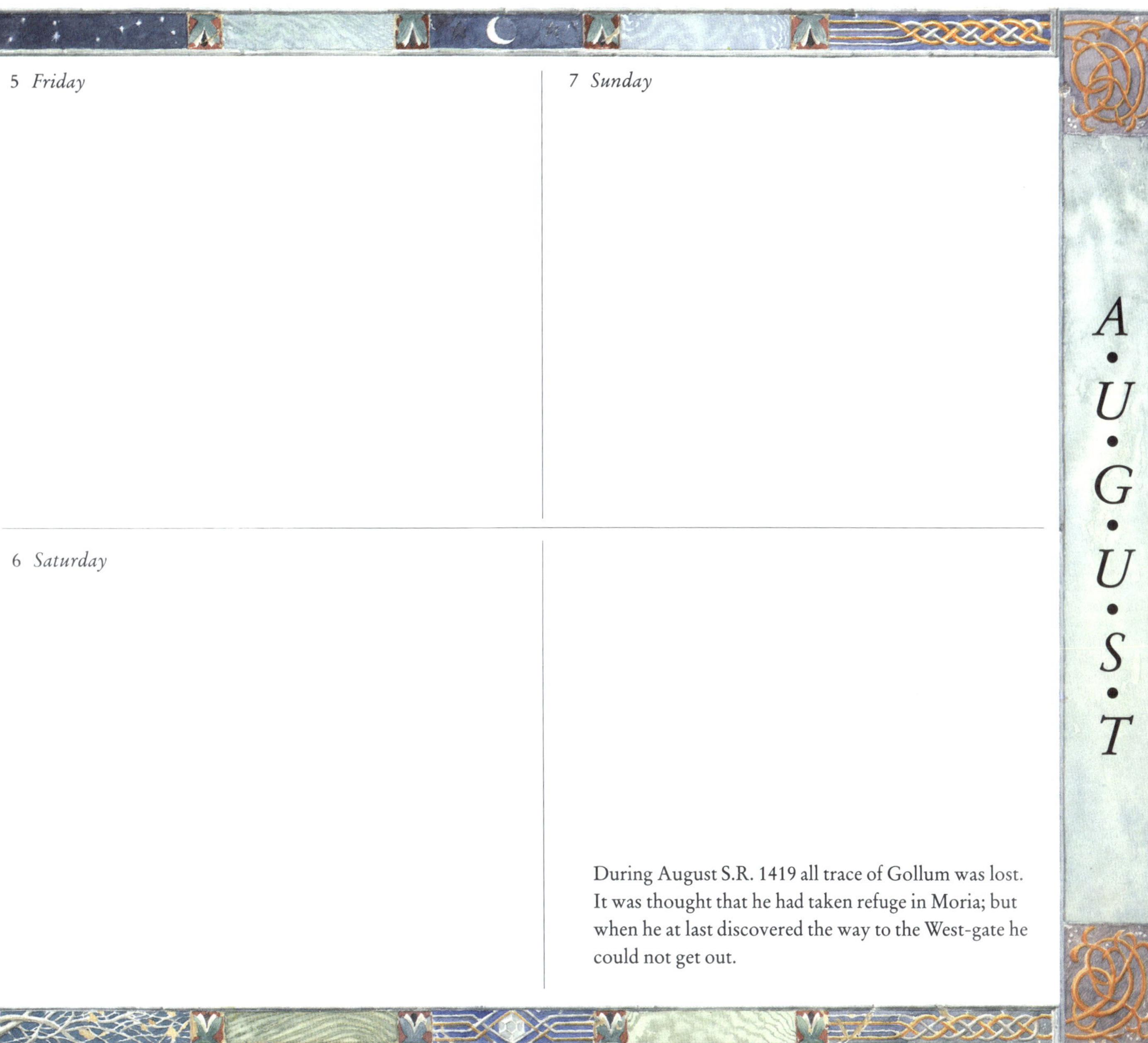

5 *Friday*

6 *Saturday*

7 *Sunday*

During August S.R. 1419 all trace of Gollum was lost. It was thought that he had taken refuge in Moria; but when he at last discovered the way to the West-gate he could not get out.

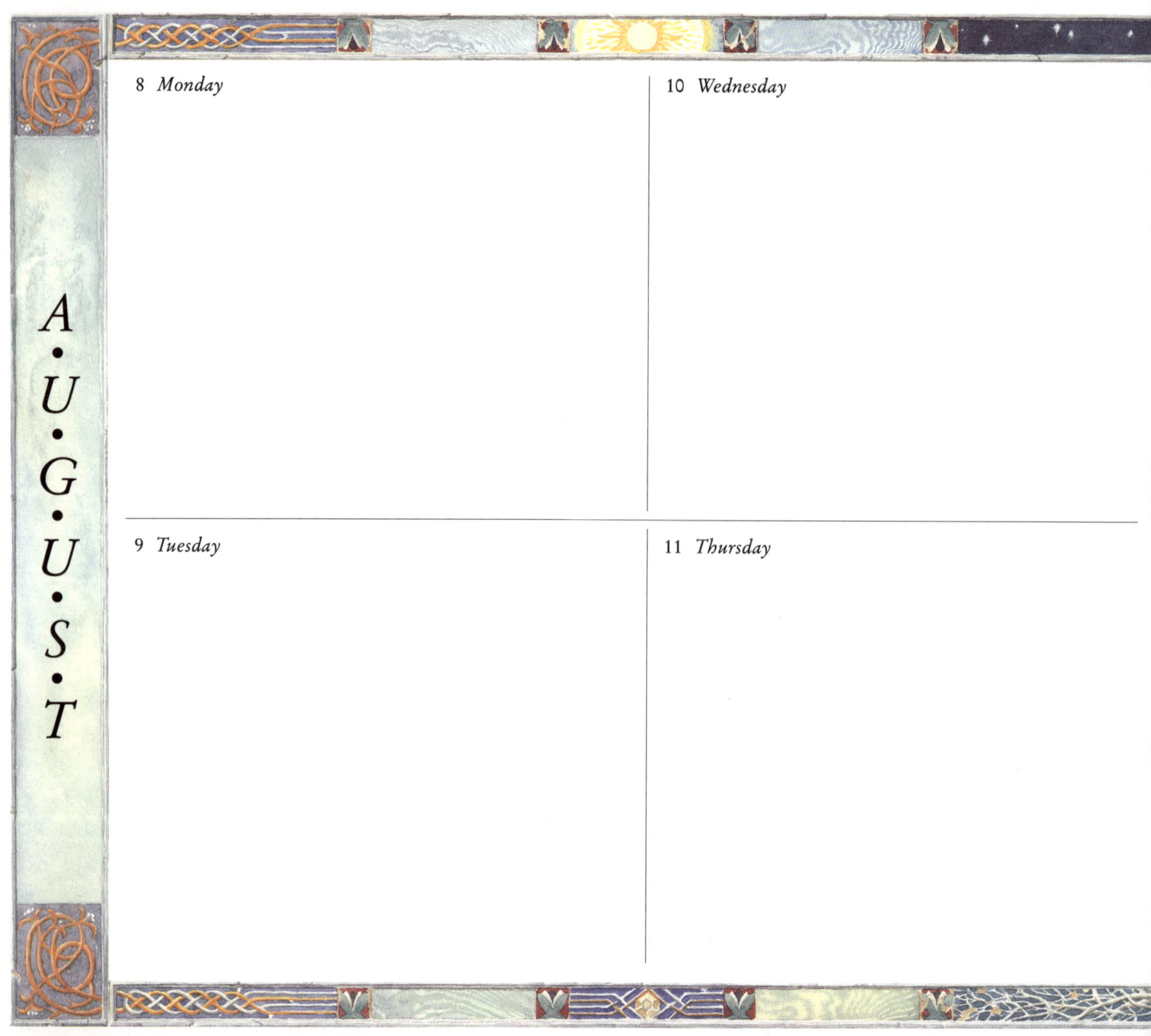

A·U·G·U·S·T

8 *Monday*

9 *Tuesday*

10 *Wednesday*

11 *Thursday*

12 *Friday*

14 *Sunday*

13 *Saturday*

The first volume of *The Lord of the Rings* was described by C.S. Lewis in *Time and Tide* as "like lightning from a clear sky… heroic romance, gorgeous, eloquent, and unashamed, has suddenly returned."

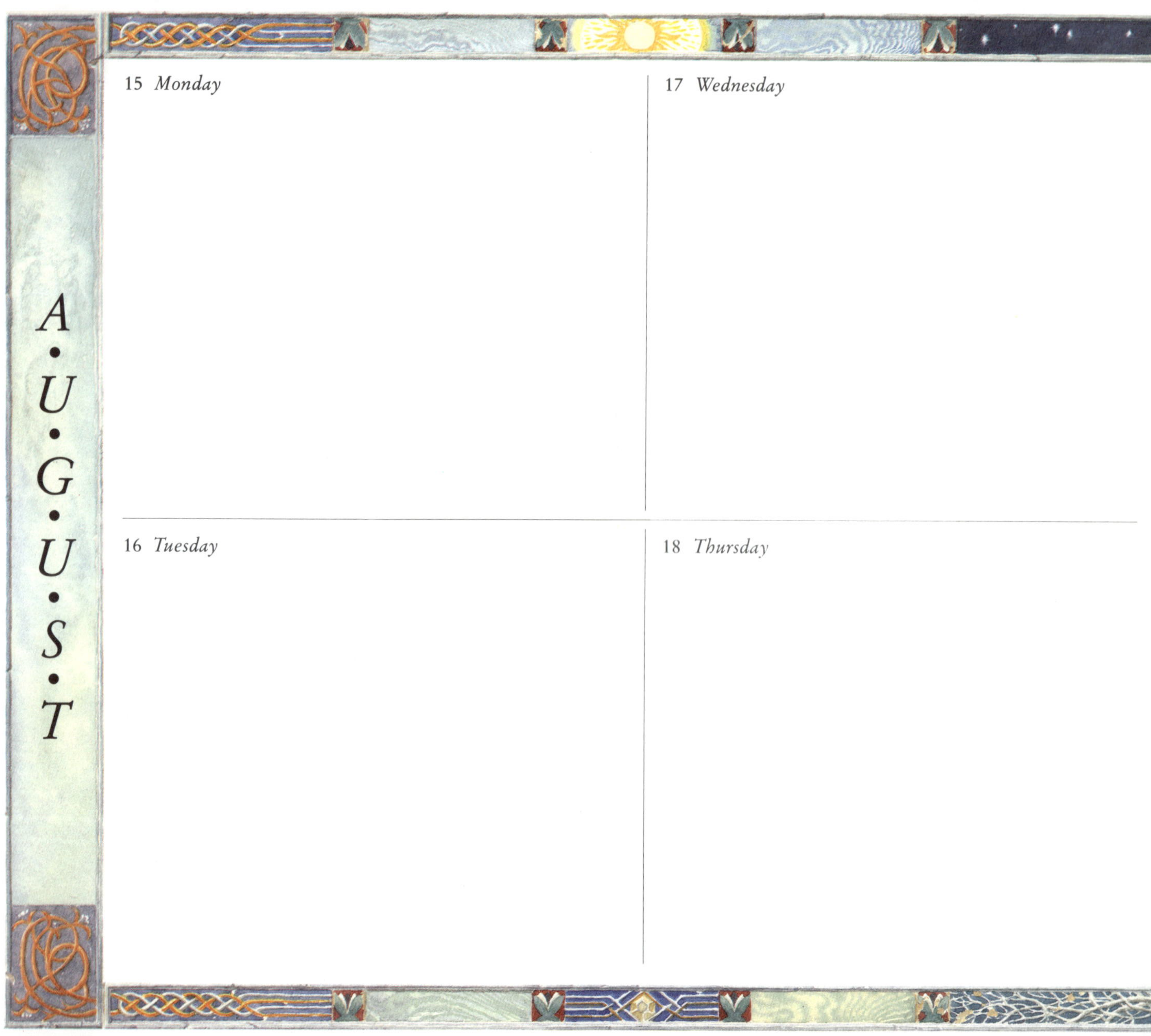

A·U·G·U·S·T

15 *Monday*

16 *Tuesday*

17 *Wednesday*

18 *Thursday*

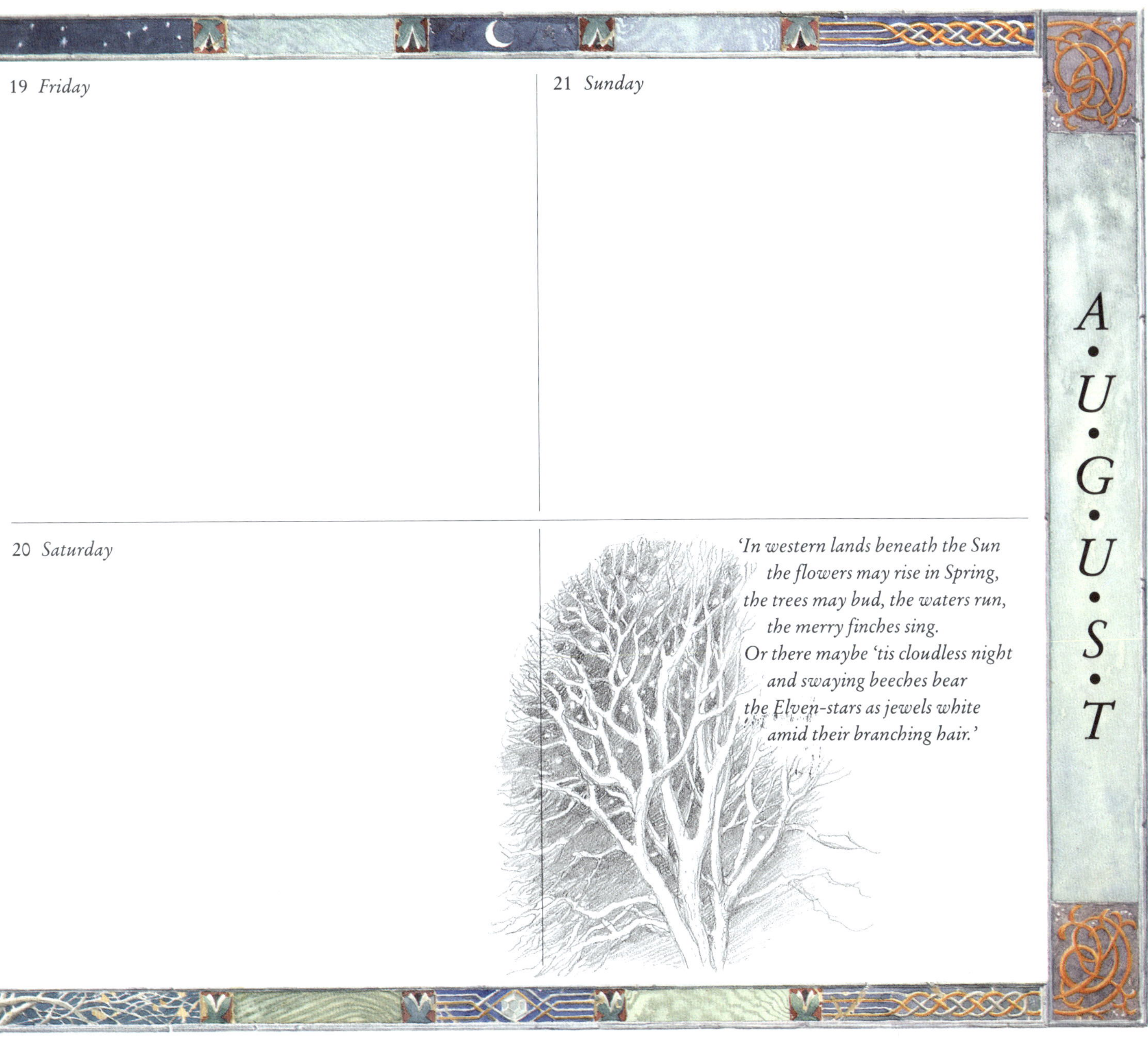

19 *Friday*

21 *Sunday*

20 *Saturday*

'In western lands beneath the Sun
the flowers may rise in Spring,
the trees may bud, the waters run,
the merry finches sing.
Or there maybe 'tis cloudless night
and swaying beeches bear
the Elven-stars as jewels white
amid their branching hair.'

A•U•G•U•S•T

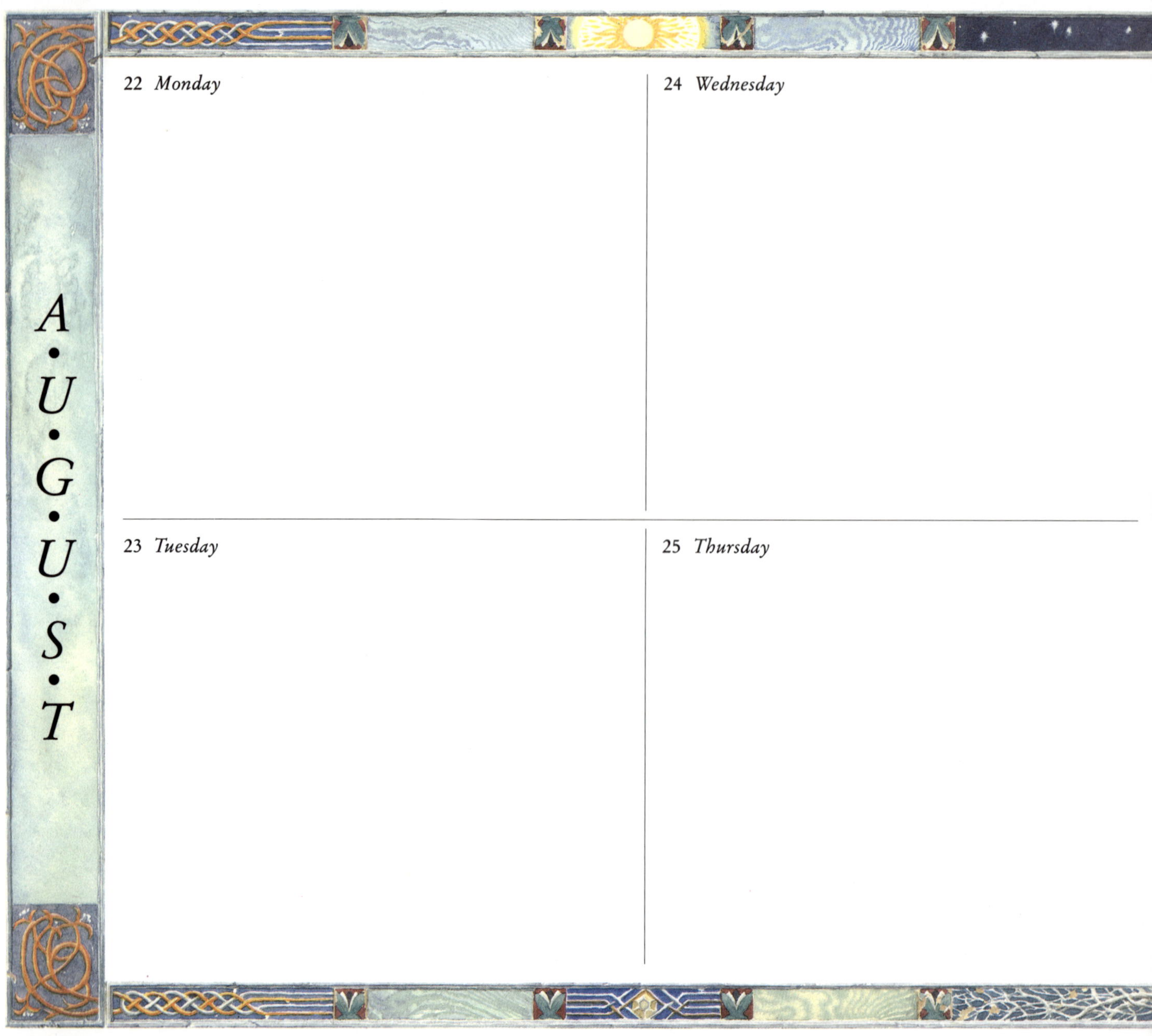

22 *Monday*

24 *Wednesday*

23 *Tuesday*

25 *Thursday*

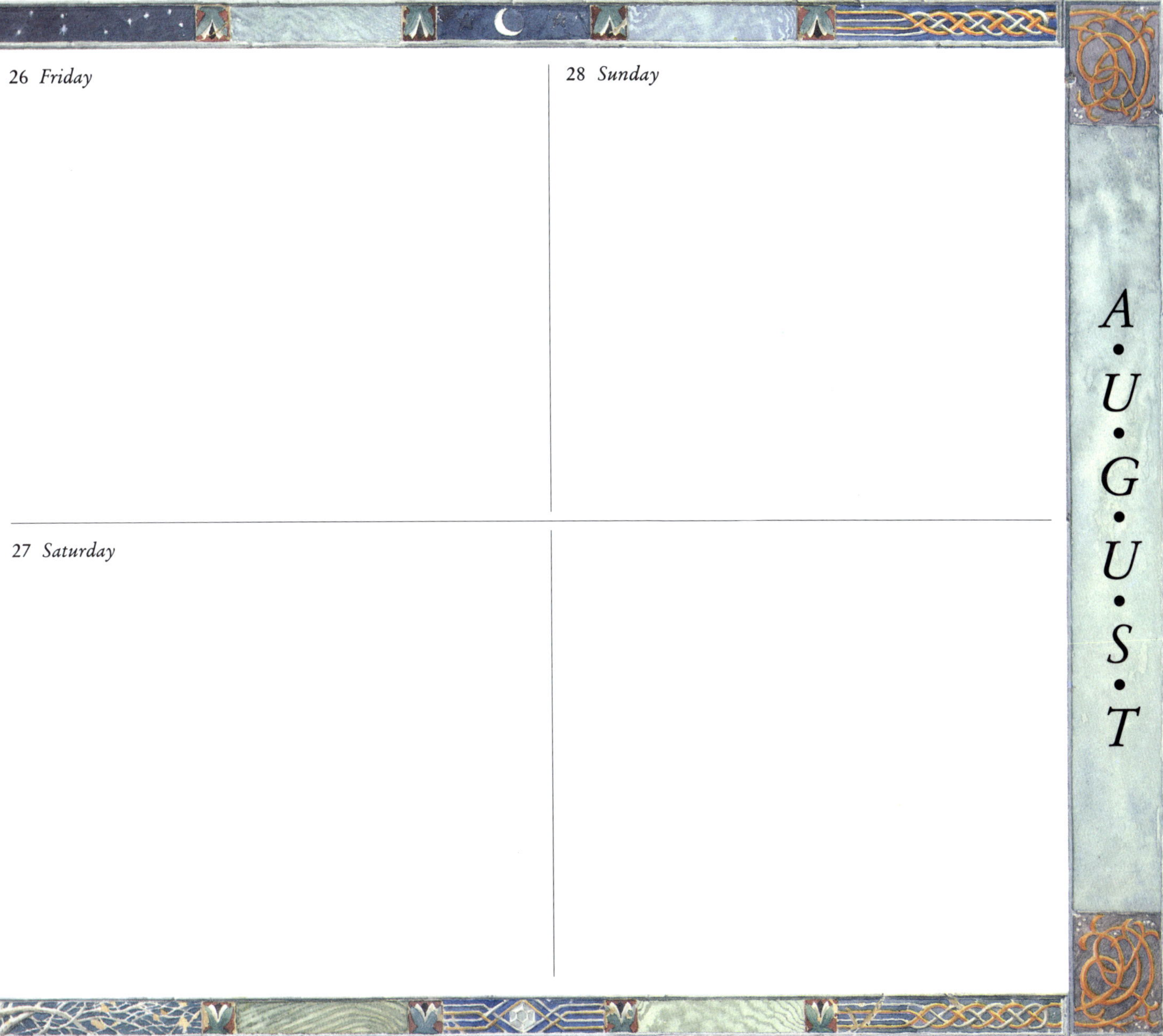

26 *Friday*

28 *Sunday*

27 *Saturday*

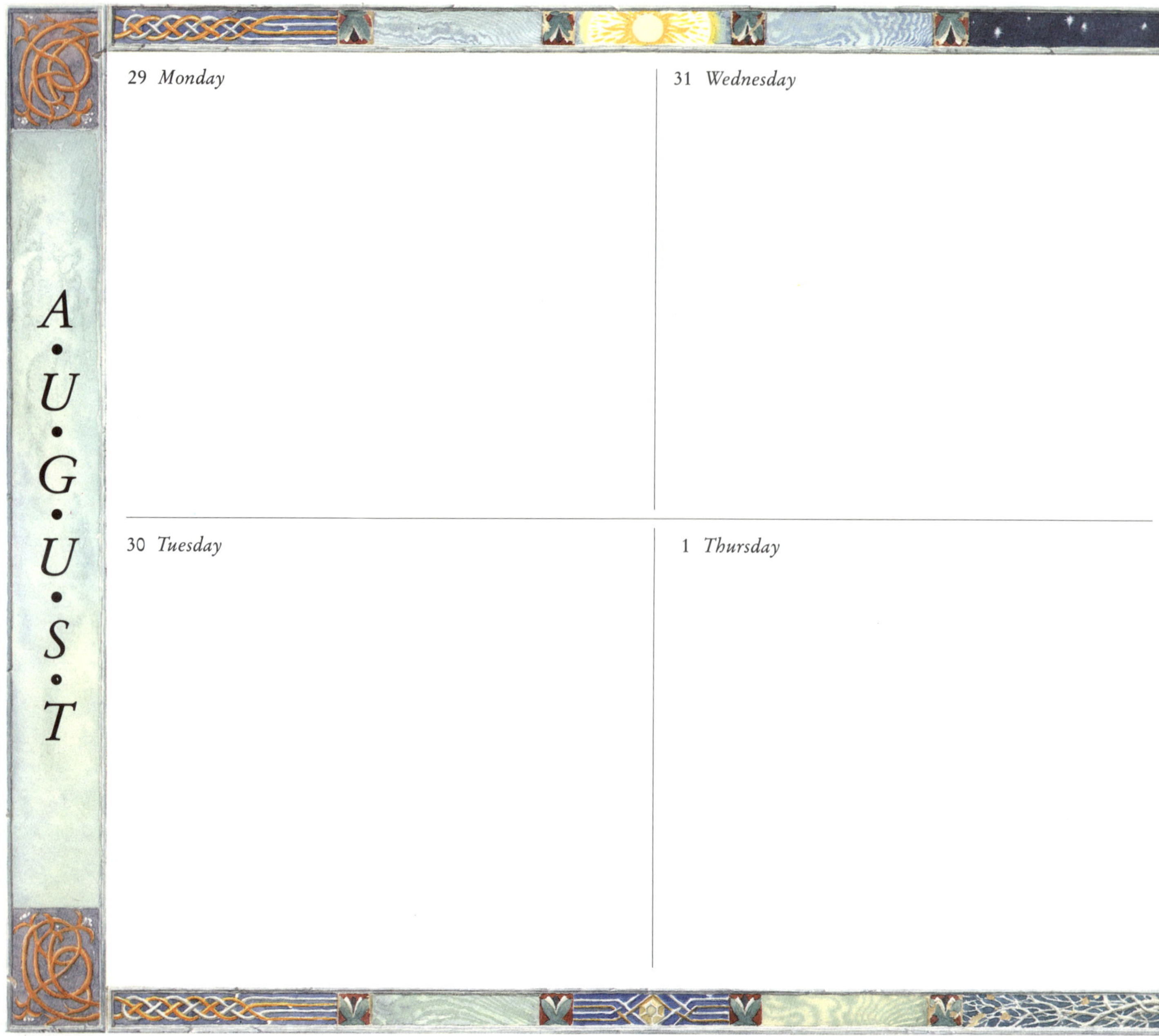

29 *Monday*

31 *Wednesday*

30 *Tuesday*

1 *Thursday*

S • E • P • T • E • M •
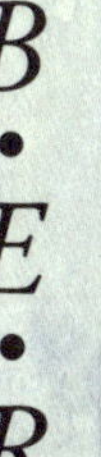
B • E • R

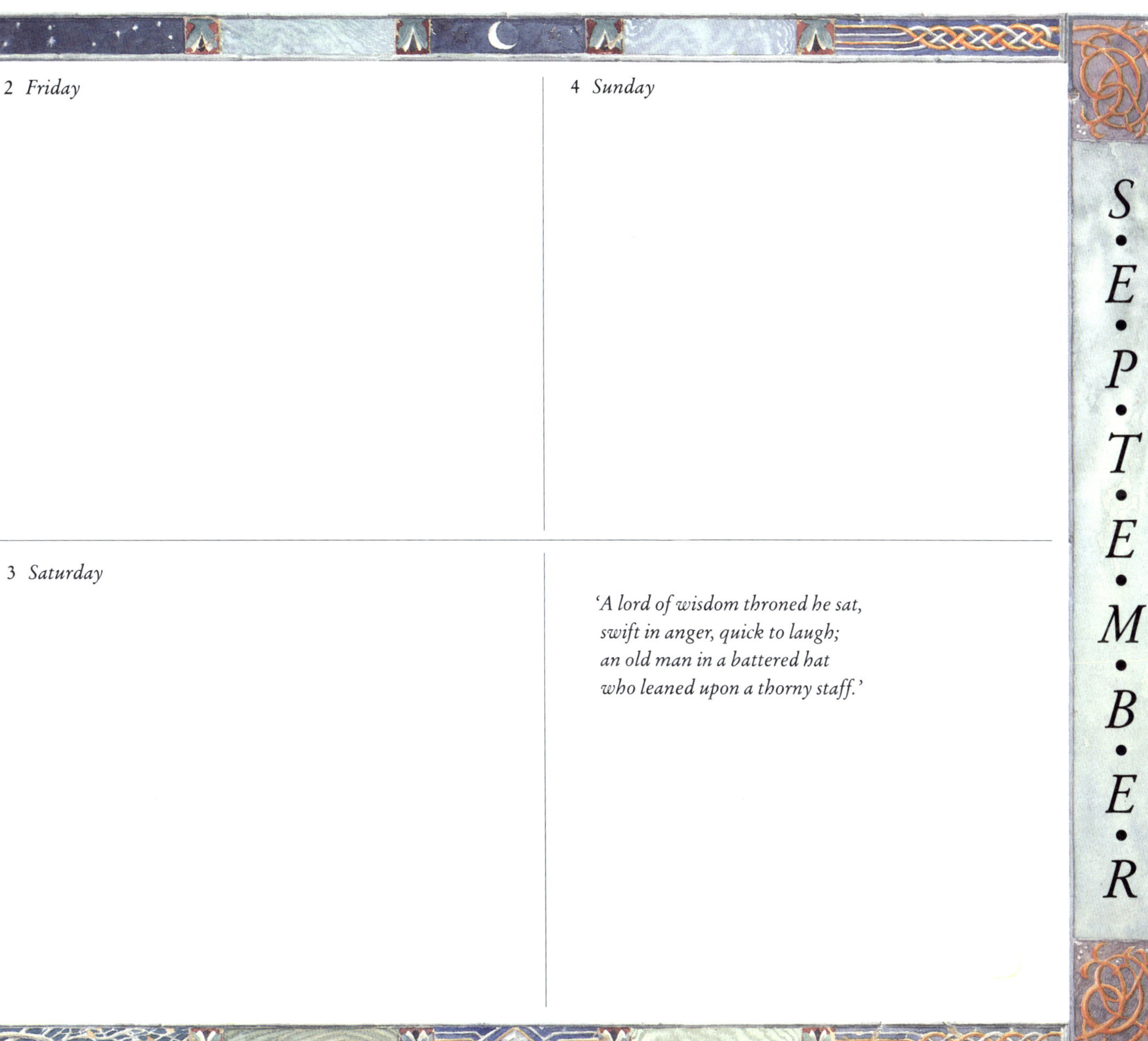

2 *Friday*

4 *Sunday*

3 *Saturday*

'A lord of wisdom throned he sat,
swift in anger, quick to laugh;
an old man in a battered hat
who leaned upon a thorny staff.'

S·E·P·T·E·M·B·E·R

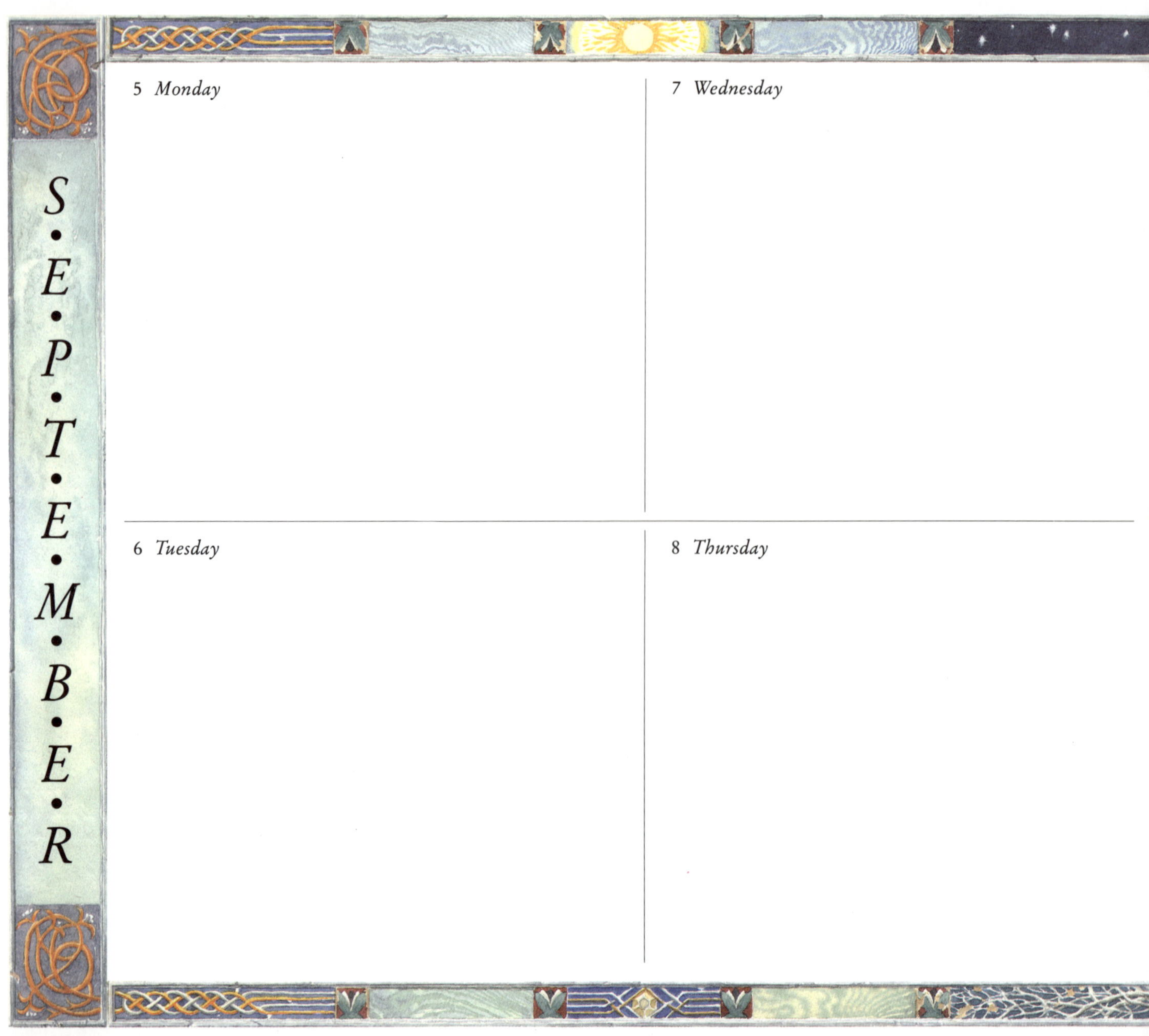

S·E·P·T·E·M·B·E·R

5 *Monday*

7 *Wednesday*

6 *Tuesday*

8 *Thursday*

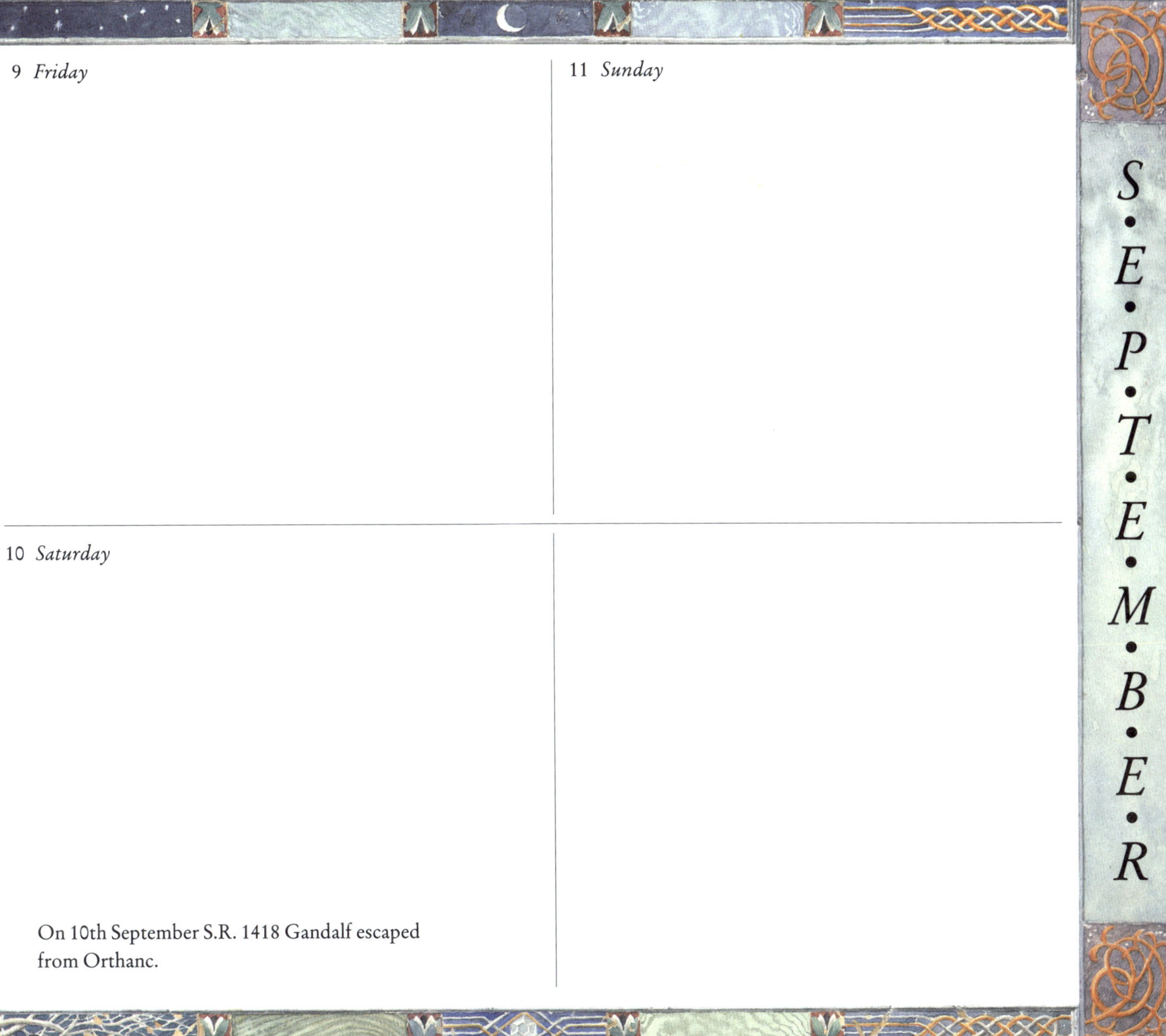

9 *Friday*

11 *Sunday*

10 *Saturday*

On 10th September S.R. 1418 Gandalf escaped from Orthanc.

S•E•P•T•E•M•B•E•R

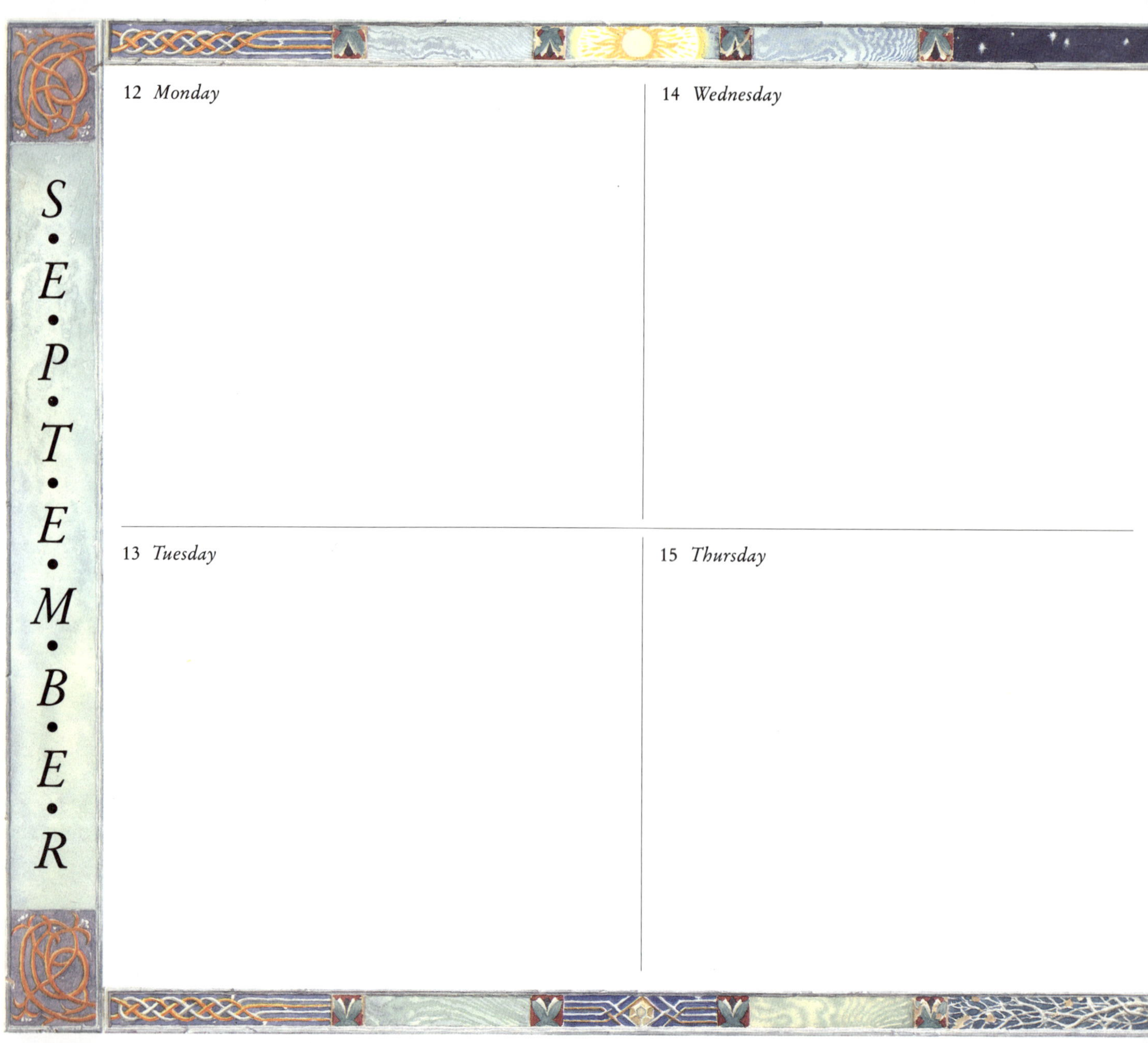

S·E·P·T·E·M·B·E·R

12 *Monday*

13 *Tuesday*

14 *Wednesday*

15 *Thursday*

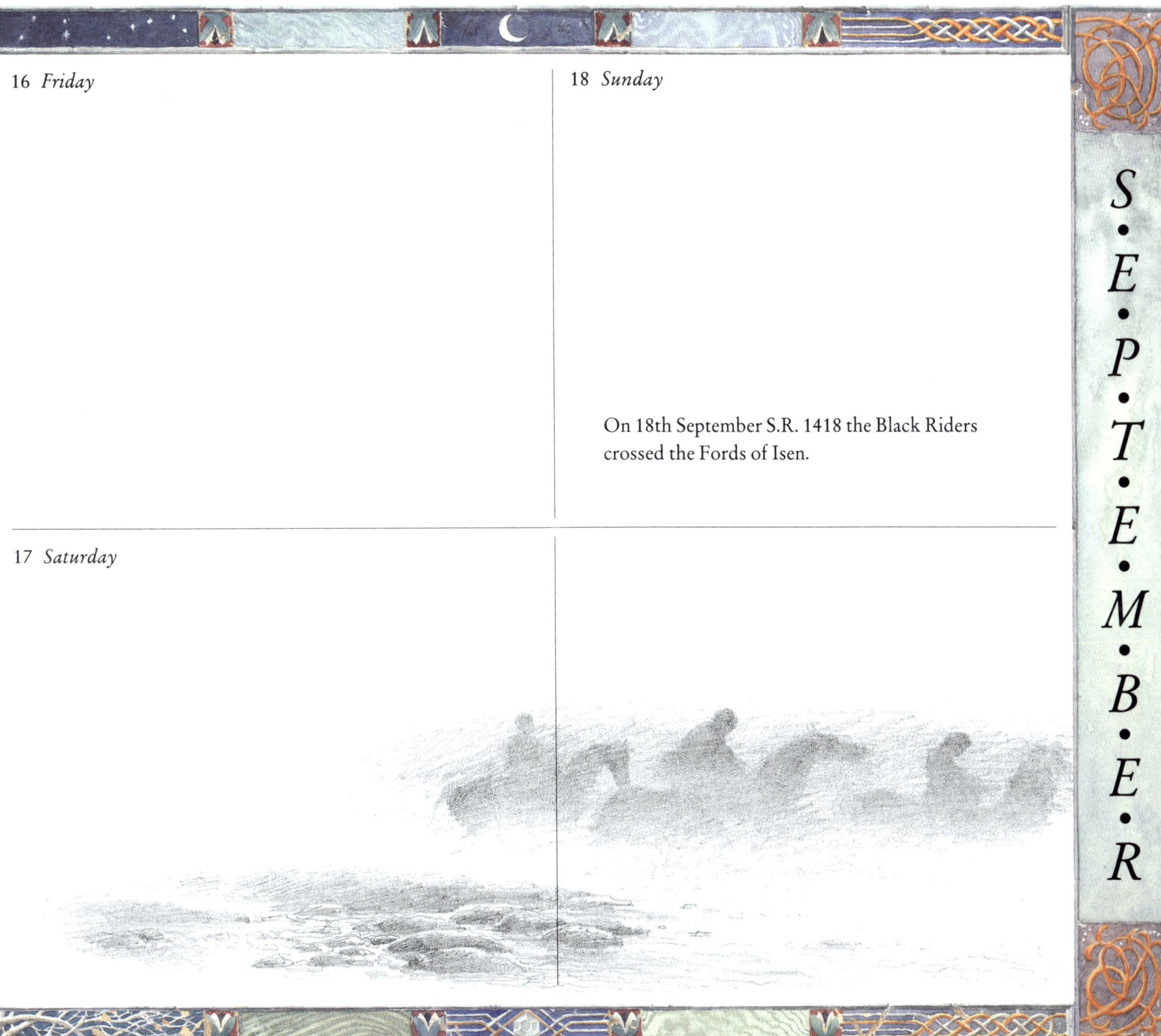

16 *Friday*

17 *Saturday*

18 *Sunday*

On 18th September S.R. 1418 the Black Riders crossed the Fords of Isen.

S•E•P•T•E•M•B•E•R

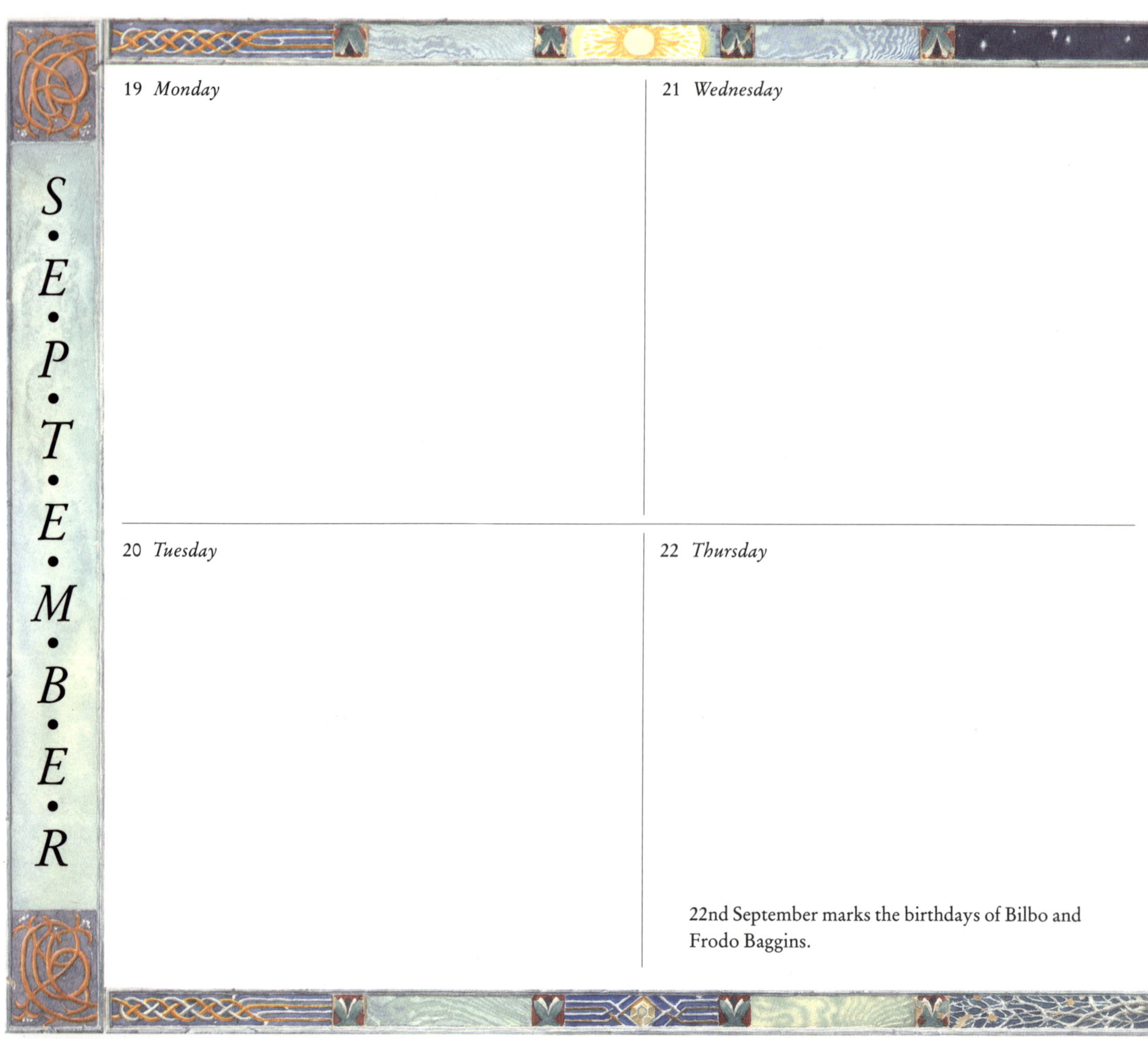

19 *Monday*

20 *Tuesday*

21 *Wednesday*

22 *Thursday*

22nd September marks the birthdays of Bilbo and Frodo Baggins.

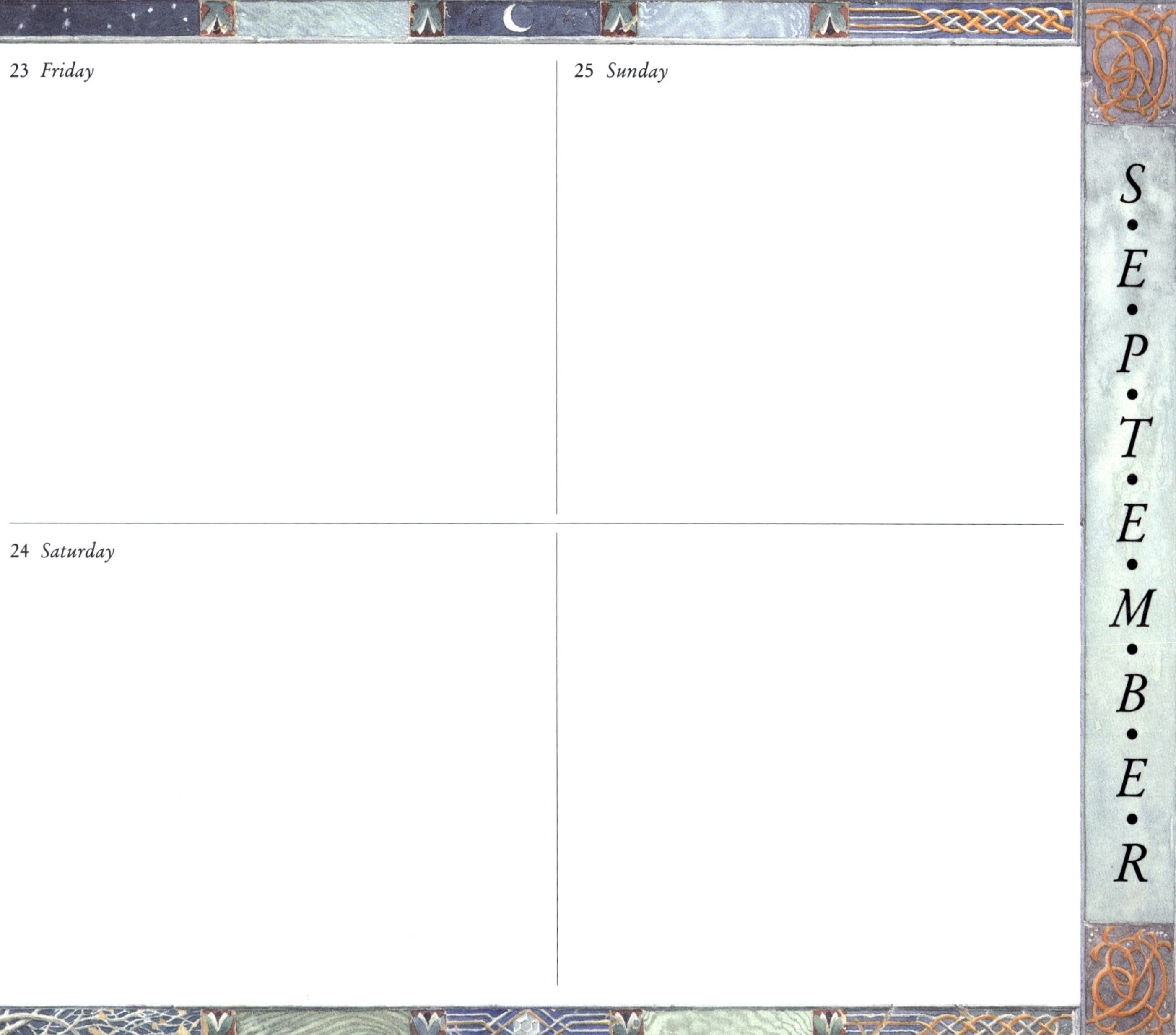

23 *Friday*

25 *Sunday*

24 *Saturday*

S•E•P•T•E•M•B•E•R

S·E·P·T·E·M·B·E·R

26 *Monday*

27 *Tuesday*

28 *Wednesday*

29 *Thursday*

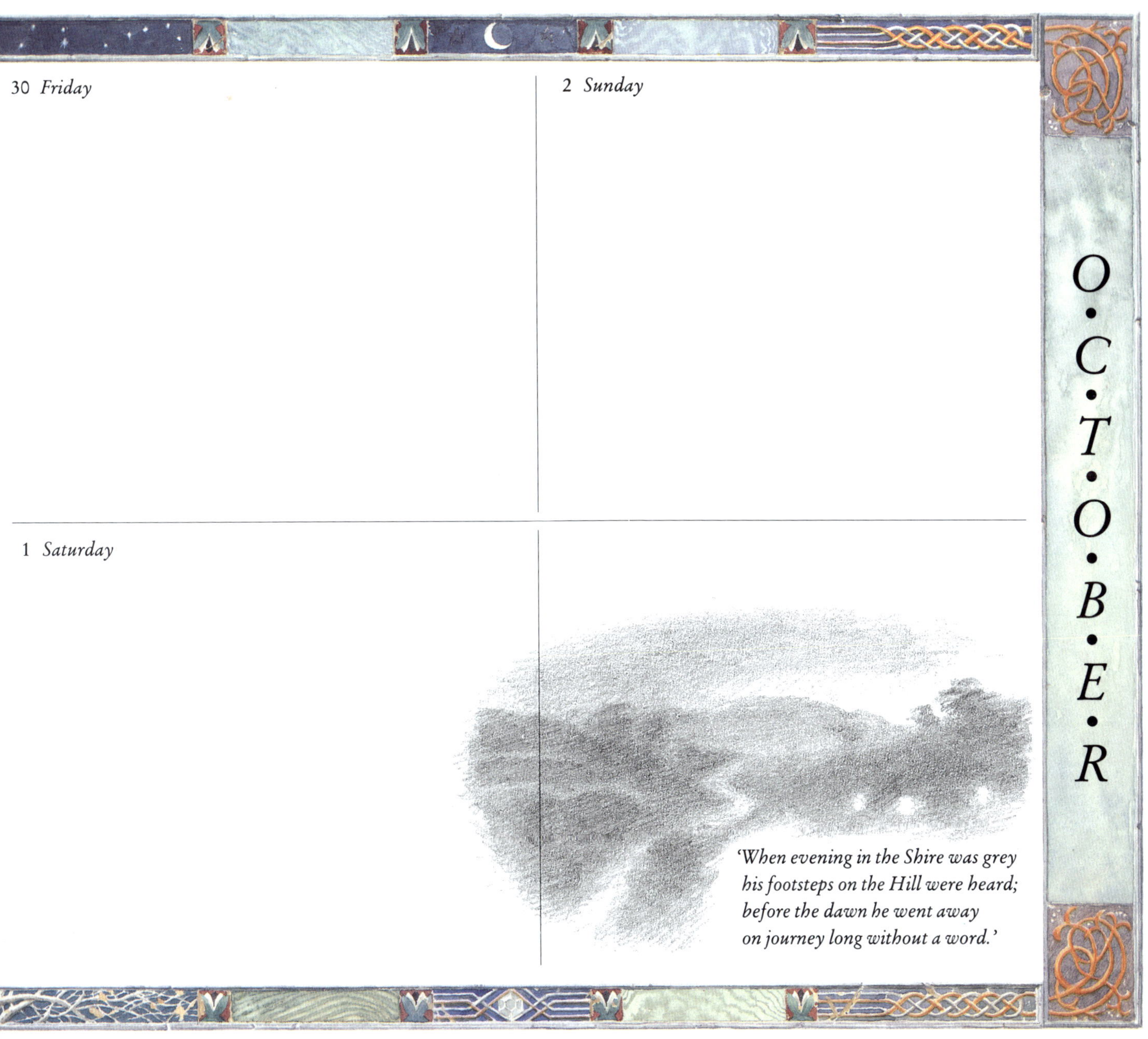

30 *Friday*

2 *Sunday*

1 *Saturday*

'When evening in the Shire was grey
his footsteps on the Hill were heard;
before the dawn he went away
on journey long without a word.'

O·C·T·O·B·E·R

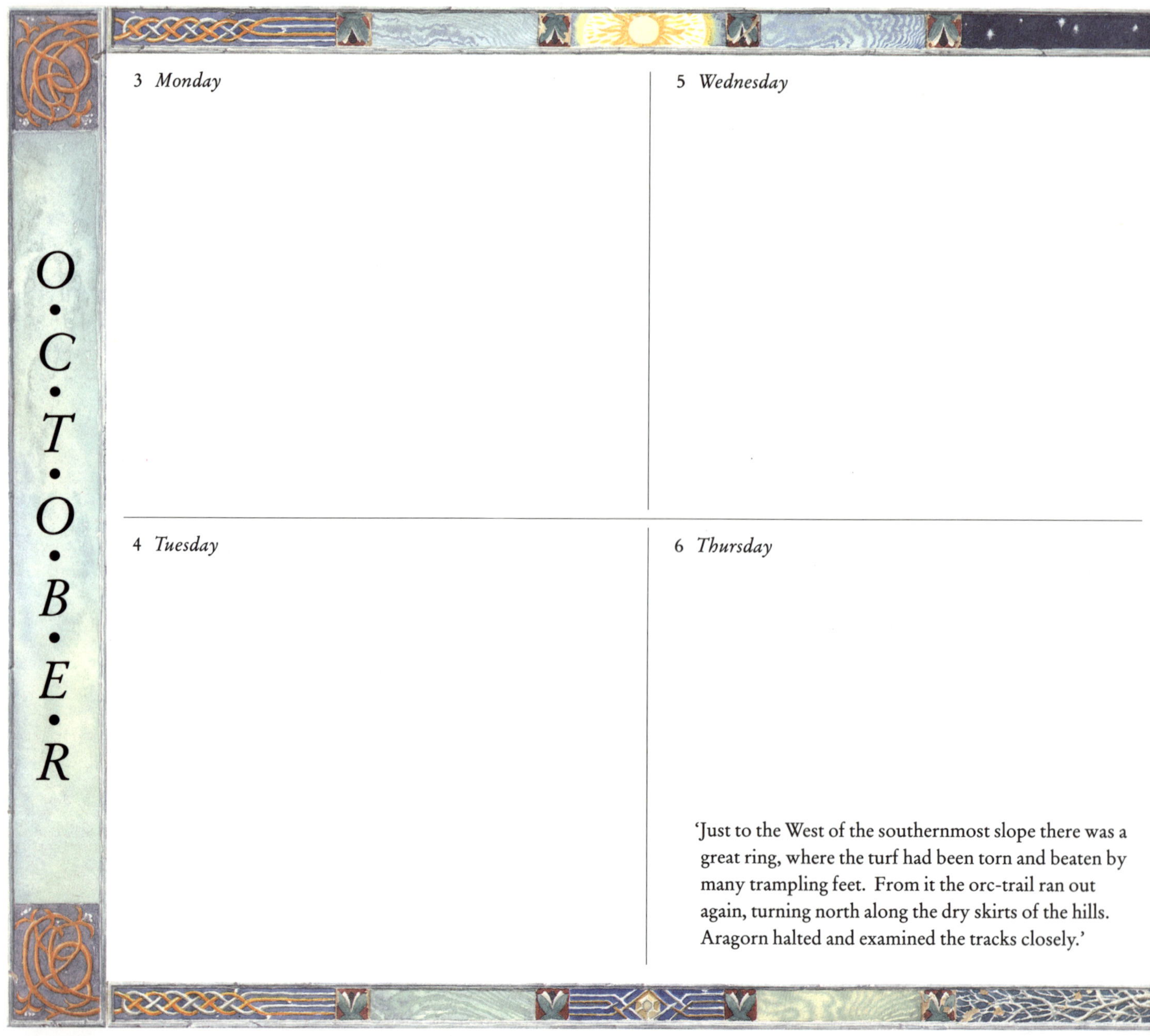

O·C·T·O·B·E·R

3 *Monday*

5 *Wednesday*

4 *Tuesday*

6 *Thursday*

'Just to the West of the southernmost slope there was a great ring, where the turf had been torn and beaten by many trampling feet. From it the orc-trail ran out again, turning north along the dry skirts of the hills. Aragorn halted and examined the tracks closely.'

O•C•T•O•B•E•R

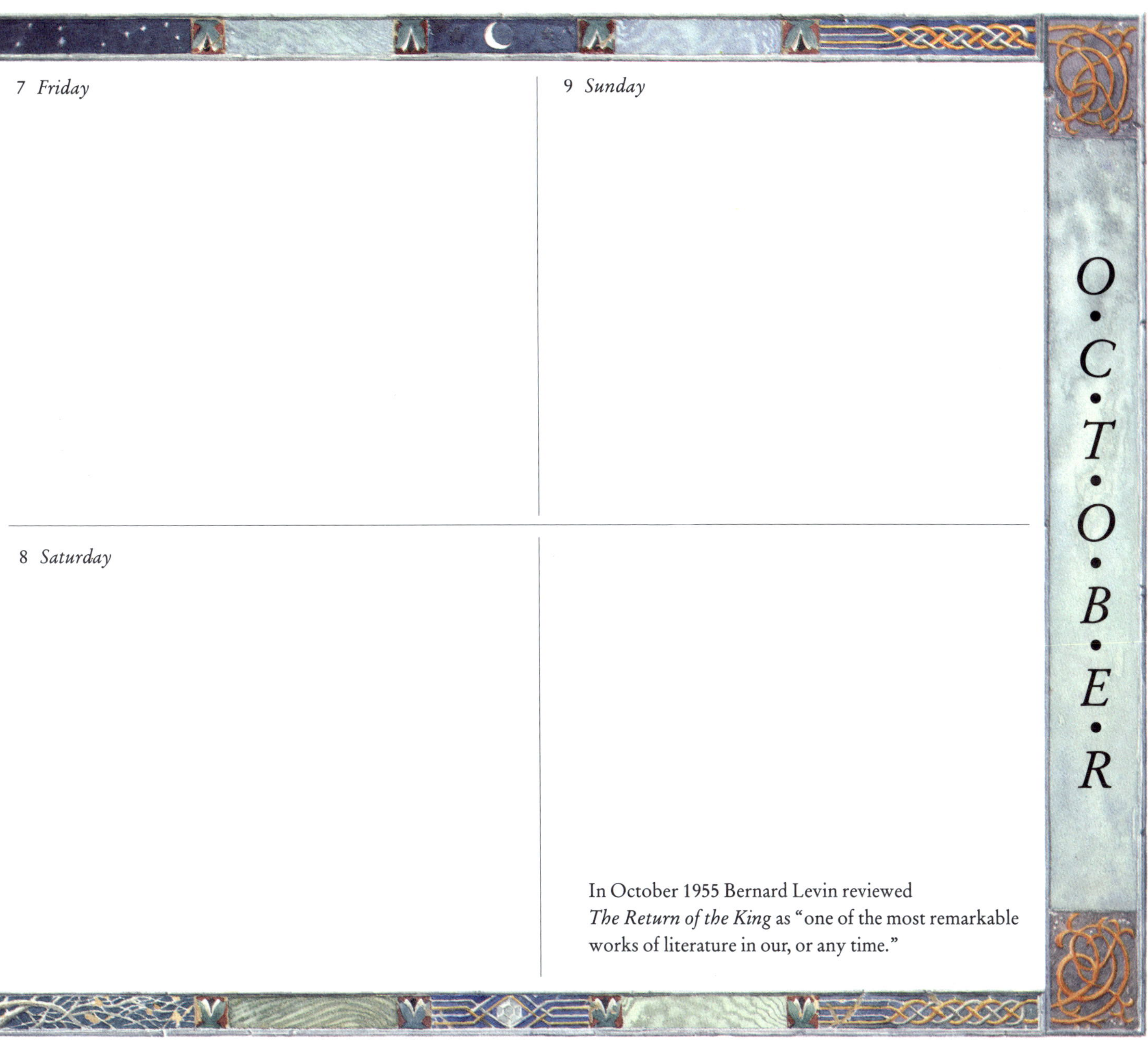

7 *Friday*

8 *Saturday*

9 *Sunday*

In October 1955 Bernard Levin reviewed *The Return of the King* as "one of the most remarkable works of literature in our, or any time."

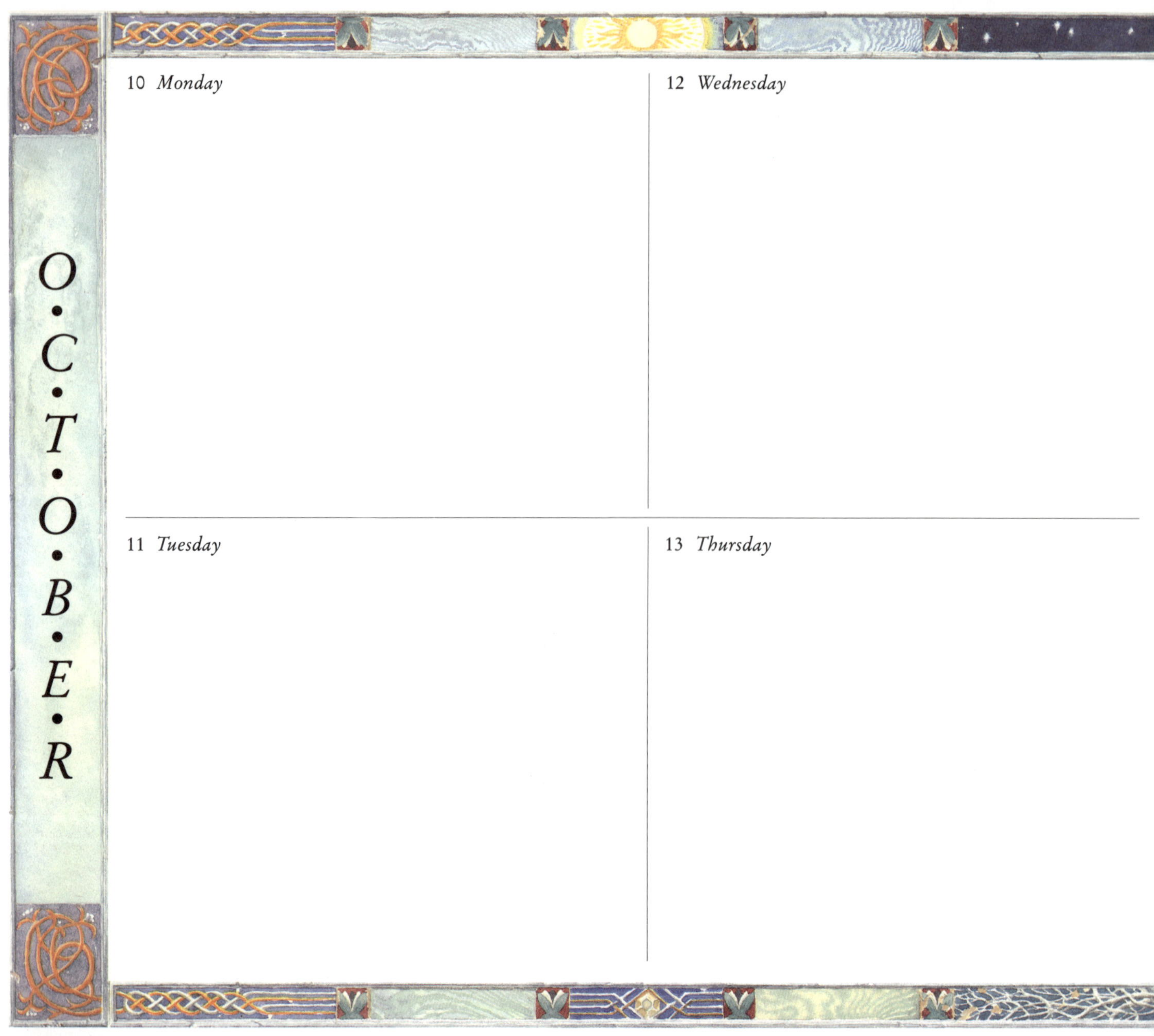

O·C·T·O·B·E·R

10 *Monday*

12 *Wednesday*

11 *Tuesday*

13 *Thursday*

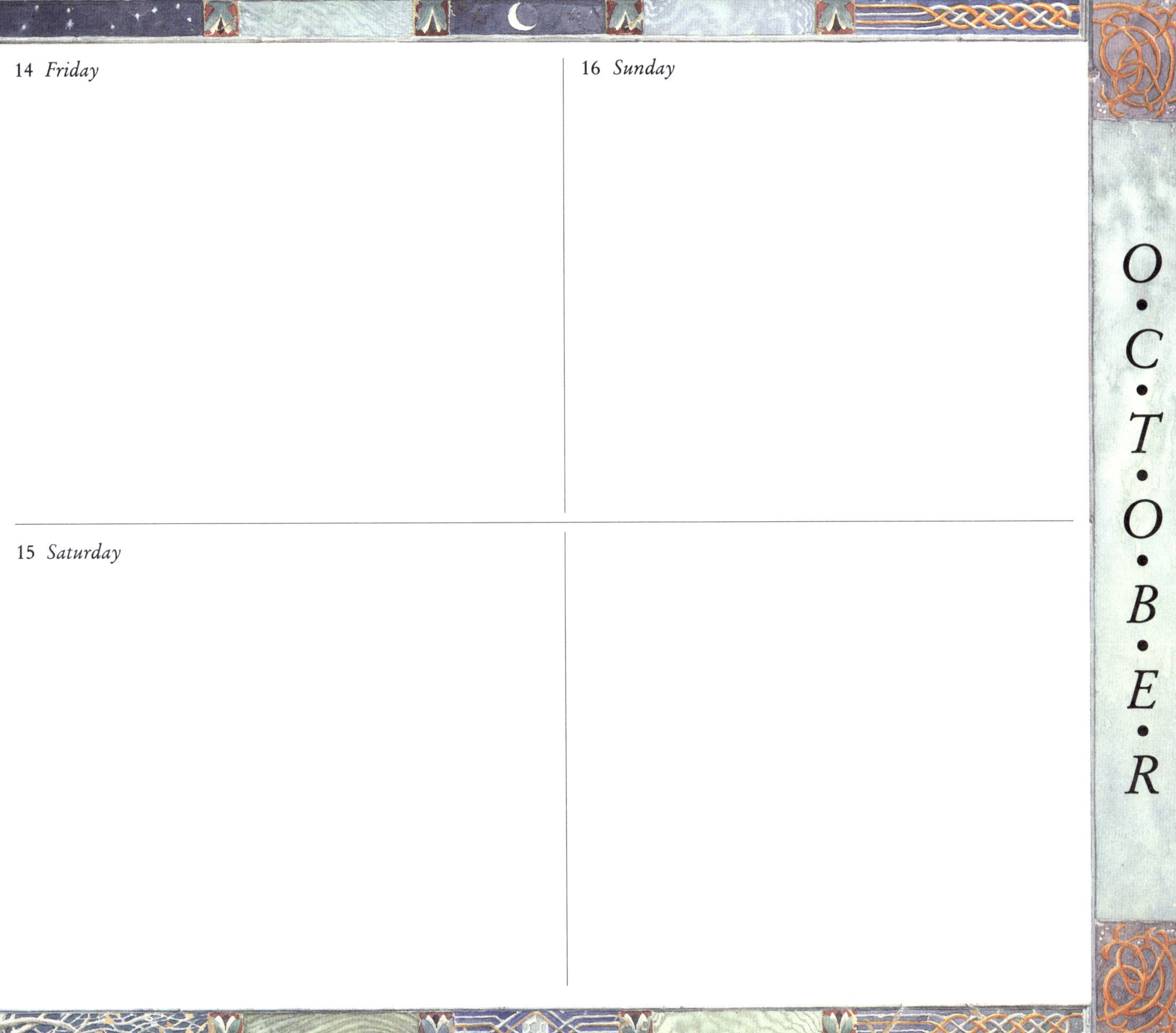

14 *Friday*

15 *Saturday*

16 *Sunday*

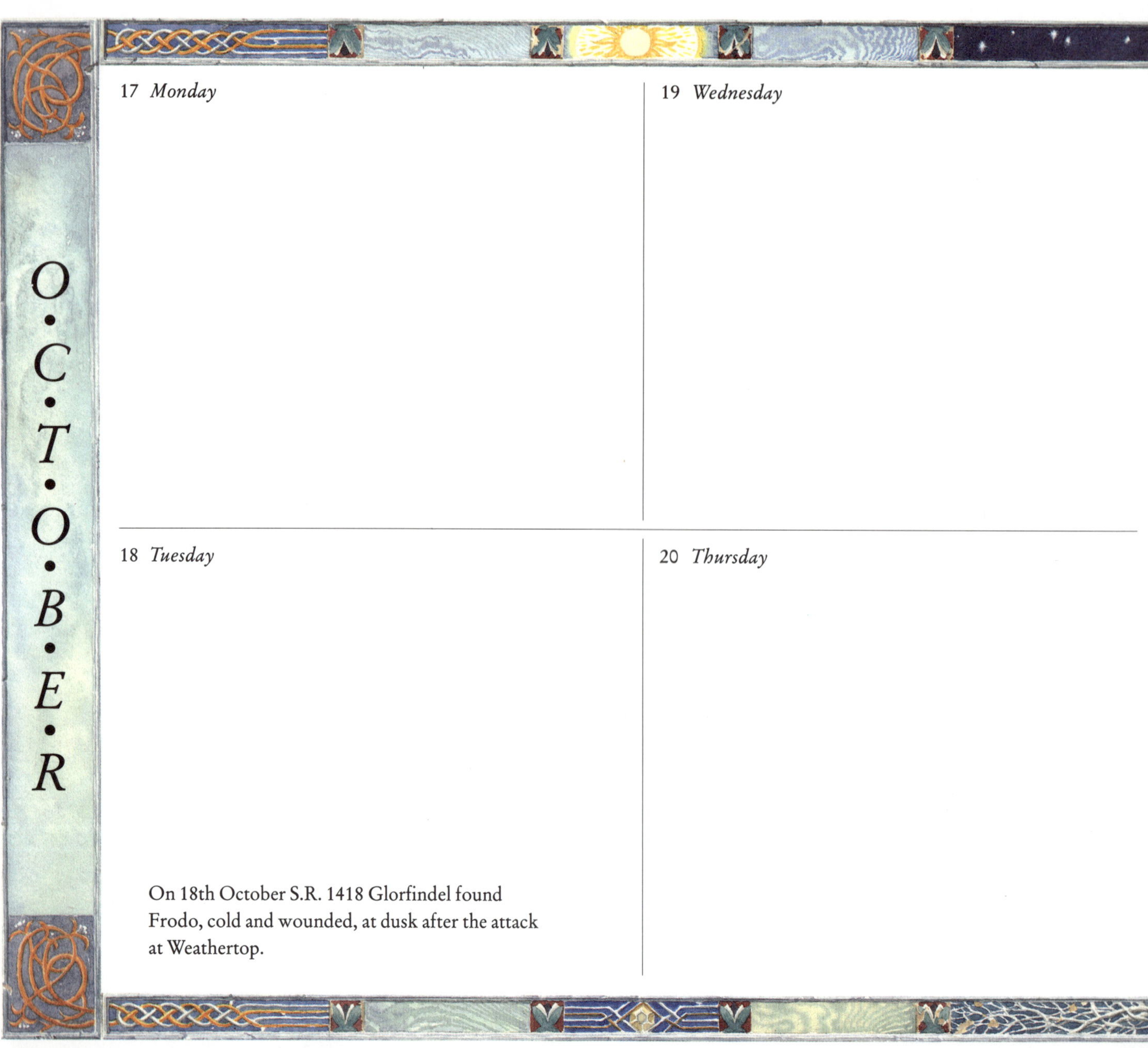

17 *Monday*

18 *Tuesday*

On 18th October S.R. 1418 Glorfindel found Frodo, cold and wounded, at dusk after the attack at Weathertop.

19 *Wednesday*

20 *Thursday*

21 *Friday*

23 *Sunday*

22 *Saturday*

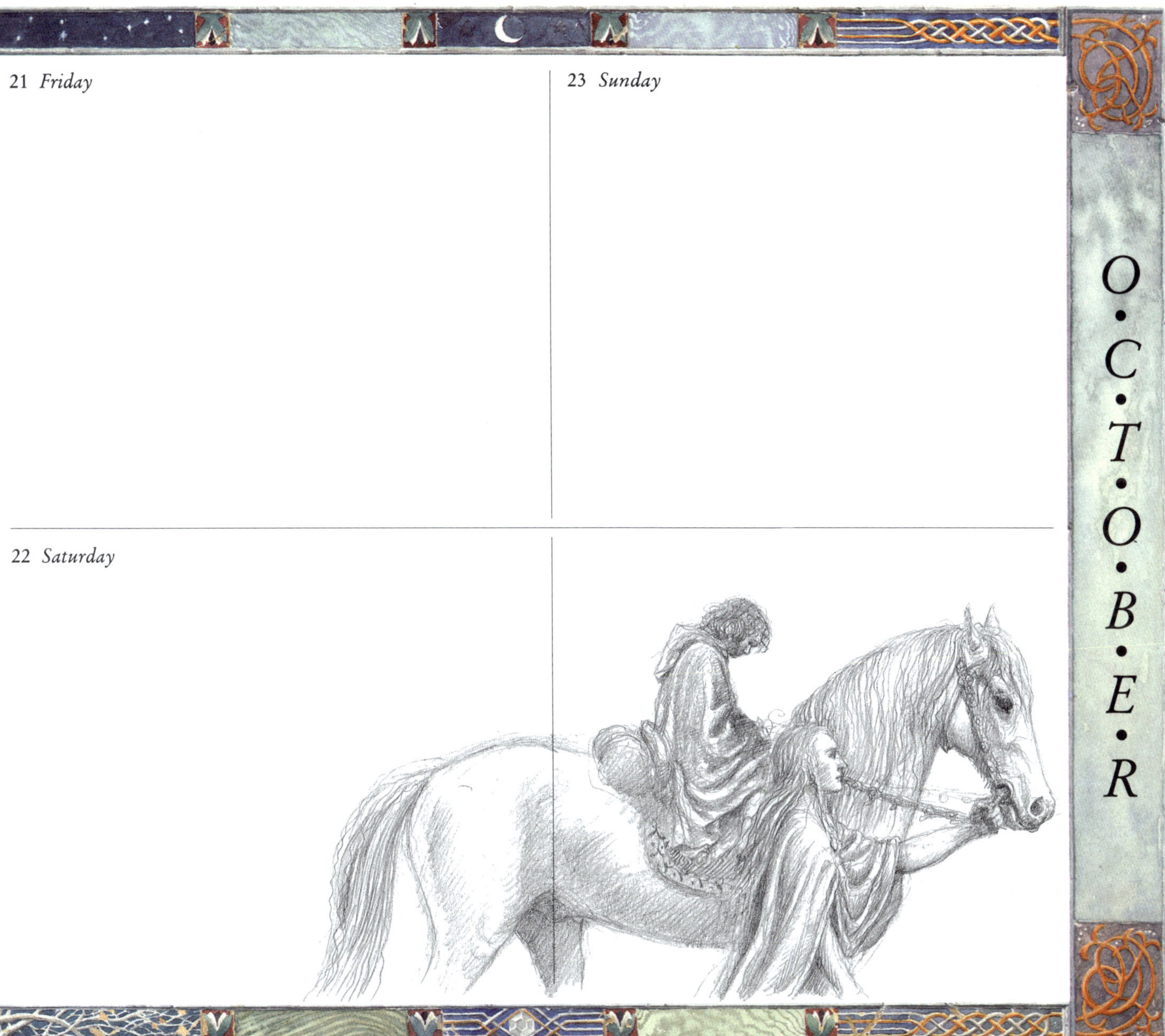

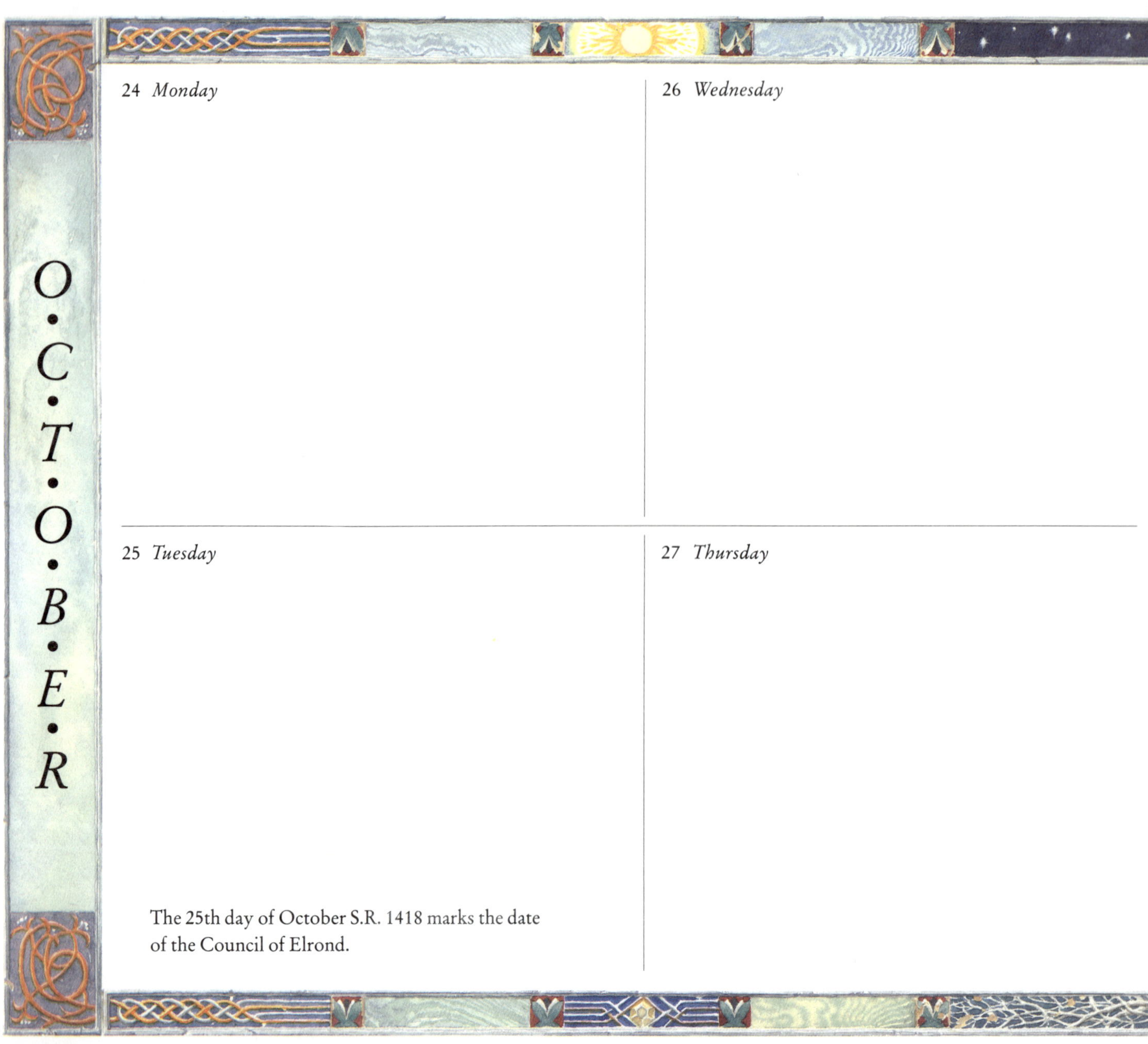

24 *Monday*

25 *Tuesday*

The 25th day of October S.R. 1418 marks the date of the Council of Elrond.

26 *Wednesday*

27 *Thursday*

28 *Friday*

30 *Sunday*

29 *Saturday*

O·C·T·O·B·E·R

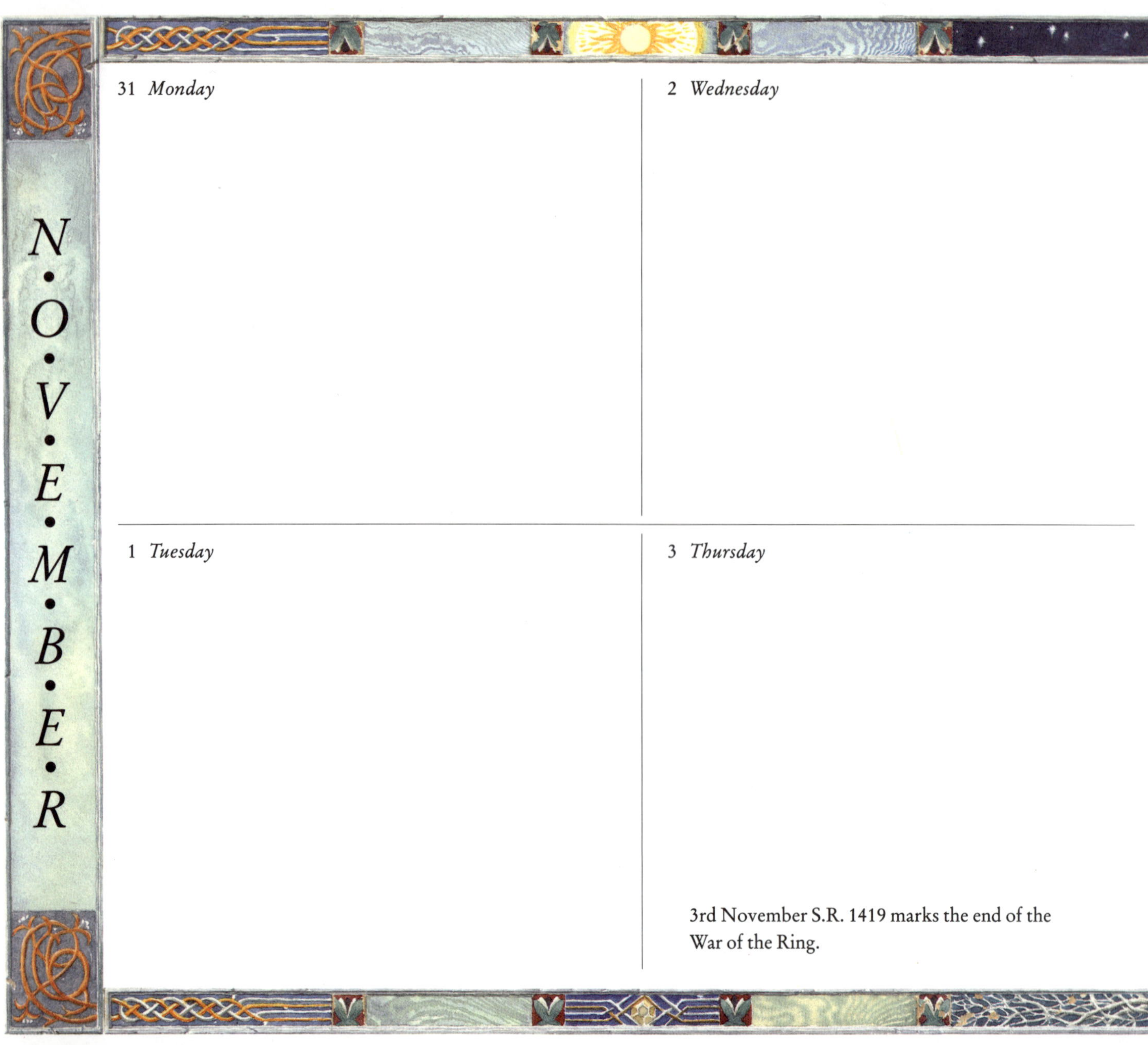

31 *Monday*

1 *Tuesday*

2 *Wednesday*

3 *Thursday*

3rd November S.R. 1419 marks the end of the War of the Ring.

N•O•V•E•M•B•E•R

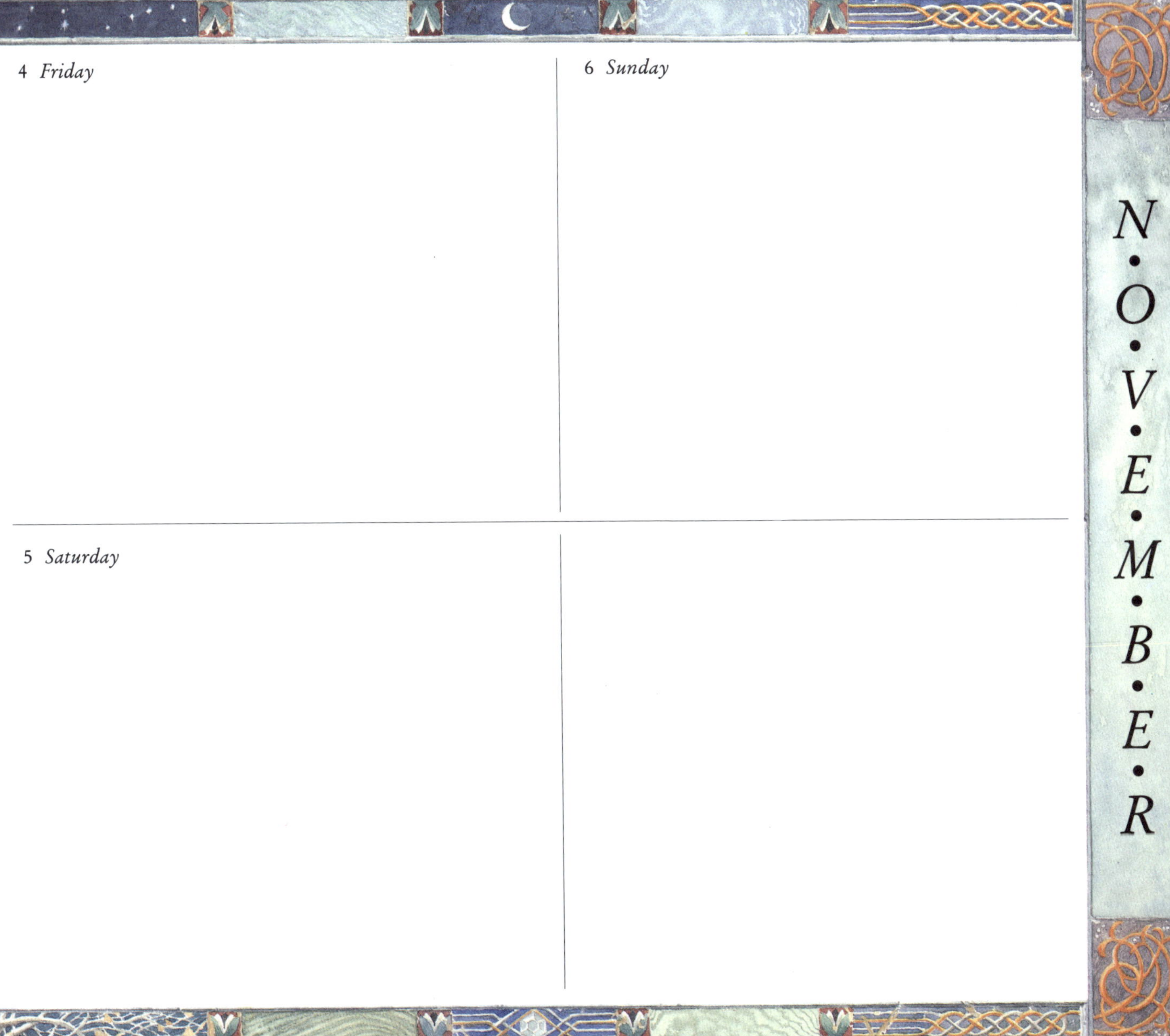

4 *Friday*

6 *Sunday*

5 *Saturday*

N·O·V·E·M·B·E·R

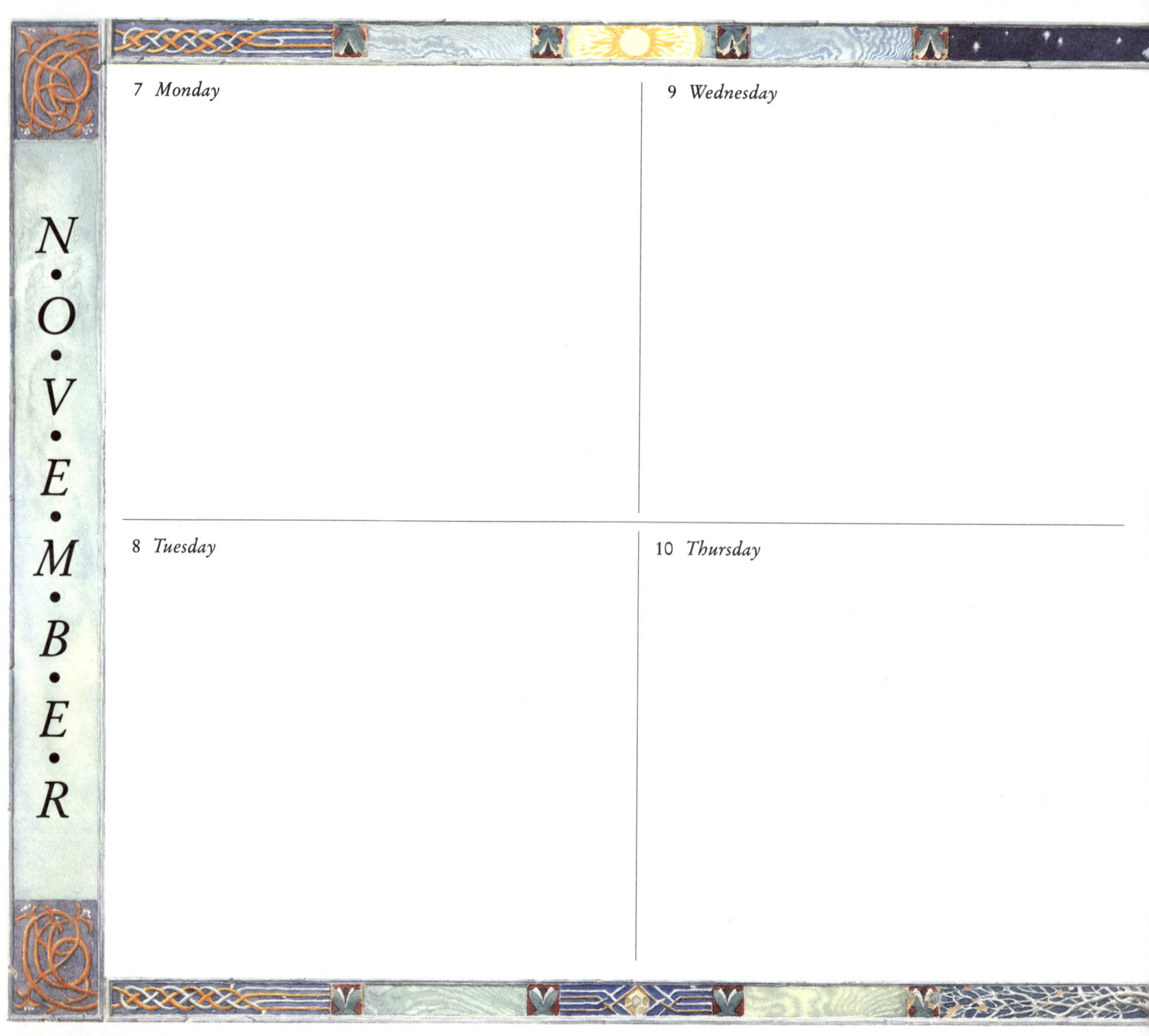

N·O·V·E·M·B·E·R

7 *Monday*

9 *Wednesday*

8 *Tuesday*

10 *Thursday*

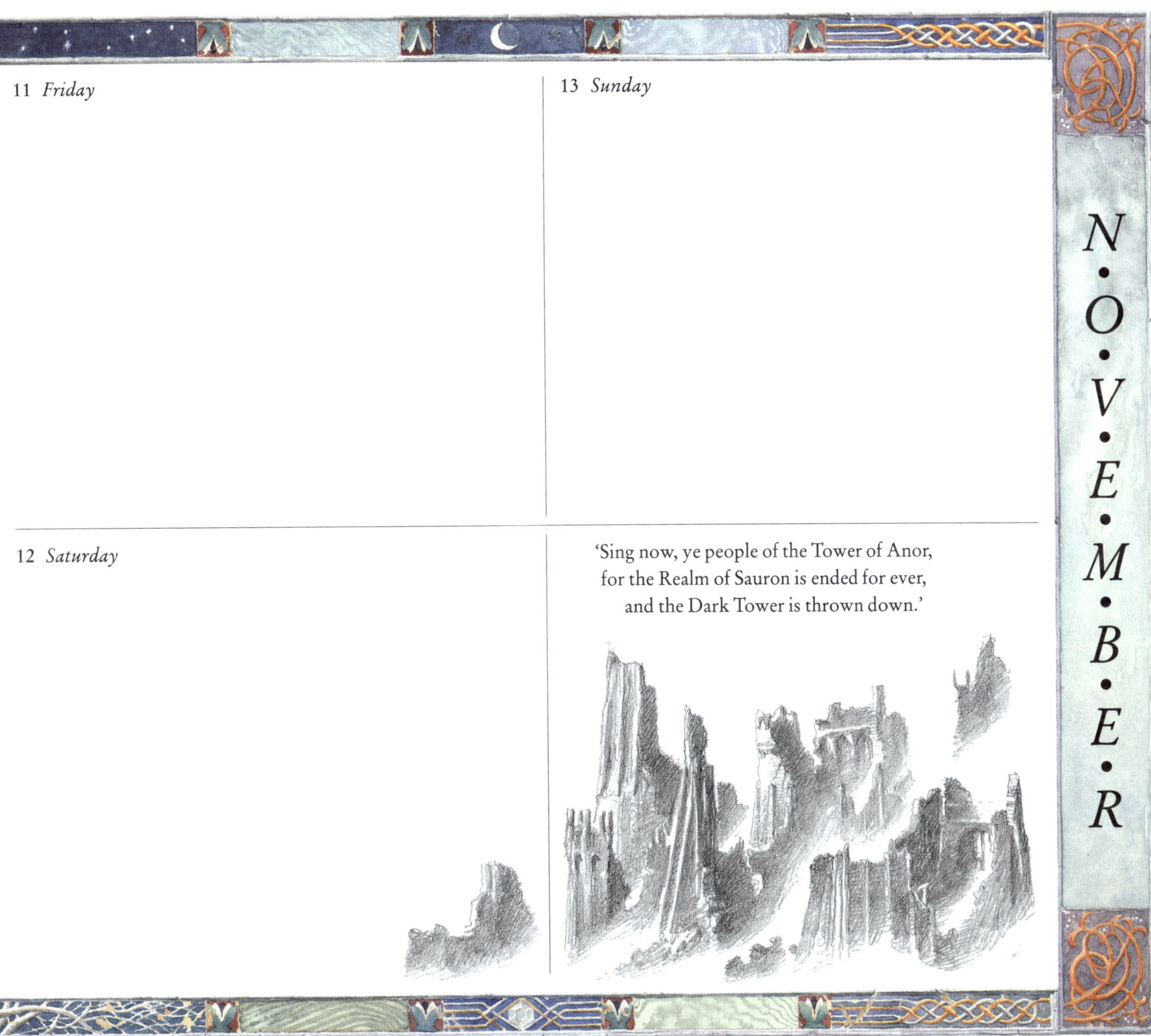

11 *Friday*

13 *Sunday*

12 *Saturday*

'Sing now, ye people of the Tower of Anor,
for the Realm of Sauron is ended for ever,
and the Dark Tower is thrown down.'

N·O·V·E·M·B·E·R

N·O·V·E·M·B·E·R

14 *Monday*

15 *Tuesday*

16 *Wednesday*

17 *Thursday*

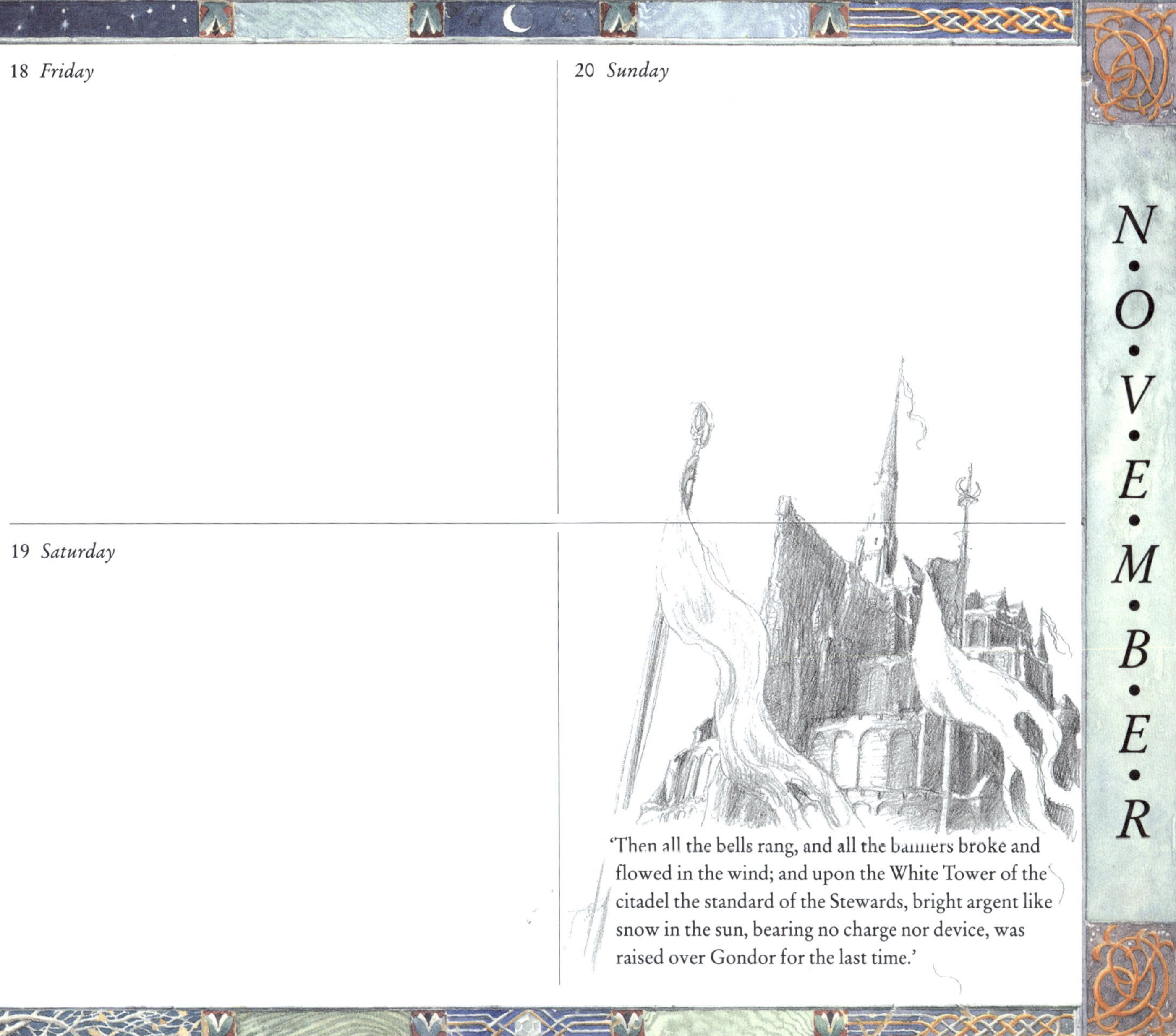

18 *Friday*

19 *Saturday*

20 *Sunday*

'Then all the bells rang, and all the banners broke and flowed in the wind; and upon the White Tower of the citadel the standard of the Stewards, bright argent like snow in the sun, bearing no charge nor device, was raised over Gondor for the last time.'

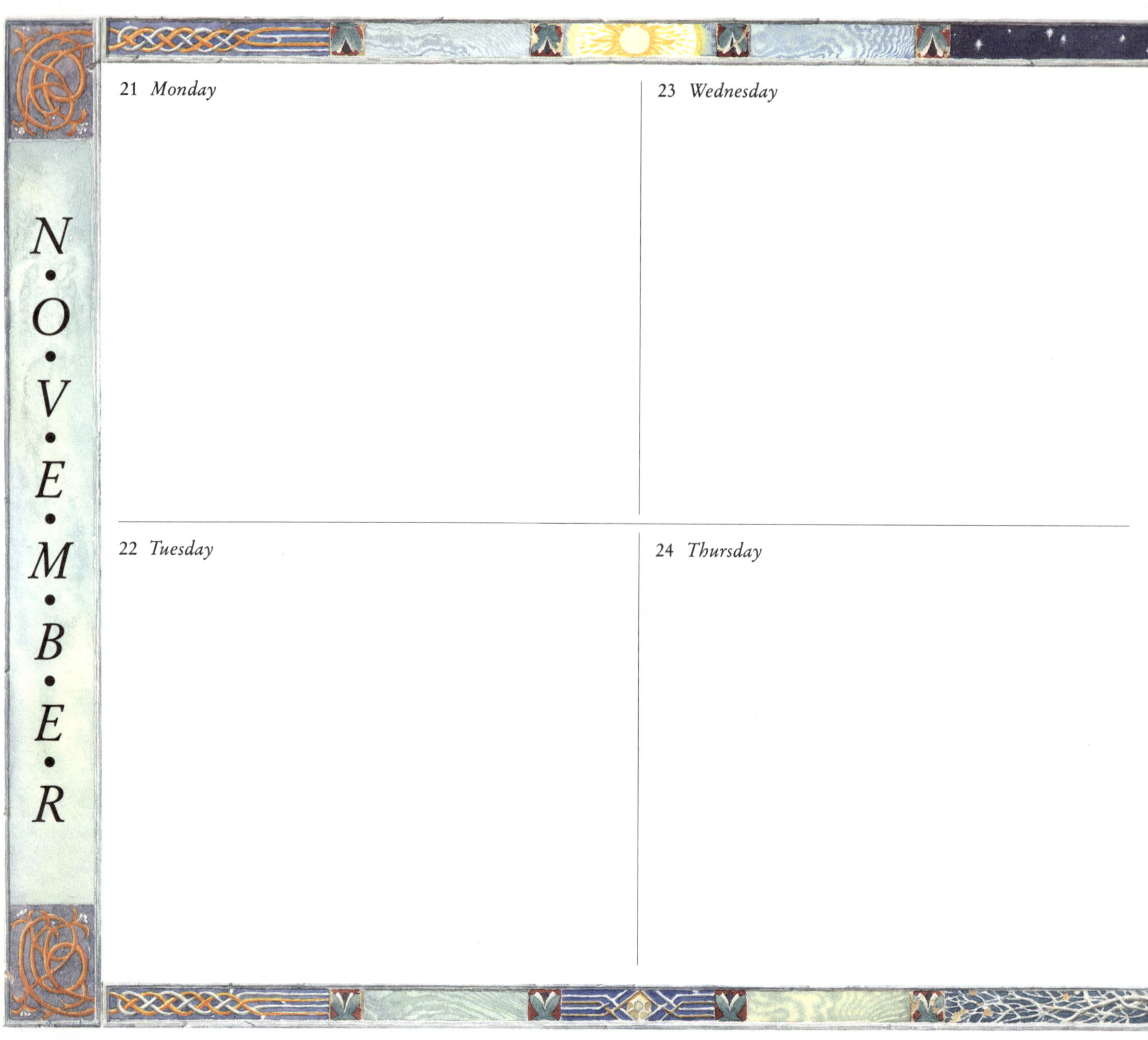

N·O·V·E·M·B·E·R

21 *Monday*

22 *Tuesday*

23 *Wednesday*

24 *Thursday*

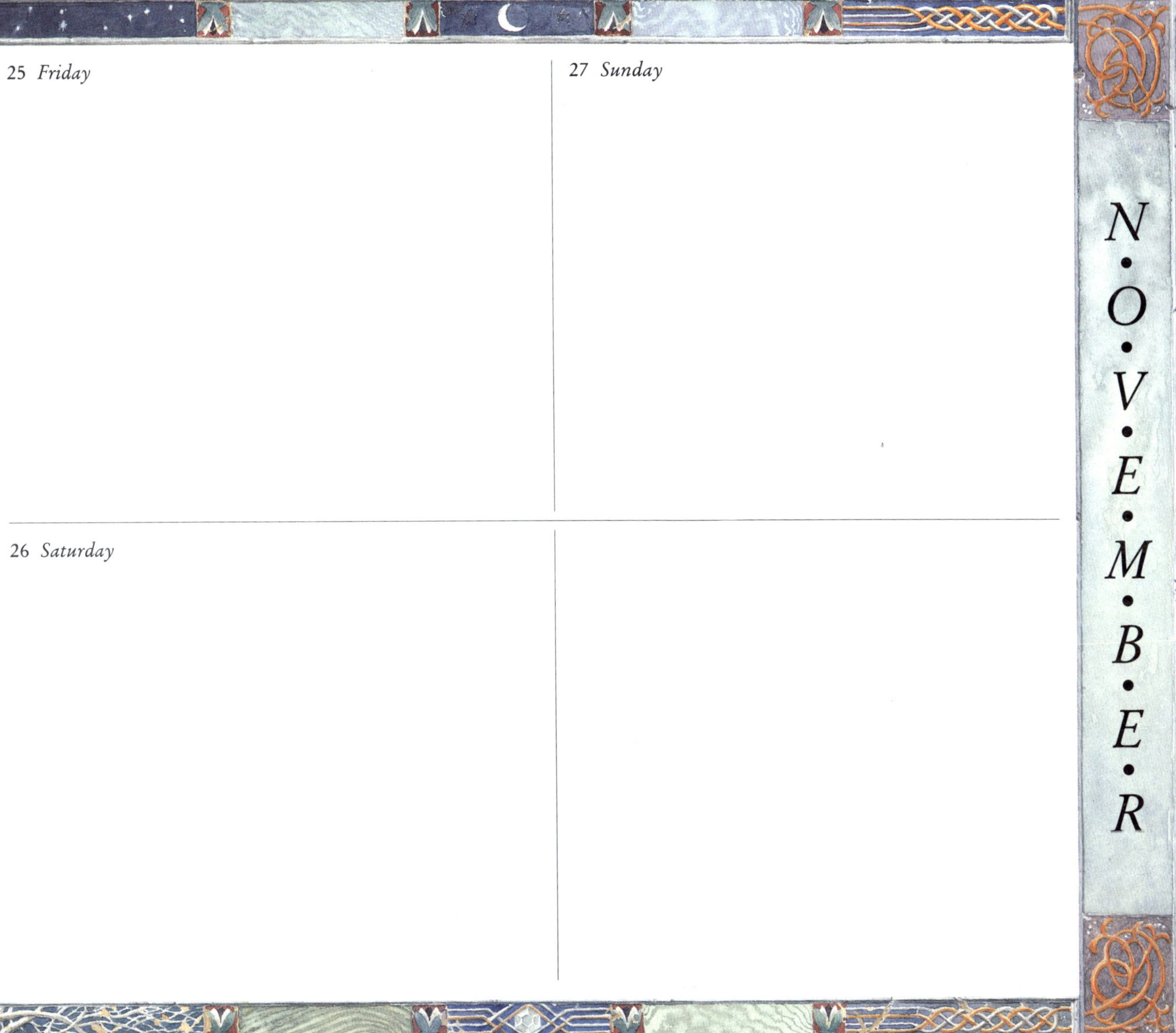

25 *Friday*

26 *Saturday*

27 *Sunday*

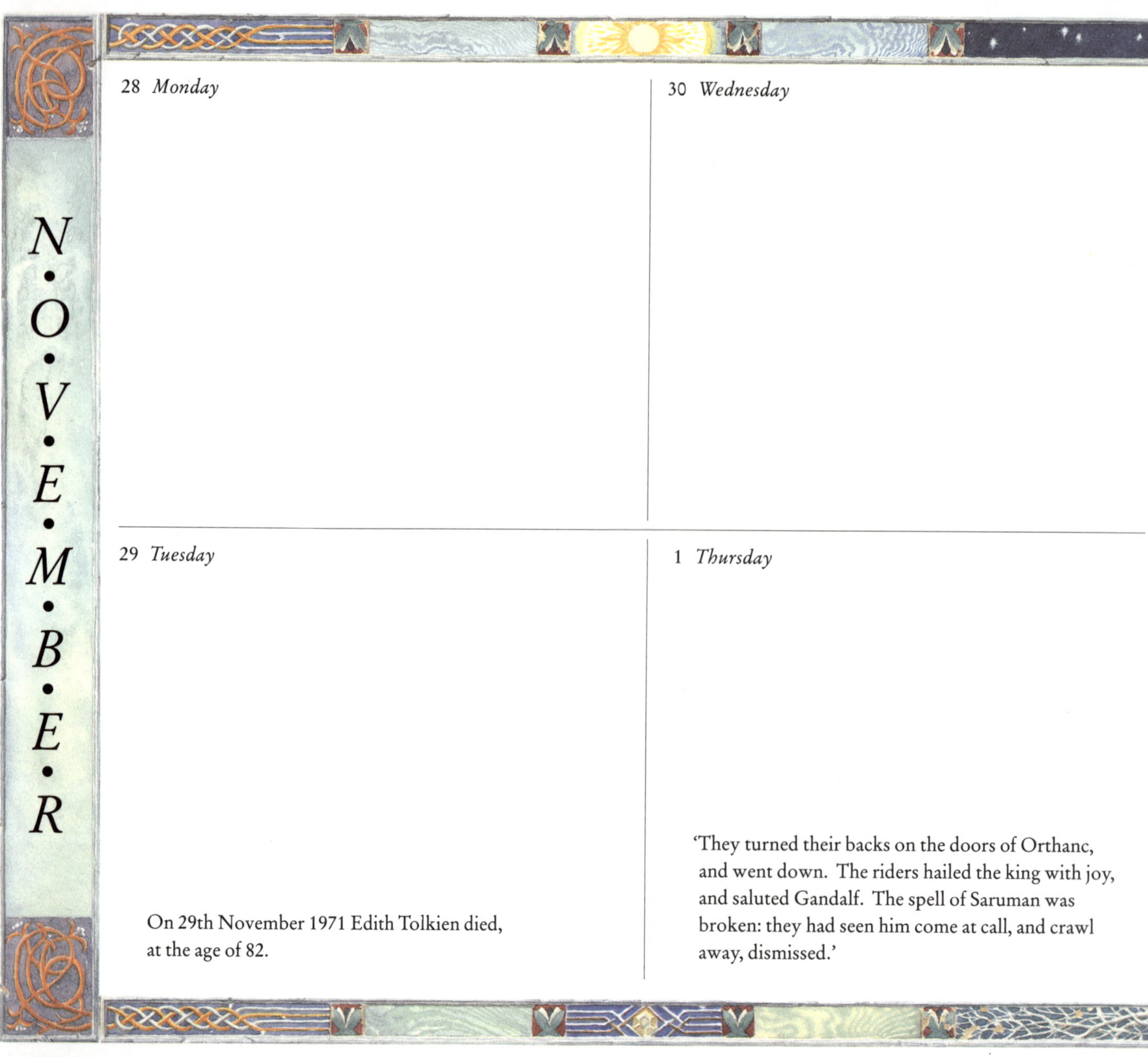

N·O·V·E·M·B·E·R

28 *Monday*

29 *Tuesday*

On 29th November 1971 Edith Tolkien died, at the age of 82.

30 *Wednesday*

1 *Thursday*

'They turned their backs on the doors of Orthanc, and went down. The riders hailed the king with joy, and saluted Gandalf. The spell of Saruman was broken: they had seen him come at call, and crawl away, dismissed.'

D•E•C•E•M•B•E•R

2 *Friday*

4 *Sunday*

3 *Saturday*

D•E•C•E•M•B•E•R

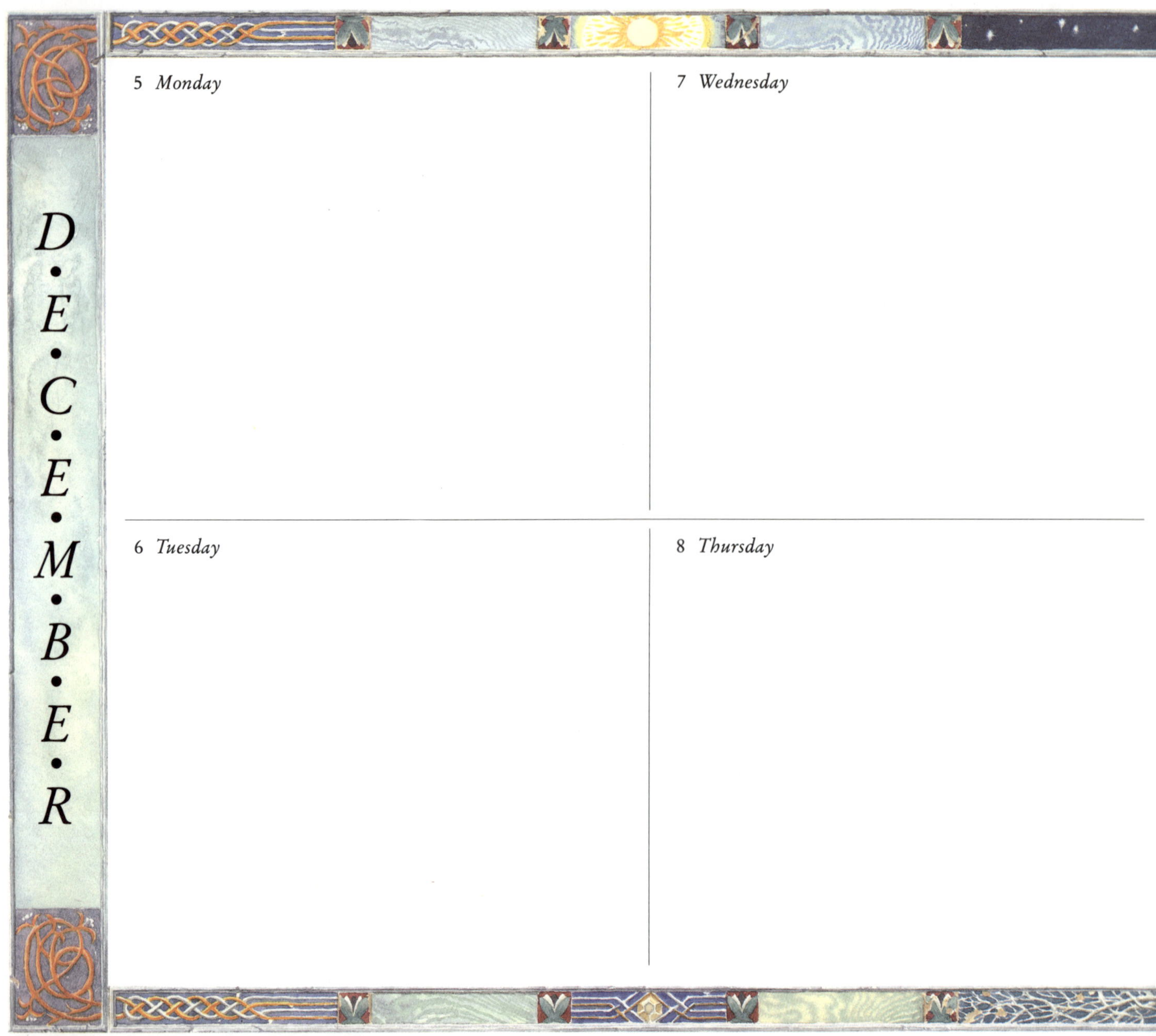

D·E·C·E·M·B·E·R

5 *Monday*

7 *Wednesday*

6 *Tuesday*

8 *Thursday*

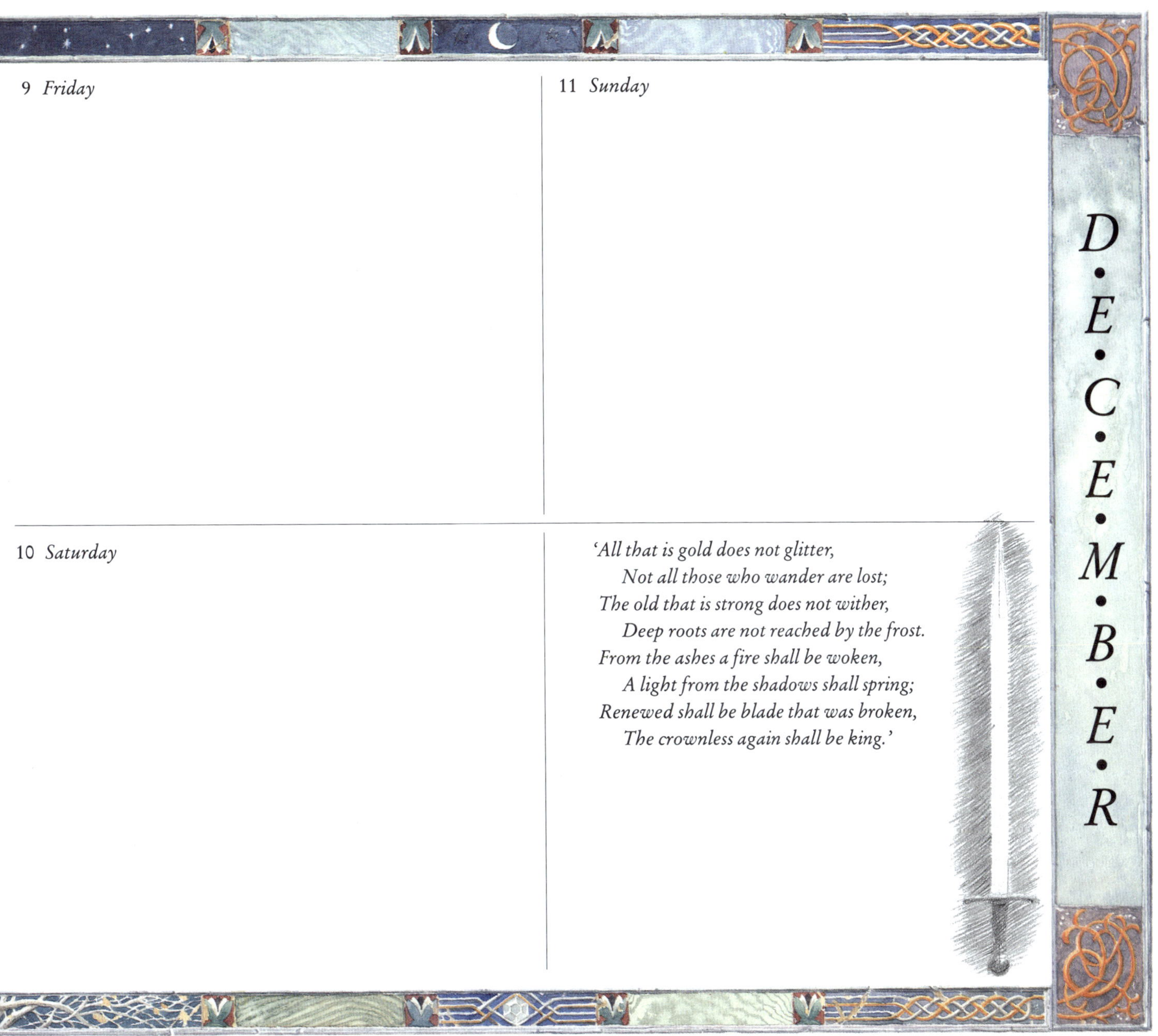

9 *Friday*

10 *Saturday*

11 *Sunday*

'All that is gold does not glitter,
Not all those who wander are lost;
The old that is strong does not wither,
Deep roots are not reached by the frost.
From the ashes a fire shall be woken,
A light from the shadows shall spring;
Renewed shall be blade that was broken,
The crownless again shall be king.'

D·E·C·E·M·B·E·R

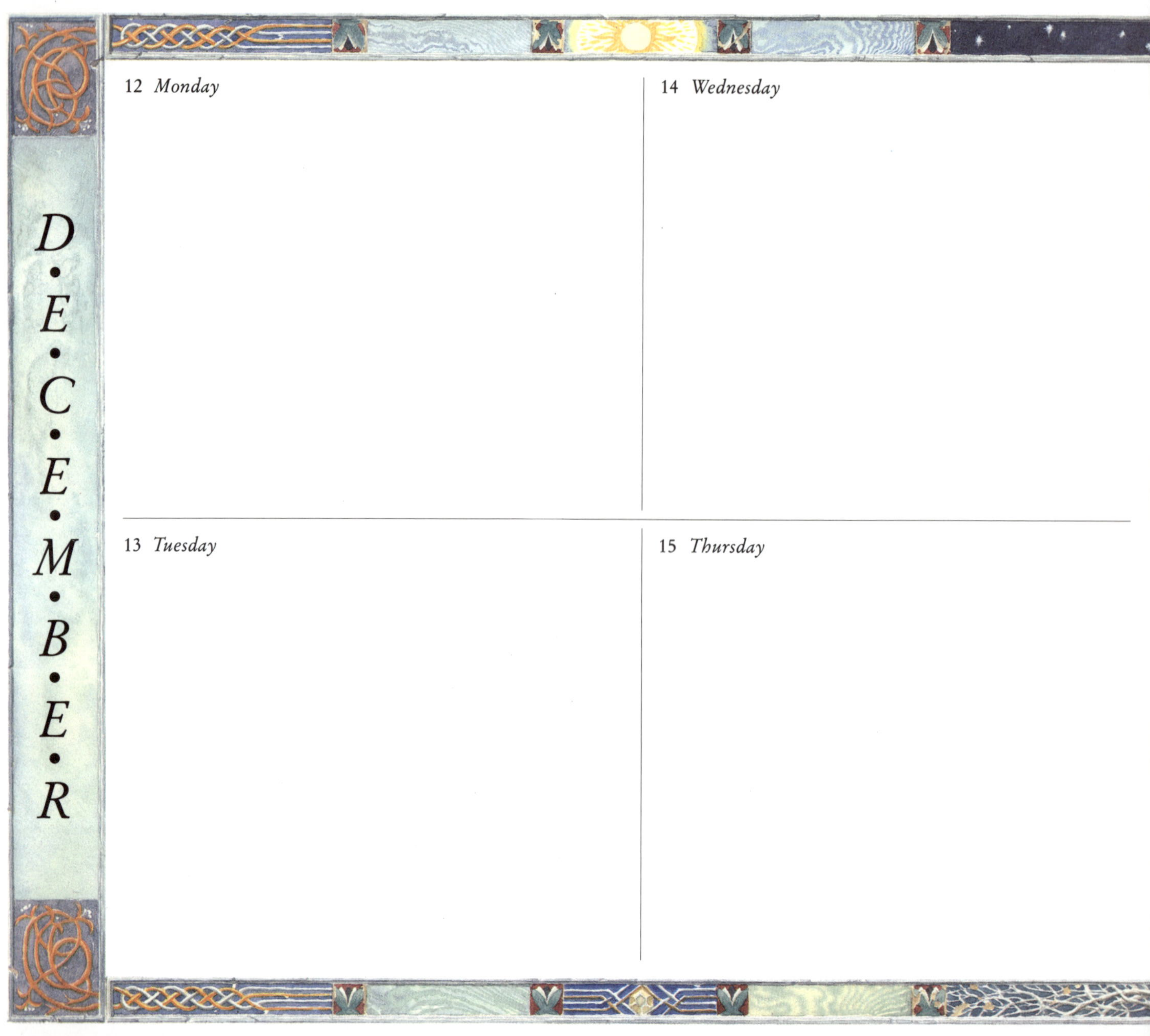

12 *Monday*

14 *Wednesday*

13 *Tuesday*

15 *Thursday*

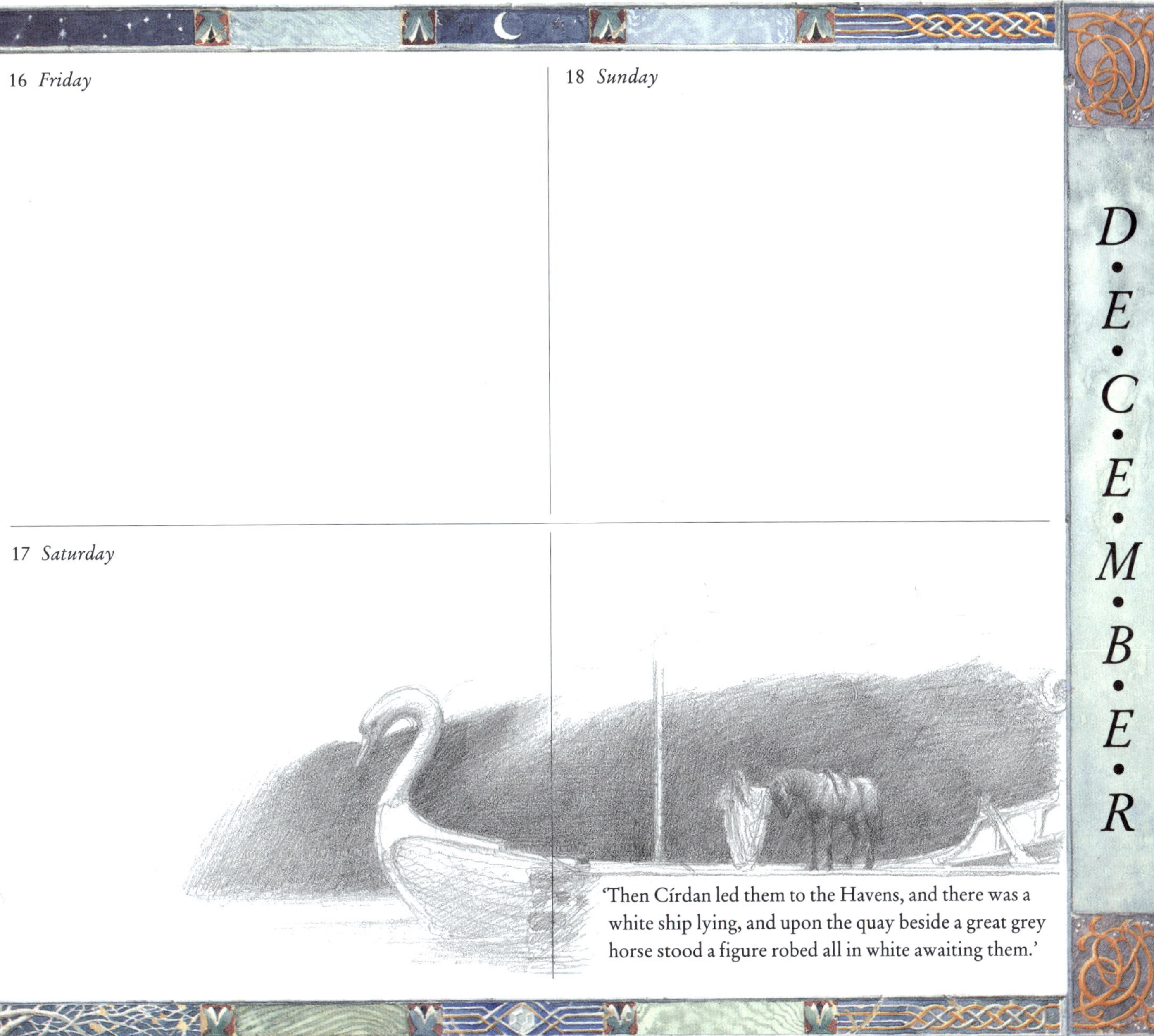

16 *Friday*

18 *Sunday*

17 *Saturday*

'Then Círdan led them to the Havens, and there was a white ship lying, and upon the quay beside a great grey horse stood a figure robed all in white awaiting them.'

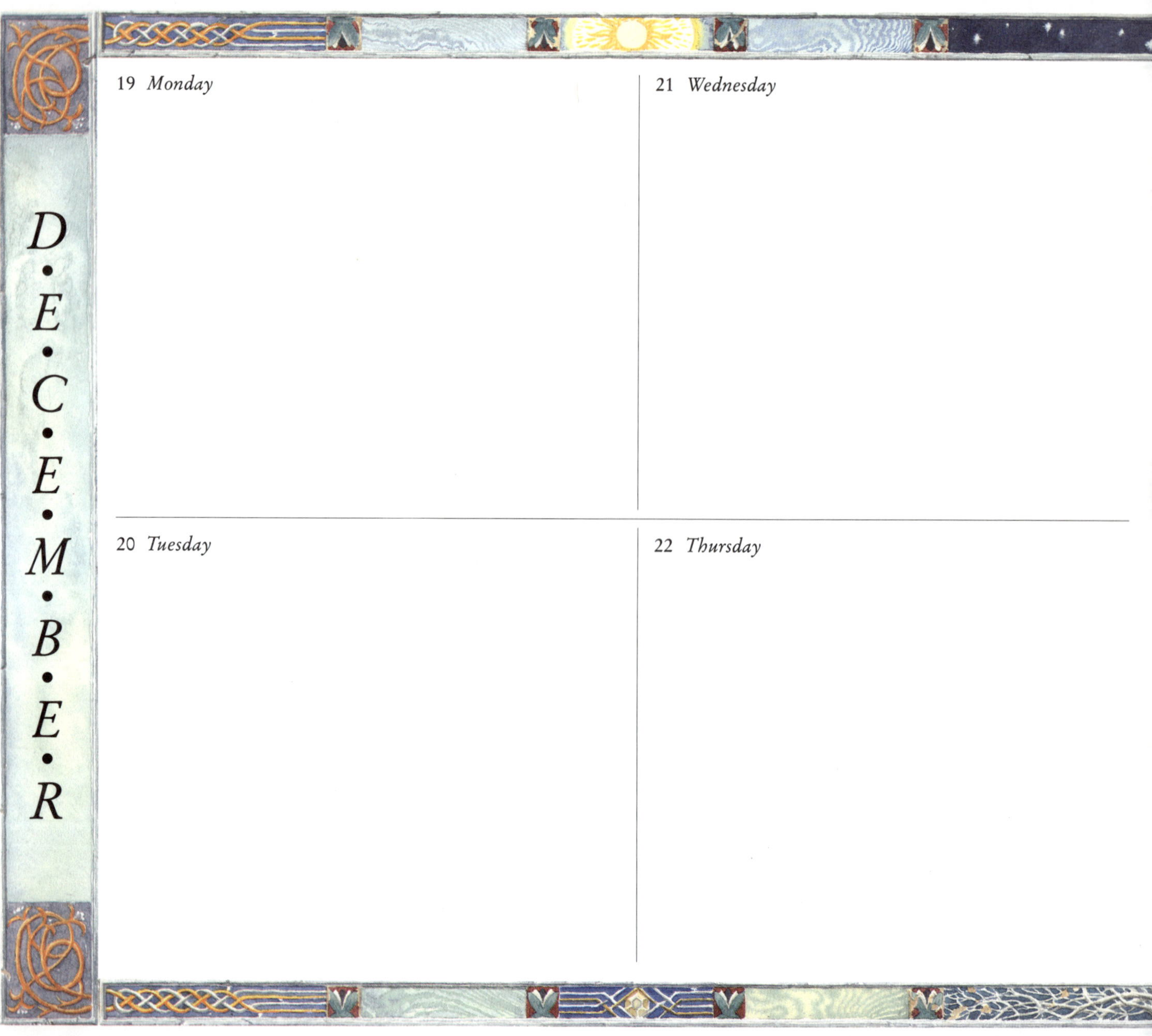

19 *Monday*

21 *Wednesday*

20 *Tuesday*

22 *Thursday*

23 *Friday*

25 *Sunday*

24 *Saturday*

D•E•C•E•M•B•E•R

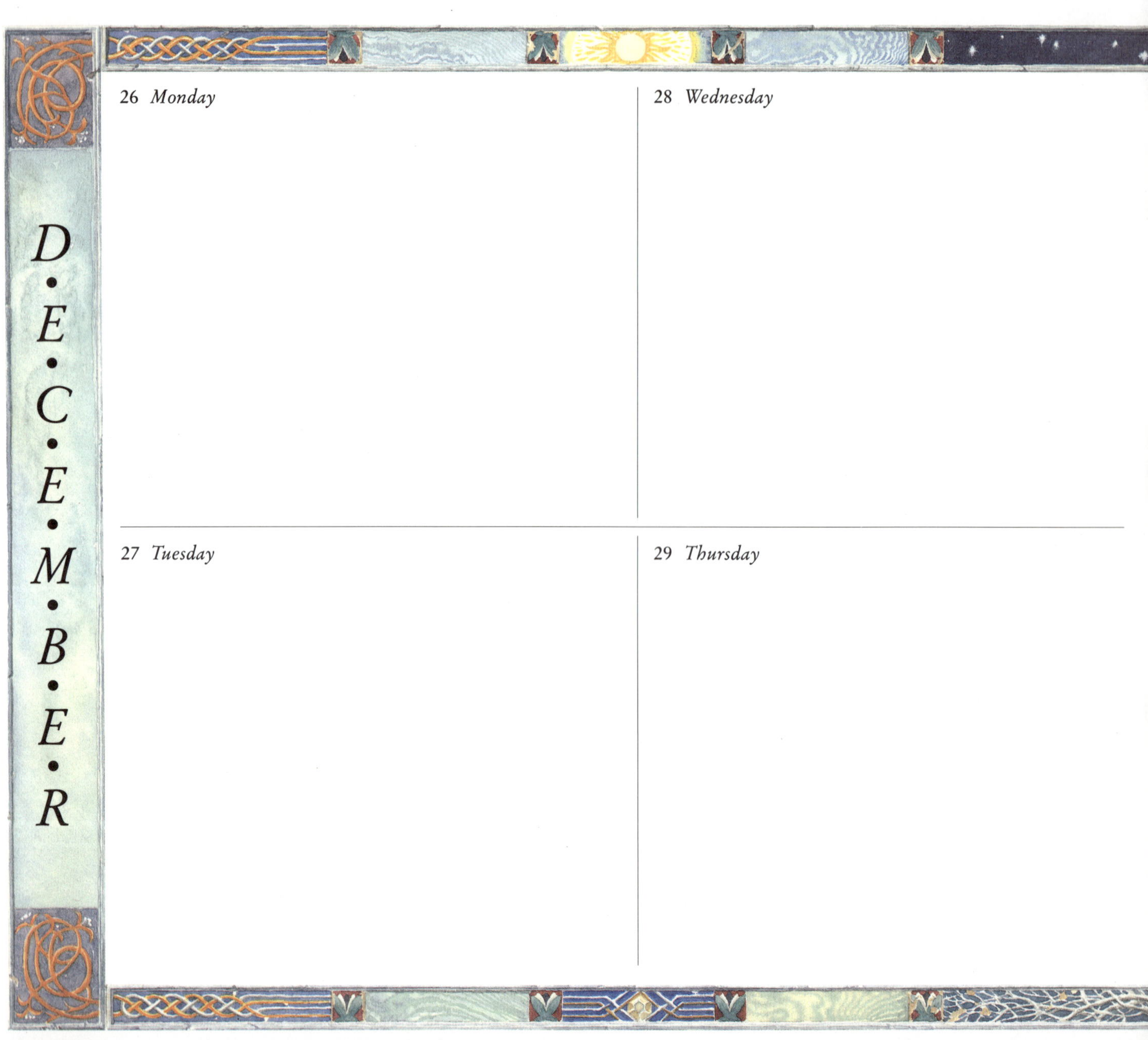

26 *Monday*

27 *Tuesday*

28 *Wednesday*

29 *Thursday*

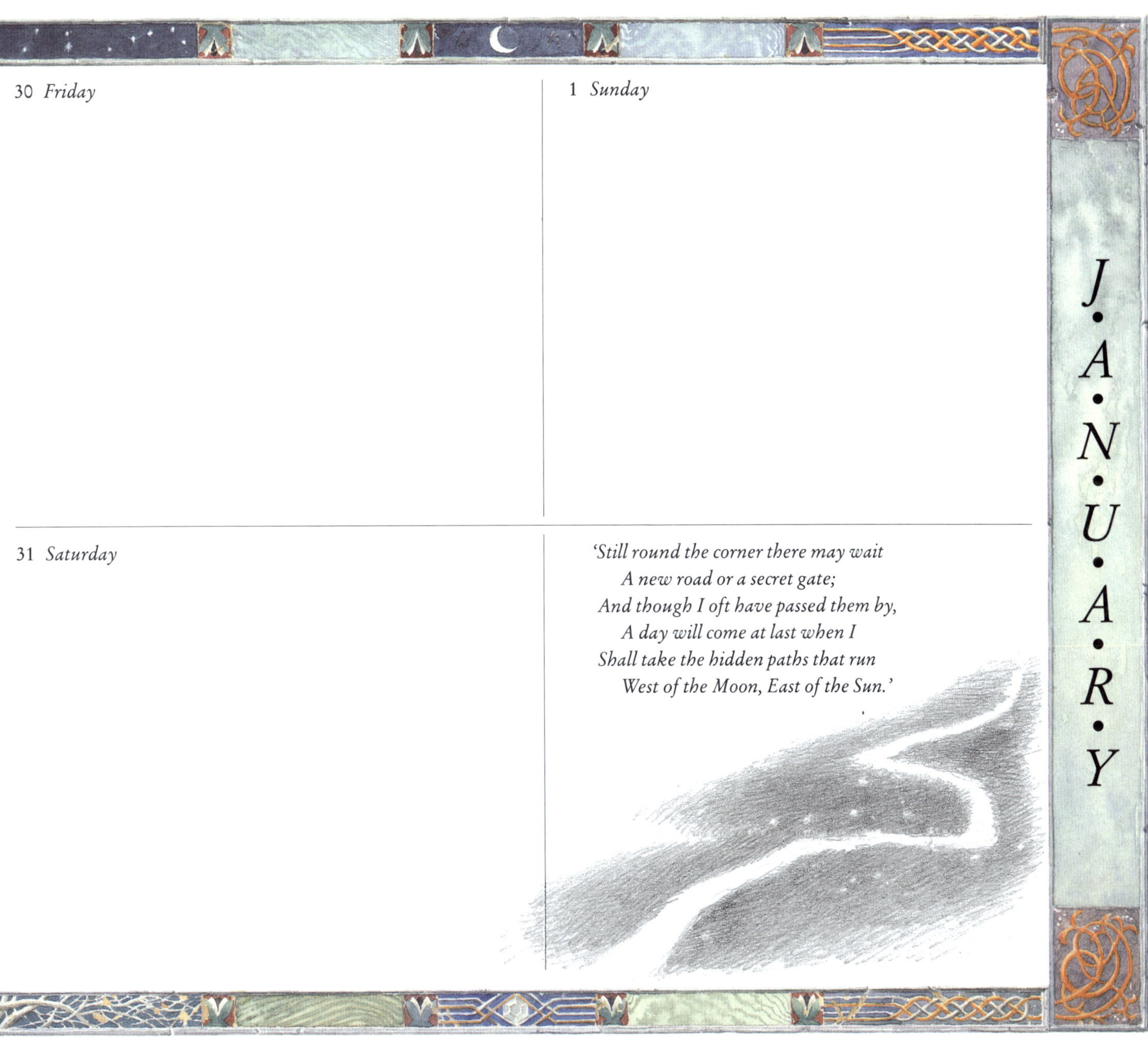

30 *Friday*

1 *Sunday*

31 *Saturday*

'Still round the corner there may wait
A new road or a secret gate;
And though I oft have passed them by,
A day will come at last when I
Shall take the hidden paths that run
West of the Moon, East of the Sun.'

J·A·N·U·A·R·Y

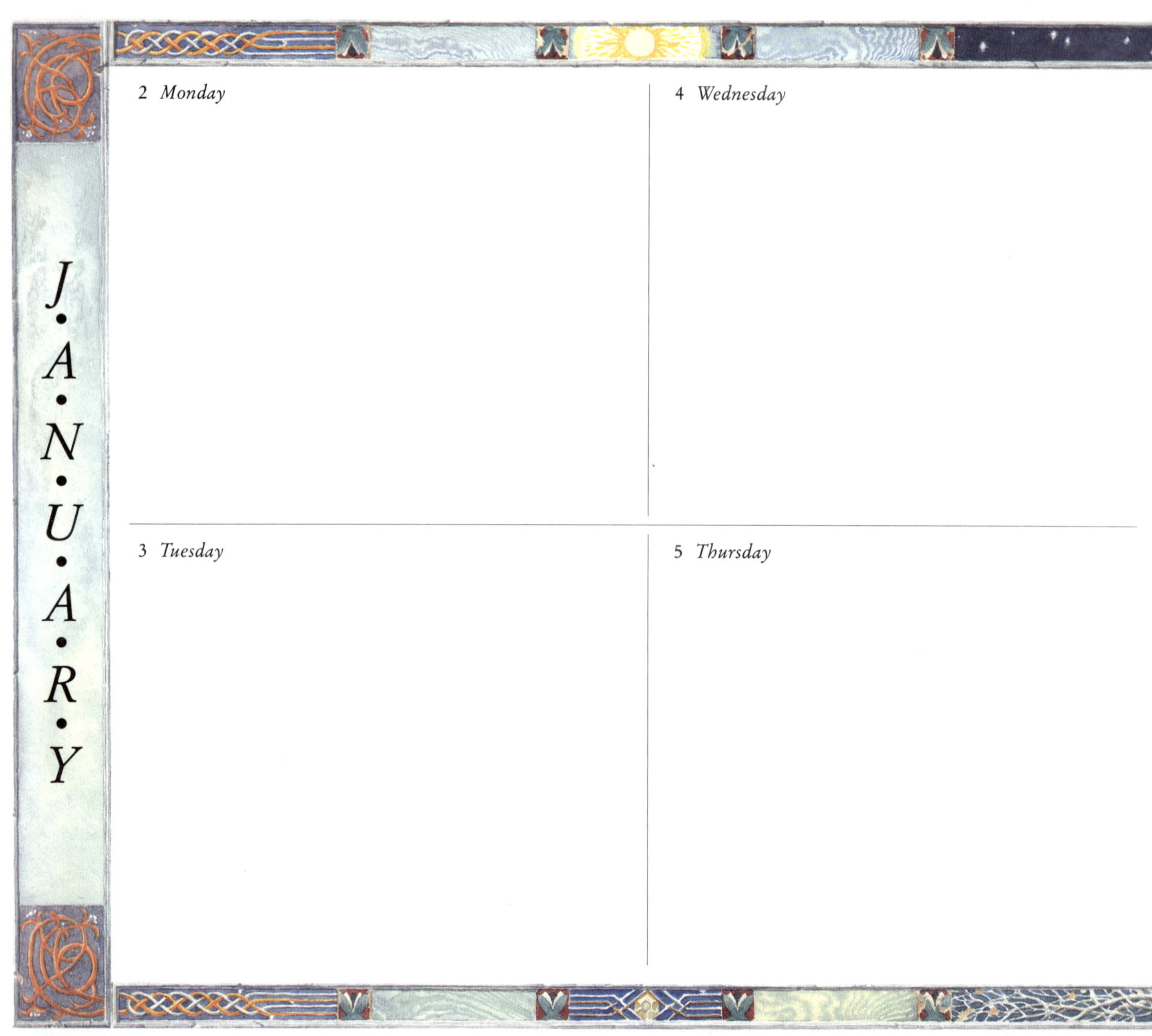

J•A•N•U•A•R•Y

2 *Monday*

3 *Tuesday*

4 *Wednesday*

5 *Thursday*

N•O•T•E•S